NAMES IN A JAR

Names in a Jar

JENNIFER GOLD

Second Story Press

Library and Archives Canada Cataloguing in Publication

Title: Names in a jar / Jennifer Gold.
Names: Gold, Jennifer, 1979- author.
Identifiers: Canadiana (print) 20210136324 | Canadiana (ebook)
  20210136421 | ISBN 9781772602074 (softcover) | ISBN
  9781772602081 (EPUB)
Subjects: LCSH: Holocaust, Jewish (1939-1945)—Juvenile fiction.
Classification: LCC PS8613.O4317 N36 2021 | DDC jC813/.6—dc23

Editor: Sarah Swartz

Cover © Talya Baldwin/www.i2iart.com

Printed and bound in Canada

*Second Story Press gratefully acknowledges the support of the Ontario Arts
Council and the Canada Council for the Arts for our publishing program.
We acknowledge the financial support of the Government of Canada through
the Canada Book Fund.*

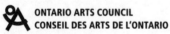

ONTARIO ARTS COUNCIL
CONSEIL DES ARTS DE L'ONTARIO

Canada Council
for the Arts

Conseil des Arts
du Canada

Funded by the Government of Canada
Financé par le gouvernement du Canada

Canada

Published by
SECOND STORY PRESS
20 Maud Street, Suite 401
Toronto, ON M5V 2M5
www.secondstorypress.ca

FSC
www.fsc.org

MIX
Paper from
responsible sources
FSC® C016245

For Adam

Part I

Prologue

ANNA
1986

I AM OLD, now, but the nightmare still plagues me, always the same. I am running in the dark and then my feet become mired in the sewage that once ran deep beneath the Warsaw ghetto.

Hurry, I urge myself. *Hurry!*

When I dream, I am still twelve. I dream of the sewage tunnels beneath the ghetto, where I once ran back and forth for food. Precious nourishment like a bit of chicken or a pat of butter. Maybe an egg. In my dreams, a Nazi soldier trails behind me.

I run faster, furious I've let myself be seen. Even asleep, I can recall the rules: Never make eye contact with anyone. Be invisible. Be a ghost. Beneath my feet, the sludge grows thicker and heavier, like a swamp.

The footsteps behind me grow louder, yet I am paralyzed. Heavy boots thumping along the sewer floor.

I try to scream, but I have no voice. It is only then that I wake up.

Chapter 1

ANNA
1939

MY NAME IS Anna-Maria Bar-Lev, but it wasn't always.

What is interesting about names is that when you change them, the person changes too. When I lived in Warsaw, Poland as Anna Krawitz, I was one girl, and when I was hidden in the Polish countryside as Maria Nowak, I was a different one. The woman I grew to be was different, too. There is some destiny in a name, though of course not every Daisy is cheerful and not every Bella is beautiful. Still, a name is a powerful thing.

I was born Anna Krawitz on September 19, 1929: the nineteenth day of the ninth month in the year 1929. In Jewish mysticism, the number nine means *emet*, or truth, which lasts forever. No matter how you multiply nine, if you add each digit of the product the sum is always nine. It is a constant. In my life I have changed in many different ways, but at my core I am still the same soul.

My mother died three days after I was born. She fell ill suddenly, according to my sister Lina, who never liked to tell that story but always understood my need to hear it. She had severely swollen ankles. Complaints of headache. Sharp pains around the middle. "Toxemia," the midwife hissed, and sent Lina for the doctor. Then a harrowing delivery with too much blood.

"How much blood?" I would ask, because I was always fascinated with the human body and because I had never known my mother other than from a photograph.

My older sister Lina would wince and tell me not to ask such awful questions, so I've never been able to understand what exactly went wrong during the delivery. A placental abruption? Retained placental fragments? An obstetrician by profession, I am haunted by this question. It is like a ghost, rearing its shadowy head in the delivery room whenever a birth I am in charge of takes a turn for the worse.

My earliest memory is sitting on the bed I shared with my sister and dressing and undressing my doll, Sara. After her school, Lina would take in mending and, when she had time and scraps of fabric, she would fashion dresses for Sara. My mother had been a dressmaker and the hole her death left in our lives was felt in every way.

"Why are you sewing that?" I scowled at the worn undergarments Lina mended. I thought she was a grown-up then—she wore her hair pinned and her skirts long—but she was only fourteen. Old enough to quit school entirely and take up dressmaking full time, but our father insisted she stay in school, even though we could certainly have used the extra money.

"Your mother wanted an education for you girls," he said, his pipe hanging out of the corner of his mouth. "Girls, boys, it didn't matter to her. It was something we both agreed on. There is nothing in life to replace learning."

I knew Lina was relieved, because she didn't really want to leave school. Lina loved to read, spending snippets of stolen time in our father's bookshop. She dreamed of one day writing books herself, but didn't think it would be possible given all her responsibilities. It was Lina who kept the house clean and made our supper. It was Lina who lit the Sabbath candles on Friday night and blessed the challah she'd kneaded and braided the day before. Lina took in the mending so there was money for essentials when sales were slow at our father's bookshop.

"Whose underthings are those, anyway?" I recall asking, wrinkling my nose in distaste as Lina painstakingly mended a tear. "Why are they so *big*?" I stared at the oversized, elaborate garment and burst out laughing.

Lina tried to hide a smile. "Shush," she said, biting her lip. "They belong to Mrs. Mendelsohn!"

"The doctor's wife?"

"Yes. It's very fine, Anna. Look at the lace, and it's made of silk." Lina smoothed out the worn fabric, gesturing at the trim.

"Hmph." Recoiling, I went back to Sara, carefully pulling a blue smock over her cloth head. "It's still underwear. And she has a very big behind."

Lina snorted, and we both laughed thinking of Mrs. Mendelsohn's substantial backside decked out in lace.

"Be polite," Lina managed finally, her laughter ceasing. She gave me a stern glance and reached to retrieve a spool of thread. "We need her money."

"Why don't we have a lot of money?" I frowned at Sara, whom I loved dearly but who was not as beautiful as Mrs. Mendelsohn's daughter's doll. Her doll had real hair and was bought from a shop. Sara, on the other hand, had been made by our mother for Lina and found its way to me, as all of Lina's old things did.

"Her husband is a doctor," explained Lina. "Doctors make more money than booksellers."

Our father, Lev Krawitz, owned a tiny bookshop on a street near the Plac Bankowy square in central Warsaw. Lina used to say his books were like our siblings, given the same love and care. Our father—we called him *Tateh* in Yiddish—understood and knew how to care for books. My sister and I, however, bewildered him. He loved us, certainly, but had very little idea of how to raise a pair of daughters.

I loved the bookshop. Wall-to-wall bookshelves, all stuffed to overflowing with volumes arranged by subject and author when they were organized, and according to Tateh's likes and dislikes when they were not. A rainbow of spines, burgundy and navy and forest green, some neat and vertical, and others haphazard and horizontal. Before I started school, I spent hours roaming the stacks, curled in corners or chatting with customers. As a baby, I slept in a cradle nestled under my father's wooden desk. Our aunt, my father's sister, would wander in and out, fussing.

"She should spend the day with me," *Tante* Rachel would say. "She should be with a woman."

My father refused.

"A bookshop is as good a place as any for a child," he'd say. "Plenty here to occupy a young mind."

"She can't read, Lev," my aunt would say. "She's chewing on fountain pens and old bindings."

My father would shrug. "She's thriving, isn't she?"

And I was. I was a healthy child, apple-cheeked and sturdy. My aunt learned to keep her grumbling to whispers behind my father's back.

Lina and I learned the business of bookselling like little apprentices, thumbing through old volumes and eavesdropping on conversations.

The customers were mainly scholars, the sort of men who would come into the shop to sell books to my father and in the process purchase several books of their own, often settling down on a chair in the corner with a volume for hours or days. I can remember one rabbi who became so engrossed he would forget to eat.

Lina and I would bring them bread and a bit of wine, and help my father sort the shelves. Later, I was good at sums and helped Tateh with his accounts, charming the customers with my mental mathematics.

"Mama would have adored you," Lina would say, ruffling my hair. "Little mathematician…."

It was Lina who introduced me to books on the body and blood and guts. What a sight we must have been, two girls amongst old men in a bookshop—Lina composing poetry and braiding my hair, and me sketching diagrams of the pancreas and doing the accounts.

It all changed in the summer of 1939.

The first time we broached the subject of war, I was repairing a book that had come undone at the spine. Lina had taught me how to sew very early, and my little hands proved deft with a needle and thread. I practiced my craft on discarded books, trying to give them a second chance at life.

I was nearly twelve. It was a hot, sticky summer, and Lina and I spent many hours in the bookshop with the shades drawn.

"You girls should be outside," Tateh said, frowning at us as we leafed through manuscripts and doodled with fountain pens. The pipe drooped from the corner of his mouth like a walrus' tusk. "Children should run around."

"I'm finished with school, Tateh," Lina would say, rolling her eyes. "I'm nineteen."

"Nineteen." Tateh stared at Lina in wonder. "I married your mother when she was nineteen."

Lina made a face. "It was a different time, Tateh. I'm too young."

"Mrs. Mendelsohn's older daughter Bella is nineteen," I piped up. "She's married. She got married at eighteen, I think. Now she's having a baby, and—"

Lina gave me a look that could have frozen water in July, and I immediately fell silent. I was a chatterbox child, the kind that regularly spoke before thinking.

"Bella is an idiot," said Lina grumpily. "She's probably never read a book in her life."

Tateh admonished her, but we could both tell he was stifling a laugh. "I won't make you get married until you're ready, Lina. I promise."

"No one's asked her, anyway," I said cheerfully, earning another scowl from my sister.

"There may not be any boys to marry for a while," said Lina casually.

Tateh rested a hand on my head and gave my sister a warning look.

I wasn't so easily quieted. "Why?" I demanded. "Where are they all going? Are they moving to America like Yitzik Sandler? I would love to see America. I heard—"

"They're not moving to America," Lina cut me off.

"Then why?" I persisted. "And don't say I'm too young."

That was their refrain for everything. It made me want to stomp my feet.

"You're too young," said Tateh. "And nothing is certain. It's all rumors."

Lina raised her eyebrows. "That's not what the newspapers say."

I put down my pen and looked from Lina to my father.

"I want to know what's going on," I said. "I'm nearly twelve."

Lina put a hand on my arm. "There may be a war. The Germans, they…."

Tateh frowned deeply and cut her off. "Lina, don't frighten Anna. She's just a child."

11

I bristled. "I am already a two-digit number," I said indignantly. "I know what war is. And I've heard about the Germans and about Hitner—"

"Hitler," corrected Lina, surprised. "Where did you hear about Hitler?"

"I work in a bookshop," I pointed out. "I listen. And I can read newspapers, remember?"

"There won't be a war," said Tateh unconvincingly. "This conversation is over."

Tateh's voice was firm, and both Lina and I quieted. When Tateh used that voice, it was best not to push.

He reached into his pocket and counted out some coins, which he thrust at Lina. "Take your sister for a lemon ice," he instructed. "And then to the zoo."

"Hurray!" I loved lemon ice, and I loved the zoo in Praga, across the Vistula river. My favorites were the elephants, and one was due to give birth.

"Maybe the elephant will have her baby," I said excitedly. "I would love to watch it come out."

"Anna!" Scandalized, Lina winced. "You can't say things like that!"

"But why not?" Puzzled, I stared at her. "It would be fascinating. It's just like with people, you know, an elephant is a mammal. The baby comes right out of the...."

A mortified Lina propelled me to the exit. My father, now an even deeper shade of red, avoided my gaze. *What had I said that was wrong?* I wondered. It was just science, wasn't it?

"Let's get a nice lemon ice, shall we?" said Lina. She was using her mother voice and not her sister one, the one she used when I made a fuss over bedtime or refused my supper. I knew better than to argue if I wanted the ice.

Outside, the air was as thick and damp. I shook my skirt to create a cooling wind as I skipped alongside my sister.

"Is there really going to be a war, Lina?" I remember feeling afraid, even then.

Lina stopped, looking serious. "I don't know, Anna," she said honestly. She took my hand in hers and squeezed it tightly. "But I can promise you I will never let anything happen to you."

Her voice shook slightly, and I blinked. I stepped back from her, wary, and tried to loosen her grip.

"You're hurting me, Lina," I said, surprised.

Lina blinked as if she'd forgotten who I was and where we were. We stayed silent until we reached the lemon ice stand.

After that, everything changed.

Chapter 2

LINA
Summer, 1939

WHEN MAMA DIED, everyone was shocked but me. I'd dreamed it months before, the sort of dream where you wake up trembling and soaked with sweat. I dreamed of a shadowy gray creature under her bed, emerging to swallow Mama whole, like a cloud of pungent smoke.

I knew immediately what it was. The Angel of Death.

I didn't tell my mother, who was not superstitious. Mama prided herself on being a "woman of science," which in her case meant she devoured any volume on the subject from Tateh's shop.

"Madame Curie would not tolerate all this nonsense over the Evil Eye," she'd scoff when the other women would fret over imagined curses and malicious slights. "Madame Marie Curie is a woman of science. Born right here in Warsaw, she won two Nobel Prizes. It could happen to you one day, Lina!"

When I was little, I imagined moving to Paris in a white lab coat. But when I started school, it was clear my talents were elsewhere. I loved to read and write, to bend the written word to my will. Words were to be arranged like flowers in a vase, and I spent hours writing poems and stories. My mother watched me with worry.

"That girl has her head in the clouds," she whispered to my father.

"She's bright enough," Tateh would say, defending me. "She's still a child. She's an excellent student and, more importantly, a good girl. So what if she likes fairy tales?"

I could never tell Mama that I checked under her bed every night for the Angel of Death. Madame Curie would never believe in such a superstitious thing. Mama's belly grew bigger and bigger. And then one day the swelling and the headaches started, and the pains came on. Three days later, she was gone and in her place we had Anna.

Before I saw Anna, I hated her for killing our mother. But once I held her, the hatred melted like butter in the sun.

"Poor baby," I whispered in her tiny pink ear. She was wrapped in a white towel, bundled tightly by the midwife. "What will we do with you?"

Anna opened her eyes and looked very serious, like she was contemplating her response. She didn't cry the way other babies did. She just stared at me with those gray eyes, and I felt something forever change within myself.

"I will protect you!" I told her fiercely.

I clutched my sister tightly. Death had undoubtedly known Anna was there, in the cradle beside the bed. He may have passed her over this time, but he could return.

❧

Anna reminded us of Mama. At first it was just her looks—the same unusual colored hair, reddish gold and very straight. The same round face, full cheeks, and one-dimpled smile. Even the almond shape of their eyes was the same, only Mama's had been blue and Anna's were the color of smoke.

I told no one what I believed: that my sister's eyes were gray because the Angel of Death had touched her when he stole Mama from us. It made me watch Anna even closer, worried that he would be back to steal her too.

"Don't touch that, Anna!" I grabbed my sister's chubby three-year-old hand and snatched the mushroom from it. We were playing in a park near the bookshop with some neighbors, who had found a rabbit and were feeding it bits of leaves.

"Bunny food," she protested, trying to reclaim it. "Mine, Lina!"

"Poison," I said, horrified. I chucked the mushroom, which Anna had plucked from the damp earth near a giant oak tree. "It's poison, Anna!"

"Bunny food," she said, stomping her foot.

"Poison," I said for the third time. My heart beat fast as I retrieved a handkerchief from inside the sleeve of my blouse. "It would make the bunny sick. And Anna, too."

Furiously, I wiped at Anna's hands with the little cloth, scrubbing back and forth until Anna screamed.

"Hurting me, Lina!" Her lower lip trembled and she yanked her hands away.

"I'm sorry." I hugged her. "I just want to keep you safe."

Anna was curious about nature and the world around her. She loved to see how things worked, to open them up and examine their contents. She watched in fascination as I cracked eggs and emptied their runny innards. When she cut her finger, she would stop crying so that she could examine the blood.

"Where does it come from, Lina?" she asked. She was six and mesmerized by a gash on her knee from climbing trees.

"The blood is pumped around the body from the heart," I said, parroting a book from Tateh's shop. "Did you know it's only red when it comes out of the body? Inside it's really almost blue."

"Blue!" Her eyes were like saucers.

"Yes." I dabbed a cotton ball with a bit of iodine. "Hold your breath, Anna, this might sting a bit."

Obediently, Anna sucked in a lungful of air, her nose wrinkling with the effort. I would have shut my eyes—I couldn't stand the sight of blood, especially my own—but Anna watched with a clinical eye as I treated her wound.

"Doesn't it hurt?" I asked. She hadn't flinched.

"It's not so bad," she said bravely. She studied me as I finished tying the ends of the bandage, tucking them under so they would not be a nuisance under her knee socks. "Thank you, Lina."

"Of course, my little love." I kissed the top of her head. "Be more careful next time."

By the time she was eight, Anna had read all the books in Tateh's library on anatomy, and he bartered for more with other booksellers. Anna also showed an early talent for numbers and assumed responsibility for Tateh's bookkeeping when most other girls her age played with dolls. It was a source of both pain and pride to me. On the one hand, she had made herself useful early on, which in a motherless household was not merely an asset but a necessity. On the other, I felt pained at her lack of a normal childhood.

I comforted myself that Anna's aptitude for science would have delighted our mother, who would have found her Madame Curie in her youngest daughter. If my interests were in the imaginary, the fantastic, and the construction of words and sentences, Anna's lay in the tangible; in living things and nature. Anna could stare for hours at a nesting bird or an anthill.

"Lina," she breathed with excitement that spring, that last spring before the war. "Lina, I think ants have some way of talking to one another!"

"Do they?" I smiled at her as I mended our neighbor's stockings. "How do you figure that?"

Squirming with anticipation, she clapped her hands together and recounted her experiment.

"I left some crumbs of bread near the anthill outside the shop and I watched because there was an ant there, and it picked up one of the crumbs and took it back down the hole." Her eyes shone. "And guess what happened?"

"What, *mamaleh?*" I asked, using the Yiddish term of endearment for "little mother."

"A whole group of ants came spilling out to get the rest

of the crumbs! The first ant must have told them. How else would they know?"

"How indeed?" I set down the stockings. "How do you think they speak? Do they have mouths?"

Anna laughed, then grew serious. "I don't know," she said thoughtfully. "I think they might speak but we can't hear or understand it. But I did it three more times and it was the same every time. I wanted to make sure it wasn't a coincidence."

I nodded, impressed. "Very clever, Anna. That's what scientists do."

She furrowed her eyebrows at me. "They watch ants?"

I laughed. "They repeat their work. To make sure it's accurate."

"Really?" She looked pleased. "I'm like a real scientist?"

"Oh, absolutely!" I reached to give her rosy cheek a squeeze and inadvertently knocked my writing journal to the ground. Anna clamored off her chair to grab it.

"Any new stories for me?" she asked.

Anna was my first reader whenever I wrote something new, which sadly was less and less often.

"Nothing yet." I tried to smile.

Anna stared at the pile of mending. "I should help you," she said guiltily. "I shouldn't be playing with ants. I could share the mending with you, and then you would have time to write." She picked up a pair of Dr. Mendelsohn's trousers.

"Don't be silly," I said sharply, tugging the trousers out of her childish hand, the fingernails appropriately caked with dirt. "You're too little."

"I'm the same age as you were when I was born," she pointed out. "I want to practice sewing anyway," she said cheerfully. "Maybe I'll be a surgeon. Cut people open and stitch them back together!"

I had a vision of Anna sliced in half and dropped the trousers.

"Lina?" She sounded worried. "Are you alright? You look a bit funny."

I snapped out of my reverie, bending to grab the trousers. "Fine, darling," I said brusquely. "Why don't you go wash up before we start dinner?"

"But...."

"Please." My tone firm, I motioned toward the door. "Be a good girl, now."

Anna stomped off, and I exhaled loudly. Unbidden thoughts of Anna injured or ill had plagued me of late. I told myself it was the newspaper headlines and the constant murmurs of war. Everyone was worried Hitler would cross into Poland. The men who remembered the last war, the Great War, insisted that cooler heads would prevail. Meanwhile in the bakery line, the women whispered nervously that Hitler could not be trusted, that he had a special hatred for Jews, and that men were always ready to go to war.

The gossip of war grew louder over the summer, an angry buzz like a disturbed hive. People moved quickly in the streets, bought more than they could afford in the shops. Fewer customers came to Tateh's store. People had less to spend on books as they stocked up on necessities like food and clothing. I took in more mending to make up the money lost and worried constantly. Tateh denied there would be another war, insisting that even Hitler would see the logic in avoiding bloodshed.

Anna improved with a needle and thread, and I reluctantly allowed her to help me with the heavier load. When she wondered aloud if she wouldn't have to return to school in the fall if the Germans came, I snapped at her, accidentally stabbing myself with a needle in the fleshy part of my palm.

"Don't be a fool!" I said furiously. "Wishing for a war so you won't have to go to school! I'm disappointed in you, Anna."

"Oh, Lina, you're always so serious." Anna flung her work down. "No one wants to go to school. Especially if there are soldiers in the street and a bomb could fall on the school, and—"

"Shush!" I tried not to think of the school in flames, and glanced down at my hand. It oozed a small bit of blood, and I averted my eyes, feeling sick.

"Let me get that." Anna leapt up and returned with the bottle of iodine and a strip of cloth. "Hold out your hand," she commanded.

I started to protest, then held it out. I didn't watch as Anna confidently cleaned and bandaged my hand.

"There," she said cheerfully.

I studied her work. "Perfect," I said. "Didn't hurt a bit."

"If there's a war, maybe I could become a nurse," she said casually.

"You will not. You will go to school and become a scientist or a doctor, like we've always talked about."

Anna sighed and rolled her eyes, stabbing the socks menacingly.

"And there isn't going to be a war." I said it convincingly, but Anna just raised her eyebrows at me.

We both knew it was a lie.

Chapter 3

ANNA
Fall, 1939

ON SEPTEMBER FIRST, we crowded around the radio to hear the news. The music I liked to hum along with and dance to while I swept under the beds had suddenly stopped, replaced by a somber voice letting Poland know that Germany had invaded.

"There's nothing to panic about," said Tateh, though I could see he was struggling to remain calm. "The Polish army is trying to fend them off."

Lina shook her head. "Men on horseback, fighting Nazis on those giant steel beasts."

"Steel beasts?" I imagined giant steel lizards, storming their way through the streets of Warsaw.

"Tanks," explained Tateh, sounding less calm. "Like huge, armored trucks."

"Oh," I said, although I didn't know exactly what armored meant for a truck. I could only think of medieval knights. I made a mental note to look it up later.

Tateh rose, reaching for his pipe the way he always did when he was flustered. "You heard the radio. We need to block the lights. Black out the windows so the Nazis won't see us when they fly over the city."

I peered out the window, but there were no German airplanes in sight. I watched the branches of the giant oak tree sway gently in the breeze. Fearfully, I imagined the old tree aflame, a conflagration of leaves and twigs.

"What can I do?" I asked, rising. "I want to help."

Lina looked at me as if she'd forgotten I existed.

"I can sew curtains to keep us out of sight from the outside," I suggested.

"Good, because I will need Lina's help with the moving." Tateh's pipe dangled from the corner of his mouth.

"The moving?" Lina frowned.

"Moving the books," said Tateh. "From the bookshop."

"Where are you moving them?" I asked.

"They'll need to be stored underground," said Tateh practically. "Less chance of them burning."

"Burning!" Lina paled.

"From the bombs," I explained to her helpfully. She stared at me, and I fell silent.

"Will the landlord let us move them to the cellar at our house, do you think?" she asked. "There's no cellar access at the shop."

We all avoided the landlord, a man with an angry temper. As the youngest and least likely to be verbally attacked, Lina sent me with the rent money each month.

"I don't know." Tateh looked worried. "The cellars will be used as bomb shelters."

Lina looked pained. "We'll have to save only the most important volumes, and pray the rest stay safe. There won't be room for everything."

Reality sank in slowly. Shelters in the cellar, in case we were bombed! I imagined our home ablaze, the flames licking at the bed I shared with Lina.

The following days were a flurry of preparation. It was strange, because it felt normal and abnormal at the same time. Outside, the sun still rose and set as usual. During the day, school remained open and I continued with my classes as if nothing had changed, though some of my friends had stopped coming. I was now glad to go to school because it was a welcome distraction from the frenzy of activity all around us, the thick blanket of panic that had descended upon our city like a fog.

It wasn't just in the Jewish quarter. In the park, where I sometimes went after school with my friend Sarah, the gentile children also spoke of frightened adults and dimmed lights and basement shelters. Roza and Agata, two girls we jumped rope with, had stories similar to ours.

"I've heard Hitler eats children," said Agata solemnly. Agata always wore her fine, flaxen hair in two tightly knit braids and was the sort of girl who told you she had a pony in her kitchen.

"That's ridiculous," I said, snorting. "No one is eating children."

"I heard it too," said Roza, who was usually the sensible one. Her hair was copper-colored like mine, worn in one long braid down her back. "I heard the Germans are going to make us their slaves."

My rope-turning hand faltered, and Agata tripped.

"Sorry!" I said, wincing. "That was an accident."

"It's alright." Agata untangled herself from the rope. "I have to go, anyway. My father is on the black out committee, so we eat supper earlier now."

"What's a black out committee?" I gathered up the rope, carefully looping it into a neat figure eight.

Agata straightened importantly. "It's men who go out at night to make sure everyone is following the black-out rules and curfew," she explained. "If they aren't, my father can arrest them."

Sarah and I bid the girls good-bye and headed back to our neighborhood.

"Do you think Hitler really eats children?" Sarah looked at me, whimpering.

"Don't be such a fool, Sarah." I rolled my eyes. "Of course not. That's just Agata being crazy. Remember she told us she had a pet horse?"

Sarah sniffed, and I sighed.

"Hitler isn't coming here, anyway," I pointed out. "Just his soldiers. Hitler is in Berlin, or Munich, or some other big German city."

Sarah's sniffling grew noisier. Irritated, I walked faster.

❧

The air raid siren sounded as we cleared the supper table. Lina froze, a statue holding plates and cutlery. I jumped and cried out. We stared at each other and at Tateh, still at the table.

"Do we go down?" Lina looked at Tateh uncertainly. "Is it time?"

"I—I think so, yes." Tateh straightened, removed his pipe from his mouth and placed it in his jacket pocket. He was trying to sound calm, but his voice shook.

"Hurry, girls. Anna, you take our coats and some bread. Lina, you get the photo of Mama and those books." He motioned to a small stack of valuable volumes.

In the hallway, we joined other families in the building rushing down to the basement, a damp, small space with a dirt floor that stank of mildew. The air was rank and thick like rancid soup from the crowd of families already crammed inside. Our building wasn't huge but it did have four floors, with at least five families to a floor. It seemed impossible we could all fit.

"We'll stay on the stairs," said Lina, backing up, gasping. "There isn't room for us."

"It's so small." I stared at the swarm of people, wondering if it was possible to run out of air.

"It looked much bigger empty," said Lina. She had a hand-kerchief at her mouth as she led us to the stairwell. I spotted Tante Rachel and waved.

Lina and Tateh had spent days down here stacking boxes

of books into a small crawlspace toward the back of the basement. They'd sealed the most valuable of Tateh's stock from the shop into crates and buried them under the dirt floor. Each day, they'd return covered in dirt, like gravediggers.

We settled on the stairwell with my aunt and her son, our cousin David, who was only a year old and crying loudly. They lived on our floor.

"Can I take him?" I loved babies. I reached out for little David, who stopped crying when he saw me and put his arms out eagerly.

"Quite the little mamaleh," commented my aunt.

"He's adorable." I made a silly face at him, and he giggled loudly.

I sat down with David perched on my lap, singing softly. Nearby, I watched another family wrangle their three-year-old twins and a cat into a semi-circle on the landing.

"The cat? Really?" Tante Rachel made a face at the black and white feline, now writhing frantically and mewing in protest at being tightly held. "Ridiculous."

"Why? I wish we had a cat." I looked hopefully at Lina, but she wasn't listening.

The stairwell teemed with families clutching their most treasured possessions, the children making a ruckus. Outside, the faint sound of sirens still warned of looming danger, but there was nothing happening.

"Where are the Freudmans?" Tante Rachel peered around the stairs like a teacher taking attendance. "Poor Masha is so far along, she could have her baby any minute."

I thought of Masha Freudman, who I'd seen yesterday panting as she climbed the stairs. "She's probably too big to move."

"Anna!" Tante Rachel looked scandalized. "You can't say that!"

I shrugged. "It's true, though."

The night wore on. The excitement waned as I grew tired and irritable. Our neighbors began to annoy me with their noise and their smells. Even little David, now sound asleep across my legs, his diaper clearly soaked.

"Lina?" I tugged at my sister's sleeve pathetically, like a much younger child. "How much longer?"

"I don't know, darling," she said. "Why don't you let me take David? I'll bet he's heavier than he looks."

"Thank you," I said gratefully as she reached for him. He woke up and shrieked loudly, dissolving into noisy sobs. I could feel everyone's eyes on me, glaring, and I stared at my shoes.

"Would you like a sweet, dear?" A neighbor tapped my arm. She lived with her husband a floor above us. In her outstretched palm was an assortment of hard candy.

"Yes!" Greedily, I plucked one from her hand, unwrapping it.

Lina nudged me.

"Thank you," I added sheepishly.

"You're very welcome." She held out her hand to Lina, who politely declined, even though I knew she loved candy.

"May I sit with you?" She smiled tentatively at Lina, who made space for her, looking wary.

"I'm Rivka Levy," she said, introducing herself. "We moved in only a month ago."

"I'm Anna," I said, sticking out my hand. "And this is my sister Lina. And my father is…."

I looked around for my father but couldn't see him. Worried, I sat up straighter.

"Tateh went to pray," Lina explained, noticing my alarm. "There's a group of men praying further down the stairwell."

I nodded. Tateh was not religious, but these were not normal times.

"My husband went as well," said Rivka. She fidgeted with the pleats of her skirt.

"Do you have children?" I asked curiously. Lina made a small sound of disapproval and I sighed, aware that I had committed some sort of minor social misdemeanor.

"It's alright," said Rivka, smiling at Lina. "I don't mind. Actually, Anna, Dov and I are expecting a baby." She touched her belly lightly, looking pleased. "I'm three months along."

I stared interestedly at her stomach, which still looked flat to me. I wondered how big an unborn baby was at three months.

Lina kicked me in the shin, and I looked away. Even I knew it wasn't polite to stare at a woman's belly.

"How old is he?" Rivka nodded shyly at David, asleep now against Lina's shoulder.

"He's one," I said. "But he's our cousin. Lina's not his mother."

Lina and Rivka were about the same age, which surprised

me. To me, Rivka was an adult, a married woman with an apartment and a baby on the way. And Lina—well, Lina was Lina. Ageless to me, both sister and mother.

Rivka seemed unsure as to what to say next, so she carefully unwrapped a candy and popped it into her mouth.

"Are you sure you wouldn't like one?" She held the remaining sweets out to Lina. "They're quite tasty. They're from Gdańsk, where I'm from. A little shop around the corner from where I used to live."

"Lina loves sweets," I told her. "She just doesn't want to be rude, I think."

"Anna!" Lina groaned and took a green one. "Thank you," she said. "I do love sweets."

"Oh, me too! My mother used to say I would rot my teeth and never find a husband." Rivka smiled wistfully.

"You must miss her," I said, "if all your family is in Gdańsk." I thought of being apart from Lina.

"Oh, I do! But she isn't there. I mean, she isn't anywhere. She passed away before my wedding." Rivka nervously twisted the remaining candy in her hands, her cheeks flushed. "I'm sorry, I talk too much when I'm nervous."

"Our mother is dead too," I informed her. "She died right after I was born."

"Oh, that's terrible!" Rivka looked frightened, and I remembered that she was pregnant. Lina gave me a sharp elbow in the ribs, and we lapsed into silence, all of us pink with embarrassment and anxiety.

Outside, there was a loud bang and a bright flash like

31

lightning lit up the small basement windows. Everyone fell quiet, exchanging terrified glances. There was more noise, a staccato of gunfire and explosions that shook the building. Instinctively, I covered my head and glanced upwards, but I could see only the ceiling. I moved closer to Lina.

Lina handed David back to his mother and gathered me in her arms as if I too were an infant. I buried my head in her armpit as another bright orange flash illuminated the stairwell.

"It will be over soon," whispered Lina soothingly. "We're safe down here."

They were white lies and I knew it, but I still felt better. I shut my eyes and focused on the rhythm of Lina's breathing until my breaths matched hers, our chests rising and falling in synch.

The noise and light stopped as abruptly as they had begun, but no one moved.

"Is it over?" Lina looked around uncertainly. "It can't go on all night, surely."

"We should wait." It was Tateh, and my heart leapt at his voice. "They may be back," he said. "Another round."

Another round? How many planes do the Germans have? The crowd murmured worriedly, echoing my thoughts.

There was more noise, but of a different sort. From above, shouts and screams and loud moans of agony. Human noises.

"What's wrong?" Tante Rachel stood, frightened. "Has something happened?"

"He's hurt!" someone shouted. "We need a doctor! Clear some space!"

We all tried to move out of the way, tripping over each other.

Lina gasped, startling me. I looked up in the direction of her gaze and saw why.

It was Mendel Freudman, husband of the very pregnant Masha. He was bleeding heavily, and in his back was a large piece of jagged metal.

"Shrapnel," I overheard someone say grimly. "It doesn't look good."

Lina looked faint. "Why was he outside? And where is Masha?"

"I'll go see if I can find Dr. Mendelsohn," said Tateh, and it was all I could do not to cry out. If Mendel had been hit with shrapnel, what was to stop my father from being struck? Lina gripped my arm tightly as our father disappeared up the stairs.

"Move him on his belly," someone shouted. The two men carried the injured man and laid him across the dirt floor. Blood pooled around him, and others rushed forward to help, tearing at sleeves and skirts to create bandages.

Mendel tried to lift his head. "Masha!" he cried. "The baby is coming! The midwife, I…."

He collapsed mid-sentence, his face hitting the floor with a sickening thud. I winced, horrified.

"He must have gone to find the midwife," said Rivka, ashen. "God in heaven, where is Masha?"

Tante Rachel handed me David. "Be a good girl, Anna, and mind your cousin." Her voice shook. "I will go find Masha."

David let out a wail, but she ignored his outstretched arms and dashed up the stairs two at a time.

"Should we remove the shrapnel?" a man asked anxiously over Mendel's unconscious form. It was Mr. Guttman.

"No!" I found myself on my feet, still holding David.

Everyone turned to look at me in surprise.

"No," I said, bolder now. I clutched at my cousin, who had begun to cry at the sound of my raised voice. "It may kill him."

"What do you know? You're just a child!" Mr. Guttman shouted back at me.

"I read it in a book," I said stubbornly. "You should wait for Dr. Mendelsohn."

"He might die while we wait!" Mr. Guttman crouched down next to Mendel and reached for his wrist. "He barely has a pulse."

"Pull it out!" someone shouted.

"Listen to my sister!" said Lina, her voice trembling. Her face was drained of all color—she couldn't stand the sight of all the blood. "She knows!"

The crowd erupted in disagreement. Anxiously, I shifted from foot to foot. If the doctor didn't arrive soon, it wouldn't matter if we removed the shrapnel or not.

Mendel's body jerked unexpectedly, and there was a collective gasp of horror from the crowd.

Mr. Guttman glared at me. "I'm taking it out."

"You're going to kill him," I snapped, glowering at him. I heard Lina's sharp intake of breath.

Mr. Guttman grasped the metal and tugged hard. In my arms, David writhed and wailed. We all held our breath, and for a long moment, nothing happened.

Then more bleeding started. Slow at first, then faster, like a rainstorm building in intensity.

"Apply pressure," someone yelled, rushing forward with a torn shirtsleeve. "Staunch the bleeding!"

They tried. Nearly everyone in the stairwell contributed clothing to try to help. I knew, though, it was no use. My eyes met Mr. Guttman's and I quickly looked away. I felt guilty now, about what I had said. I didn't blame him, not really. With injuries that severe, Mendel probably never had a chance.

By the time Tateh returned safely with Dr. Mendelsohn, Mendel was dead.

"He's passed," said Dr. Mendelsohn gently, kneeling next to Mr. Guttman, who was still clutching at a torn piece of clothing, holding it tightly against Mendel's back. Mr. Guttman didn't move, his shoes and trousers soaked with blood.

"His injuries were—they were not compatible with life." Dr. Mendelsohn put a hand on Mr. Guttman's shoulder. It unfroze the man, and he wept into the doctor's shoulder like a small boy.

The men convened to pray for the second time that night. As they chanted the mourner's *Kaddish*, the prayer for the dead, we all joined in. At least one woman had fainted, and others, like Rivka and Lina, were close. Very few had ever seen so much blood.

The blood didn't bother me, but the body did; the lifelessness of it. It had been Mendel, and then it wasn't anymore. He was gone.

He was the first person I saw die. I didn't know then there would be many more.

Chapter 4

LINA
Winter, 1940

THE HAZE OF DEATH was everywhere. The casualties of war were piling up: Masha's husband, her baby who had been born with the cord around her neck and had died at birth. There were dozens of others who hadn't found shelter when the bombs fell. I went quiet, avoiding conversation with anyone besides Anna and Tateh. Rivka, the pregnant girl from the stairwell, made me more anxious as she tried to befriend me. All I could see was Masha's poor dead infant. Eventually, we went back to our own flats.

"You don't really like Rivka, do you?" Anna said one afternoon after we'd seen Rivka in the butcher line. "Why? She's really nice and she's trying so hard to be your friend."

"I do like her," I said quickly. "Why would you say that?"

Anna raised her eyebrows. "You always seem like you're in a rush to get away from her," she said. "Like she's got the flu and you're going to catch it."

"It's just the war," I said brusquely. "I'm too anxious to stand around and chat. Best to get home quickly."

"Okay," said Anna, shrugging. I knew she was far from satisfied with my response, but for once she held her tongue.

Then came the laws against the Jews and what happened to Mr. Guttman. The laws revoked all our rights as Jewish citizens of Poland and forced us to wear yellow stars affixed to our clothes. Tateh's bookshop, like other Jewish businesses, was abruptly closed, and rumors swirled about beatings by soldiers and confiscation of property. Even the mending we took in dwindled as our customers could no longer afford to send out their laundry. Tateh and I worried how we would pay our rent and feed ourselves.

Mr. Guttman was walking home from the evening service at the synagogue when they attacked him. The attackers were two Nazis and a Pole, according to the story told later in whispers. The Pole was our neighbor, a man who owned a repair shop. A man to whom we'd brought our broken radios. A man who had previously greeted us in the streets.

The three men, all in various states of drunkenness, had targeted Mr. Guttman, first with jeering insults and then with fists and boots.

They had taken turns kicking him in the head. When he finally stopped breathing, the soldier to kick last had been declared the winner and thus the recipient of Mr. Guttman's only valuable possession, a slender gold wedding band. The body had been left in the road, like an animal. The *chevra kadisha*, the group of Jews who volunteer to prepare the dead for burial, had retrieved his broken body hours later. It was said he was recognizable to his wife only by a birthmark on his arm.

Mrs. Guttman had not even sat her week of *shiva*, the traditional period of Jewish mourning, when the announcement was made: We would all be leaving our homes. All Jews were to be confined to a small area of the city. We were to be evicted immediately and permitted to take only what we could carry ourselves to our new quarters.

"It's not a big enough quarter for the entire Jewish population." My father, who had a book of maps, spread out the pages showing Warsaw on our dining table. "Where will we all go?"

"I'm sure it's bigger than you think, Tateh," I said unconvincingly, trying to remain upbeat for Anna. "Probably there are more apartments, only smaller."

Tateh's eyes met mine over Anna's head. "Perhaps," agreed Tateh quietly. He placed his pipe back in his mouth and looked away. I resumed packing our suitcases with Anna's assistance, gently reminding her to take only what was necessary.

"We can't possibly carry all those books, darling," I told her as she loaded up a case with anatomy texts. "We'll keep them safe for after the war."

Anna looked agitated. "But Lina, I need them!"

"I'm sorry, Anna, but we can't. It won't be forever. You can take one."

Anna's hands curled into fists of frustration.

"How long do you think it will last?" She clutched the edge of one of her hardcover books, reluctant to part with it. "The war."

"It can't last very long, now that Britain and France have declared war on Germany," I reassured her, parroting what I'd heard on the streets. "I'm sure it will be over in six months."

"I hate this!" Anna picked up the book and threw it violently to the ground. "It's not fair!"

I sighed and, rather than reprimand her over the book, I pulled her close.

"I'm sorry," I murmured into her hair. "I hate it, too."

"My friend Roza wouldn't play with me," she said then, and burst into tears. "At the park. She said her parents said to stay away from Jews."

"Oh, Anna." I hugged her tighter. "I'm so sorry."

"We were friends!" She pulled back and stared at me, her face a mess of tears and fury. "She told me Jews just cause trouble. I never caused her any trouble. Now I hate her!"

"I know," I whispered. "I know."

We packed what we could in six suitcases, two apiece. Our entire life's belongings crammed into six small bags. I tucked the picture of Mama into my own suitcase, along with one nightdress of hers. If I pressed my face into it, I could still smell her: rosewater mixed with baking bread and melted candle wax. I folded it neatly along the bottom of my suitcase along with one of Anna's books and the leaded-glass picture frame. It was the heaviest suitcase, but the most important one, and I clutched tightly at the handle as we left our home for the last time.

❧

Tateh was right about the Jewish quarter; the ghetto, as it quickly came to be called. There was simply not enough room.

"My God," I hissed, sucking in my breath as we reached our new quarters.

We were to live in a space much smaller than our flat, and we shared it with other families from our old building: the widow Masha Freudman who'd lost both her husband and her baby, and pregnant Rivka and her husband Dov. The building itself was also older and smaller than the one we'd left behind, and didn't look as if it had been lived in for some time. Windowpanes were cracked, bricks were missing or crumbling, and I could see holes in the walls, which rats could easily make use of.

We stood in the doorway together, staring at our tiny allotment of space. No one moved or spoke. Two rooms; one a bedroom, the other a tiny kitchen and living space combined. The paint on the walls was chipped and peeled, and the floor was scuffed and uneven. The light fixtures didn't work, and the scratched windowpanes let in precious little light. Masha walked over to the sink and turned the faucet. A hissing noise, then a rush of brown water. We all stared in horror until it ran clear.

"No one has lived here in ages," she said.

"Rivka and Dov should take the bedroom," said Tateh, finally. "The rest of us can use the floor in here."

"No, no," Dov shook his head, his hat slightly askew. "That hardly seems fair."

"You'll need your own space with the baby, when it comes," said Tateh reasonably. At the mention of the baby, we all avoided looking at Masha.

"I suppose we should…clean and unpack?" Rivka's voice trembled, but she was trying to sound cheerful. "It's not so terrible, really."

No one answered. I looked around, taking in the particulars of our new home beyond its inadequate size. There was a thin layer of dirt covering every surface as if the entire apartment were a jelly donut dusted with filth in lieu of powdered sugar. The air was stale and smelled strongly of mildew.

I ran my hand lightly along the doorframe. Masha glanced at my blackened fingertips but said nothing, her gaze hard. Since she'd lost both her husband and baby, Masha had said little.

"Where's the toilet?" Anna, the only one of us to casually drop her bags and wander the small square of space, looked at me, frowning.

I breathed deeply with exaggerated slowness to try to smother my growing panic. The air stank.

"I don't think the building has indoor plumbing," I said, affecting nonchalance. "There will be an outhouse in the back, I think."

Anna's eyes went wide. We'd been lucky enough to have indoor plumbing in our old building. I swallowed and felt the growing lump in my throat as I silently counted how many of us might be using the same outdoor lavatory.

Looking around, Rivka let out a stifled sob, and Dov set his bags down on the floor to put a comforting arm around her.

Only Masha didn't flinch. She had one suitcase, and she set it down with a hard thud and snapped it open. "We'll need a broom," she said matter-of-factly. Her gray eyes had the look of steel as she rummaged purposefully through her bag. "And rags. We can cut up clothing if necessary. I hardly need any clothing anymore."

"Masha…." Rivka reached out to try to put a hand on the other woman's arm, but Masha bristled and pulled away.

"Whatever you're going to say, Rivka—please. Don't." Her voice was cold. She turned to the rest of us. "Just find me a broom."

She yanked a blouse from her bag and tore it into two.

⁂

Before the ghetto, I often would complain good-naturedly of hunger at the end of a long day.

"I could eat a horse," I would joke as I quartered a chicken or trimmed the fat from a side of beef. Anna, who ate like a bird and never cleaned her plate, was the opposite, making faces as Tateh and I implored her to eat.

"One more bite of chicken, Anna," I'd say in a wheedling voice. "Just one more."

It was strange to think of it now, as our lives became slowly consumed by the thought of food: obsessing over it, wishing for it, never having enough of it. The hollow pain of an empty belly coupled with the worry over those whose nutrition was clearly sorely lacking—the children, the expecting mothers—dominated our every moment. We relied on the Germans for rations of food that were scarcely enough to keep us alive. We divided our own morsels of bread and potatoes and flour so that pregnant Rivka and growing Anna could have the largest shares, particularly the meager monthly ration of meat and margarine. It left our bodies weak and our minds confused. The days blended into one another in a fog, and I wondered how long we could possibly survive in this state.

"We need more food." Masha, who often disappeared from the flat for hours at a time, stood in the doorway, one hand on an increasingly slender hip: she no longer looked as if she were with child. Her tone was matter of fact, devoid of all affect, and she spoke to the room at large but looked straight at Dov. "Unless she gets more food, Rivka and the unborn child are going to die."

Dov flinched as if he'd been slapped. He stared at his wife, who now spent most of her time asleep on a cot.

"Where?" he said helplessly. "How will we get it?"

Dov had descended into a separate fog of his own, sapped of energy and hope. Rather than help with foraging for scraps of food or cleaning or finding work, Dov simply spent his days next to his sleeping wife, his head in his hands or staring at something only he could see.

"You need to pull yourself together, Dov," said Masha calmly, and I envied her ability to voice what the rest of us were thinking. "There are ways. Bartering. You are a carpenter. There are ways to make things and smuggle them out for food."

Was this true? I caught Masha's eye, and she nodded.

Tateh stood up. "I can help," he offered. "I can do whatever is needed."

"And me," I said quickly. "I want to help."

"Me, too." Anna appeared behind Masha in the doorway, having heard most of the conversation. She attended a makeshift school now with other Jewish children, though how they focused on their studies on so little food I couldn't understand.

"You're only a child," I said to Anna, feeling tired.

"Who do you think is doing the smuggling?" Anna stood next to Masha now and I felt taken aback by her fierce expression.

"Absolutely not," I said, my voice trembling. "No."

"But Lina...."

"No!"

"How will you forbid it?" Masha frowned at me. "She's not a baby, Lina."

"Let someone else's child go," I snapped. I looked at Tateh beseechingly, but he shook his head.

"If Anna wants to go, I don't think we can or should prevent it," he said quietly. His hand went for his pipe, but there was no tobacco, not anymore. Tateh fingered the useless pipe briefly, then gestured at Rivka's sleeping form. "How will the baby survive if we aren't able to get enough food?"

"It's a mitzvah," Anna offered, invoking the Hebrew term for "good deed." "The Torah says—"

"The Torah says the few should never be sacrificed for the many," I interrupted her, my voice shaking. I grabbed the edge of an old, cracked chair for support. It buckled under the sudden weight and the back snapped clear in two.

I looked down at the splintered chair and at my hand, which oozed tiny droplets of blood.

"Are you okay, Lina?" Anna looked at me, concerned. "Let me look at it."

"I'm fine," I whispered. I rushed for the door, nearly knocking my sister over as I fled.

Chapter 5

ANNA
Winter, 1940

SIGNS FLANKED the ghetto on both the inside and outside, the wording the same for both: *"Jews who leave the ghetto without permission are liable to the death penalty. The same penalty awaits any person who knowingly gives shelter to such Jews."*

Not that leaving was easy. The Germans had been thorough in sealing off the ghetto. The wall didn't leave much room to slip in or out, and the tops of the walls were fixed with barbed wire and broken glass.

But still, there were ways, if one knew where to look. There were tunnels and sewers. There were houses on the borders. And there were cars and trucks that went in and out through the gates of the ghetto where a small child could hide.

Lina was terrified. She was sure I'd end up in the *Gęsiówka*, the Jewish prison inside the ghetto.

"You could be shot," she whispered when I returned late from smuggling outside the ghetto, slipping in while the others slept. "The Nazis shoot children."

"But Lina, look." I reached into my pocket excitedly.

"Is that…?" Lina stopped her fretting and stared.

"Butter," I said triumphantly, doing a little twirl. "Go wake everyone!"

I came back several nights a week with my spoils. Sometimes it was staples like butter or milk. Other times it was luxuries like honey. Lina may not have liked my smuggling, but she couldn't deny we benefited from the risk. Rivka was up and moving again, and we could see her fetus kicking. We looked through the anatomy book together, and I showed her what her baby looked like.

"It'll be here soon, now," I told her.

Behind Rivka's back, Masha fretted.

"Her belly is too small," she whispered to Lina.

"The baby is kicking, though," replied Lina, but she looked worried.

"She needs more than bread," said Masha. "She needs meat."

Masha had introduced me to a man I knew only as Sam, and it was Sam who told me when, where, and how to meet those outside the walls of the ghetto who would barter for food and medicine using the cash, jewelry, and other valuables Jews had smuggled into the ghetto hidden in babies' diapers and sewed inside skirts. He had a network of children—most of whom were smaller than me—who could slip in and out of the ghetto without notice. He redistributed the food to those who needed it, and no doubt took a cut for himself, too. Before the war, he had owned a factory. He wasn't a bad man, really, but he was rude and bossed people around.

"You're a bit old," he told me at our first meeting. "You need to be small to fit through the openings in the wall. To get through the sewers. Most of the kids are under eight." He waved a cigarette at me, and I coughed, annoyed. *Where is he getting his cigarettes?*

"How old are you? Nine?"

"Ten," I lied smoothly. I was small and thin for twelve. "But I can pass for Polish. My hair is light, my eyes are gray, and I speak Polish."

"Do you?" He looked interested and reached over and touched my hair, holding a strand up to the light.

"Yes, I do," I replied in perfect Polish.

Sam looked thoughtful. "We'll get you a school uniform," he said, thinking aloud. "So you don't attract attention on the outside. The other children look like urchins, no one pays them any mind. And you'll need to learn some prayers, in case some-one stops you."

"Prayers?" I asked, confused.

"Catholic ones. In Latin. You'll pretend to be a Polish girl, in Catholic school. Do you know the *paternoster*, the Catholic prayer?"

"I'll learn," I said bravely.

"Will she fit through the wall gaps?" asked Masha.

"She's a bit big for the gaps. We'll send her to the trucks or the sewer tunnels. Mind you don't get too filthy." Sam gave me a hard stare. "If you stink, you'll attract attention."

I bristled at the notion of stinking and glared at him. "I'll be careful."

And I was. I learned the paternoster until I could mutter it backwards. I practiced my Polish until it was unaccented. Three times a week, I would clean and press the Catholic school uniform that had been mysteriously procured "at great cost." Sam's gruff words, as he thrust the wrapped package at me without ever looking me directly in the eye. The hardest part of the sewers was trying not to dirty the uniform; the second hardest was trying to make it outside the ghetto unseen. Once outside, I looked for my contacts to trade whatever wares or money I'd been given in exchange for whatever we needed inside the ghetto. These were traded for things we hadn't seen since we'd been shut inside its walls: meat and butter. Sugar and eggs. Medicine.

The day after I'd heard Lina and Masha whispering, I bravely approached Sam.

"It's not your day," he said abruptly, barely looking at me. "Go home."

"My…cousin needs meat." I refused to move. "She's pregnant. Let me go find her some."

"It's not your day," he repeated. He stopped writing and looked at me. "What do you think? You can just sneak out and someone hands you a chicken?" His voice was tinged with acid.

I felt a surge of anger. "I don't even know why I'm here," I hissed, trying not to raise my voice. "I don't need your permission to do anything."

He glared at me. "You're going to get yourself and others killed, Anna. Do as you're told."

"Rivka needs meat and I'm going to get it for her," I said. "With or without your help."

"Good luck," he said, shrugging. "I won't stop you."

That afternoon, I pressed my uniform and braided my hair. We were lucky enough to have a mirror, Rivka having stashed one in her suitcase. Masha had snorted at it initially as unnecessary, but it was useful. To properly mimic a Polish schoolgirl, I needed to look the part, with perfectly braided hair and a face free of grime and dirt. Lina watched me out of the corner of her eye as she worked to turn one potato into a meal for six.

"You don't usually go Thursdays," she said quietly, stirring.

I fastened the end of my braid with a pin. "Change of plans," I said.

Lina regarded me shrewdly. "Be careful, Anna. Don't get cocky. You're just as likely to get shot this time as your first time."

I wanted to argue with her, but I bit my tongue and nodded. "I'm always careful."

I finished my second braid and stabbed a pin at it, frowning at my reflection.

"It's crooked," confirmed Lina. "Let me help."

I hesitated, then nodded. "Thank you."

Lina washed and dried her hands and came over, silently taking the comb. I knelt in front of her, and she loosened the second braid and gently brushed my hair.

I closed my eyes and enjoyed the sensation of Lina tugging the comb through my tangled locks. If I concentrated hard, I could pretend we were back in the bedroom Lina and I had shared in better times. A pantry full of food, and a toilet and sink of our own. Rugs on the floors that were soft against our feet.

"There you go," said Lina, pushing the pin back in place. "Much better. You look like that little Polish girl you used to play with. What was her name?"

"Roza," I said abruptly. "Roza, whose parents told her to stay away from Jews."

Lina winced. "Right."

"I wonder what she's doing now," I said, thinking aloud. *Is her life going on as normal?* I hadn't thought of her at all since we'd moved here. It was hard to picture the park existing now, let alone Roza playing there, skipping rope. "Do you think she still gets to go to the park?"

Lina looked stricken. "No," she said decisively. "No. It's too dangerous so she stays home."

I knew she was just trying to make me feel better, but I nodded, satisfied.

Lina put down the comb and reached around her neck. "Anna, take this and get some meat for Rivka." She removed the thin gold chain she always wore, the necklace that was once our mother's.

Once I would have told her no. Once I would have said nothing was worth trading that meaningful keepsake.

Now, I pocketed it silently and stared at my sister.

"I'm so worried something is going to happen to you." Lina's voice broke, the calm façade she affected suddenly cracked wide open. "I couldn't bear it."

"I'll be fine," I said breezily. "Nothing is going to happen to me."

It was dark in the sewers even with precious matches—it took several trips to learn where to jump, where not to step, and where to hold one's breath. Now, I moved quickly and quietly, my motions fluid and my senses sharp, feeling for holes with the tips of my shoes and breathing through my mouth.

There was skill, too, in coming out the other side. I had to know where to go so I didn't exit the tunnels in the middle of the road and be seen. I had to pick the right path, and scout my surroundings. Force my way out only an inch or so at a time.

The stink of the sewers was worse than usual that night, and I had to use my mouth to breathe nearly the entire way. It felt unnatural and my heart beat faster as I navigated the landscape. I worried my uniform would stink and give me away once I came out the other side. Why should a schoolgirl smell so bad?

I tried not to look down in the tunnels. The garbage and sewage did not bother me so much anymore, but the insects still scared me. Shiny black beasts with tiny horns; hairy monsters with too many legs. If you weren't fast enough, they would crawl across your shoes or brush against your ankles. And you couldn't scream.

Cautiously, I emerged from the rank tunnels into a quiet side street, the sewer cover obscured by a huge oak tree. I straightened my pleated skirt and smoothed the escaped strands of damp hair. Nearby, a cat watched me, sniffing as I walked by.

I had nearly reached the high street when I felt someone behind me. I could sense him before I heard the fall of boots against the pavement or smelled the alcohol on his clothes. The tiny hairs on the back of my neck rose. I walked faster, but then so did he, and that's when I started to run.

"*Fräulein!*" he shouted behind me, and I ran faster, terrified.

"Fräulein!" He was closer now, and tears pricked the corners of my eyes.

"Come on, pretty girl," he slurred. "Come give me a kiss, eh?"

Revolted, I turned the corner to the high street, panting. The man staggered up behind me, grabbing my arm for support. It was a Nazi soldier, and he was very drunk.

"Kiss me," he said again, angry now. "Kiss me now, you Polish—"

He stopped speaking abruptly and slid to the ground, like a snake slithering down a garden fence. Stunned, I stared at his collapsed form and came face to face with a serious-looking young man about Lina's age.

"You shouldn't be around here," he snapped in Polish, breathing heavily. He looked at the drunken soldier, then at his own hand, which was clutching a large textbook. "Oh Lord, he's dead. I'll be shot for sure."

"He's not dead," I said quickly. "He's still breathing. He's just drunk." I longed to kick the soldier, but dared not. "Did anyone see you?" I was afraid to turn around.

He craned his neck and had a furtive look. "I don't think so. Dare we move him?"

I considered it. "No," I said finally. "Better people think he just collapsed drunk. Let's get out of here."

We walked hurriedly, the Polish boy staring at me curiously. "How old are you?" he asked.

"Does it matter?"

"I figured you were older, the way he was shouting at you, but you're just a child." He shook his head. "What are you doing here, near the ghetto? It isn't safe."

"What are *you* doing here?" I countered. "How old are *you*?"

"I'm nineteen," he said, irritated, and he turned a deep red. The hand that wasn't holding the book formed a small, defensive fist.

"Flat feet," he said shortly. "That's why I couldn't fight. I'm not a coward, you know."

"Coward?" I squinted at him, trying to understand. "Who said you were?"

"I couldn't join the army," he explained. "I wanted to."

"You might be dead now, if you did," I pointed out. Now that the soldier was behind us, I felt calmer. "Or in a German labor camp." We'd heard that's where many of the Polish army prisoners ended up. "Having flat feet seems like a blessing to me."

He didn't answer, and I could see from the flush in his cheeks he was ashamed for *not* being dead or in a camp. Boys, I decided, could be very strange.

"Never mind," he said. "What are you doing here?"

I looked him over again, weighing my options. *Could he be trusted? Is he the sort who'd turn someone in for trying to trade on the black market?* I hesitated, then made a decision. He'd knocked a Nazi flat out with a book, after all.

"I'm trading," I said boldly. We were on the main street now, crowded even for the time of day and falling rain. At the far end of the street, I could see a group of Nazi soldiers. I wondered how long it would be before they found their friend.

"Trading?"

"I have gold. I need meat." I reached into my pocket and pulled out Mama's chain. It hurt to look at it, to imagine it around someone else's neck. "Do you know anyone who could help me?"

It was a tricky business, trading. Usually, Sam told me where to go and who to see. He had ways, Masha said evasively, of communicating to those on the outside.

The boy shook his head slowly. "You need the black market for that," he said. He looked uncomfortable.

Frustrated, I shoved the necklace back in my pocket. I supposed that's how Sam made his connections. I was foolish to come on my own, I realized. I felt a surge of hot shame and anger.

"If it's meat you need, though, I can get you some." He gave me a sideways glance, and I could see pity in his eyes as he sized up my scrawny frame. "My uncle is a butcher. I may be able to get you some scraps."

I stared at him. Overwhelmed with gratitude, I was unable to speak. "Thank you," I whispered.

"I can't promise anything good," he said, looking embarrassed. "The Nazis take all the good meat for themselves."

"Of course," I said quickly. I didn't want him to realize who I was or that I had come from the ghetto. "I just—my cousin is pregnant, and the baby seems small. Her belly, I mean. It should be bigger by now."

"Come with me."

I followed him through the streets, half expecting a group of Nazis to jump out and catch me for sneaking out of the ghetto, for attacking an officer, for being a Jew. I wondered, too, whether following a stranger down small streets was foolish. I reconsidered my earlier judgment. *Who is this boy?* How did I know he was trustworthy? He seemed nice enough, but what if he planned to turn me in? Could he possibly tell I was Jewish? Would he have helped me if he'd known? I stared at him, my mind racing.

He looked over at me as if he could feel my gaze. "I know what you're thinking," he blurted as we crossed a puddle-soaked corner together. "I'm not a coward. I wanted to fight the Nazis. These stupid feet." He breathed deeply, then continued. "My brother went, and he's missing. Probably in a work camp, like you said. We haven't had a letter from him. My other cousin, too."

"I'm sorry," I said, exhaling. He didn't seem like he was

plotting to turn me in. "That must be very hard. I have a sister, and I would find it terrible to be separated from her."

"It is," he said quietly. He peered at me. "Did your father or brothers go off to fight?"

I blinked, startled. "I have no brothers," I said truthfully. "And my father was too old."

He bowed his head. "Mine is dead."

"My mother is dead."

Our eyes met and we both nodded, a kinship in our mutual losses. I was no longer worried he was a murdering lunatic or planning to turn me in. He walked faster after that, as if propelled by nervous energy, and I had to rush to keep up.

"It's just around here," he said, motioning. "My cousin should still be there, cleaning up."

We passed by an older man closing up a tobacco shop for the night. The boy said hello to him, but the man stared at us contemptuously and said nothing, turning away.

"He and my uncle don't get along," whispered the boy. "My name is Jerzy, by the way."

"Anna," I said, then immediately regretted it. What was wrong with me, not making up a name?

Jerzy pushed the door open, where a boy his age with similar features was mopping a mess of blood and entrails. The smell was terrible, and I went back to breathing through my mouth.

He paused, leaning against his mop for support. "Jerzy," he said, frowning. "What are you doing here? And who's the little girl?"

I bristled at "little girl" but said nothing.

"This is Anna. She's looking for some meat scraps. Her cousin is pregnant, and the baby isn't growing. Anna, this is my cousin Pavel."

"Hello," I said bravely, trying to sound older. "We would be very grateful for whatever you can spare."

I noticed immediately that Pavel's face had softened when Jerzy mentioned the baby.

"My mother is expecting, too," he said. "The rations aren't enough." He shook his head, waving the mop in synch. "I don't have much, but I can give you something. Follow me."

Pavel leaned his mop against the counter, and I followed him to the back, my shoes squeaking against the damp floor.

"This is all I have," he said apologetically. He gestured to a small mound of something squiggly and pink on a block of wood at the back. "My father trades this for extra bread. In the old days, we gave it to the dogs." He scooped a few tablespoons' worth into some brown butcher's paper and began to wrap it.

"I'm sorry, but any more and my father will notice and beat me."

"Of course," I said hastily. "This is so very kind of you."

"What is it?" asked Jerzy, leaning in curiously. "It doesn't even look like meat."

"Entrails," said Pavel matter-of-factly. "Pig intestines."

Pig intestines. I felt nauseated. In my heart, I'd never been religious—nor had Lina or Tateh—but we had always followed the Jewish dietary customs. No milk with meat, no pork. I took a deep breath, forgetting not to use my nose. The smell of fresh blood was pungent, and my stomach heaved.

"Are you alright?" Jerzy looked concerned. "You look pale."

"Yes," I managed. "I'm sorry, I'm not used to the smell." I inhaled deeply through my mouth and composed myself. I was sure I had learned in my Jewish studies that to save a person's life, you were allowed to overlook the commandments.

I wouldn't tell anyone it was pork.

"Ah." Pavel nodded knowingly. "The blood." He handed me the small package.

"Thank you," I whispered. I reached into my pocket for the necklace and thrust it at him. "Please, take this as a token of my family's thanks."

Pavel looked down at the gold chain and recoiled. "Oh, no," he said, pushing my hand away. "I'm doing what any good Christian would do." Stammering my thanks, I wondered briefly if he'd have given me the meat if he'd known I was Jewish. I thought of Roza on the playground. People could act strangely when they were scared.

I followed Jerzy out as we both slipped slightly on the damp cobblestones.

"I should walk you home," he said, glancing at the sky. "It's getting dark."

Panicked, I pulled away, wracking my brain for an excuse; he couldn't know where I had come from.

"You've helped enough," I said hastily. "I've already taken up so much of your time."

"I insist," he said firmly. "You really shouldn't be out on your own. That wasn't the only drunk Nazi out tonight."

"I'm fine." I began to walk faster. "You should go home.

You hit that soldier, after all," I said. "They may be looking for you."

"I don't care." Jerzy hurried to keep pace with me. "I should make sure you get home. Where do you live?"

"I—my father said not to tell anyone where I live," I improvised. "I'll be in trouble."

"Well, alright then." Jerzy looked unconvinced but resigned. "If you need anything, just come back to Pavel here at the butcher shop. He'll know where to find me."

"Thank you," I said, relieved. "I really am grateful."

As soon as his back was turned, I dashed off into the night.

Chapter 6

LINA
Spring, 1940

THE TYPHOID FEVER came down like an army invading the Warsaw ghetto. Overcrowded and starving, we were an easy target. Tante Rachel was the first person close to me to die, and I anxiously hovered over Anna and Tateh, who thankfully showed no signs of illness.

"Why do you look at me like that?" Tateh appraised me three days after we loaded the body of Tante Rachel onto a cart bound for somewhere outside the ghetto walls. We were no longer able to bury our dead properly, but we could still sit shiva, the seven days of mourning for the Jewish dead. My father sat on the floor of our small room. Usually, one would tear a piece of clothing when a close relative died, and Tateh was Rachel's brother. This was no longer necessary now that our clothes were already tattered. Tateh rolled up a ripped sleeve and studied me.

"No reason," I said quickly. Only immediate relatives sat shiva; I kept my father company but continued with my responsibilities, cleaning and cooking and caring for Rivka. With the typhoid pandemic everywhere, I worried that she would get it, too. I stared across the room where she lay silently, asleep.

"I'm frightened for Rivka and the unborn baby," I said, not wanting to admit I had nightmares of his and Anna's death.

Anna was out again, God knows where, skulking through sewer tunnels for bread and meat. The meat she brought last had tasted unlike any kind I'd had before.

"Veal, I think," she'd answered vaguely when prompted. "Or maybe duck? I'm not sure."

I had never had pork, but I knew this must be what we were eating. I said nothing, though—why tell the others? Masha's eyes met mine, and I knew she must know as well. We were long past worrying about Jewish kosher laws—the animals whose meat was smuggled in from beyond the walls could not have been blessed by a proper rabbi. Still, eating pork felt different. It felt final, somehow, a tacit acknowledgment that our lives were never going back to being what they had been.

"I will rise tomorrow from shiva," my father said abruptly. He stared at his hands, but I could still see the sad expression in his hazel eyes.

"Tomorrow?" I was taken aback. "But it isn't yet seven days."

"These aren't normal times." My father shrugged, and I noticed how tired he looked. How old. He fingered his pipe sadly. Though we'd long since run out of tobacco, he still kept it close, like a talisman.

"I'm needed. I can still work. I don't want to sit here, useless but eating the food." His tone was firm.

"I can understand that," I said finally, nodding.

"Yes," he agreed. "At least I can be useful."

Tateh had become a librarian and teacher of sorts, cataloguing books that had been brought into the ghetto. He worked with children, mostly, and I knew the work was key to keeping his spirits up.

"How is the library?" I asked.

His demeanor brightened.

"It's growing," he said, looking pleased. "More people than you might expect brought books with them into the ghetto."

I nodded, and we fell silent. I thought of the books buried deep in the basement of our old home. *Would we ever see them again? Would anyone ever find them?*

Masha came in, noisily breaking the silence. She had a way of entering and exiting that demanded acknowledgment, the opposite of how Anna slipped in and out like a cat.

"How's Rivka?" she asked.

I shook my head. "She's still asleep."

Masha muttered something that sounded like a curse. I admired Masha's transformation. She had gone from pleasant, docile housewife to strong and fierce leader, someone to rely on and look up to. She held a bottle of white liquid tightly in her right hand.

"Is that milk?" My voice was breathless, trembling slightly. We so rarely had any. There were no cows in the ghetto and our rations were meager.

"Yes."

I waited for her to elaborate, but she said nothing.

"Half for Rivka, and half for Anna," said Masha, and she looked beadily at Tateh and me as if we might argue and drink the milk ourselves.

"Of course," I said. Tateh said nothing.

Masha walked toward Rivka, her boots heavy and wet on the floor. I gritted my teeth at the marks she left behind but said nothing, resigned to my domestic role while Masha and Anna came and went. Where did Masha get milk? And how? She certainly wasn't small enough to slip through the gates or the sewers.

"Rivkale," Masha whispered, laying a gentle hand on Rivka's shoulder. "Rivka. Wake up."

Rivka made a soft mewling sound, like a kitten. Masha frowned, and placed a hand on Rivka's forehead and neck in quick succession.

"She's burning up!" Masha nearly dropped the precious milk but recovered and thrust it in my direction. I grabbed it, cradling it like a newborn.

"She's got the fever?" Alarmed, I set down the milk. "We need to find the doctor."

Masha didn't answer immediately, deep in thought.

"She'll never make it," she said finally.

"Masha! We need to help her."

"What we need to do," said Masha evenly, "is make the baby come."

"Oh, my God." I shook my head, frightened. "Masha, no!"

"Should we let them both die then?" Masha's lips were thin and tight. She looked grim but resolved. I stared down at Rivka, who I could now see was flushed with fever.

I turned to Masha. "What do we need to do?"

She shook her head. "I don't know. I'm going to find a midwife."

"Not a doctor?"

She laughed mirthlessly. "The doctors are all men. They don't know the secrets women share. A midwife will know how to save the baby."

She disappeared as loudly and suddenly as she had arrived, the door slamming behind her.

"Tateh?" I realized he had been quiet the entire time Masha had been there.

He said nothing, regarding me thoughtfully. I felt uneasy.

"Tateh?" I said again.

"Masha," he said finally. "You realize what she is? Where she gets all the extra food?"

"No," I admitted, embarrassed. I had never bothered to think about it.

He exhaled loudly. "She's involved with the *Judenrat*," he said. "That's how she does all this." He gestured at the milk.

The Judenrat. The Jewish Council responsible for the day-to-day running of the ghetto, the link between us and the Nazis. I felt cold. I knew they tried to do good things—like redistribute food and medicine to those who most needed them—but they also policed us. It was impossible to speak about the Judenrat without a degree of mistrust. Did Masha really work for the Judenrat?

"How do you know?"

"Everyone knows," he said pityingly.

I bristled. "Is that why you don't speak to her!" I stared at the bottle of milk in my hand.

"The Council doesn't like some of what I do with the children and the books," he said. "We have…philosophical differences on culture and teaching."

Philosophical differences? I closed my eyes, a throbbing deep in my temples.

"I would never work for the Judenrat," he continued. "But someone has to do it. We shouldn't judge her too harshly. Still, you should know."

I nodded mutely. I should know. I should have known already.

"Don't judge yourself either, Lina," said Tateh gently, and I didn't have to ask what he meant. I'd been so focused on our family and Rivka and keeping everyone alive, I hadn't turned my mind much to what was going on outside. The bigger picture. It wasn't like me, but it was how I kept my sanity.

Across the room, Rivka moaned softly in her sleep, and Tateh and I glanced at each other worriedly.

"Are we doing the right thing?" I asked out loud.

Tateh put a hand on my arm. "There is no right thing anymore," he said.

We waited in silence for Masha to come back. Rivka grew steadily worse over the next few hours. Masha returned with Chana, a midwife in her fifties, Anna close on their heels.

"What's happening?" Anna's cheeks were flushed with the night air. "Is Rivka having the baby?"

"Something like that," I said grimly. I eyed my sister. "Where have you been all this time?"

Anna ignored my question but handed me a parcel.

"Eggs!" she sang out.

"Eggs!" I cradled them gently. "Oh Anna, three of them! How…?"

She shrugged. "I may have kept an extra. Don't tell Sam."

I looked worriedly over at Masha, but she wasn't listening.

"Where is that useless husband of Rivka's?" asked Masha instead, looking around disgustedly.

"He's been forced to work at the clothing factory," said Tateh softly. "But I think you know that, Masha."

I stared from one to the other, uncomprehending. Then it dawned on me. Masha knew exactly where Dov was and had planned the timing accordingly.

So he couldn't stop her.

"Masha…," I began, reaching to put my arm out as if to stop her. The horror in my eyes must have been evident, because she brushed me aside and cut me off immediately.

"Better that they should both die?" she asked harshly. "Another day, she'll be one more body on the wagon, the baby dead inside her."

I shuddered, my stomach roiling.

"Masha, what is it you plan to do?" I thought back to the night that her own husband had died, blood spattered over the basement of the old building. I stared at Chana. *Would she really do this?*

"I have...things," Chana said grimly. "Things that will make the baby come."

"Things?" I stared at her. "In the ghetto?"

"We had one suitcase," she said simply. "I brought what I knew would be needed."

Chana pulled a small glass vial of something from a battered leather bag.

"I'll help," said Anna grimly, walking over to Chana.

"No!" I cried out.

"I. Will. Help," said Anna. She said each word slowly, enunciating.

I looked at my baby sister and felt a mixture of emotions. Horror at the situation. Pride at her bravery. And worst of all a small twinge of satisfaction that Rivka's share of the milk would go to Anna. Immediately, I was ashamed by my feelings and I blinked hard, shaking my head as if to exorcise such terrible thoughts.

"Anna," I said, staring at her boldly. "Before you do anything. There is milk over there. Please go drink it."

"But...," she twisted to look at me, her face full of protest. "We'll need it for the baby, when it comes."

The baby. Of course. It would have no mother to nurse it. How would we feed it? How would it survive, when Rivka died? We had one tiny bottle of milk.

I cast a desperate glance at Masha as Chana busied herself stirring her witch's brew. It had a vaguely alcoholic scent, mixed with something citrusy and sweet.

"Who will nurse the baby?" I ventured. "Is there someone here who can take her in?"

Masha looked away. "Yes," she said shortly. "There is a woman across the road who will take her. Her own baby was stillborn last night."

"Oh," I said. I felt awkward, remembering Masha and her own dead infant.

Anna was watching Chana with frank curiosity. "What's that? That you're mixing?"

Chana looked at Anna, surprised.

"Lemon verbena," she answered. "And mineral oil. It will bring on contractions." She regarded Anna appraisingly. "Planning to be a midwife?"

Anna squared her shoulders proudly. "A scientist, actually," she informed her. "Like Madame Curie."

We all stood dumbly while Chana spooned the mixture into Rivka's mouth. Her lips were parched with fever, cracked and marked with deep cuts like incisions.

"How long will it take?" asked Anna.

"Usually within a day," answered Chana, dripping the last of the liquid onto Rivka's protruding tongue. "Faster, I suspect, since she's ill and malnourished."

Anna nodded, as if this made sense to her, and perhaps it did. I had never paid much attention to her book about the human body. Maybe it contained all sorts of useful information, all the secrets of life and medicine.

We settled in to wait. I thought of praying but decided against it.

Hours passed in near silence. We ate the thin, weak soup I had prepared, sharing it with Chana though there was not even enough for four. Masha's eyes drifted nervously to the door from time to time, clearly concerned about Dov's return, and I too wondered where he was. Shouldn't he be here by now?

Suddenly, there was a great howl from across the room, a primal sort of sound. I jumped, shaken at its intensity. Rivka's back arched as she cried out, her arms and legs flailing. Chana rushed over in time to thrust a rusted bedpan beneath her. We all turned away except Anna and Masha as Chana hunched over Rivka, oblivious to the sounds and smells.

"It is getting closer," she said grimly. "She's nearly ready. Anna, please fetch some towels or cloths. Lina, please boil the water. We need everything to be sterile."

I nodded swiftly, grateful to have a job. I found my saucepan and got to work. Anna obediently found an armful of rags and brought them to me, looking frightened but brave. One by one, we dipped the rags in the frothing water and carefully hung them to dry. Chana soon motioned and we brought her several, which she used to clean poor Rivka. I had never seen someone in labor and was shocked at the mess.

"It's normal," Anna said, seeing my face. "To soil yourself. During labor."

"You're too smart for me," I answered honestly. "How do you know everything?"

Anna didn't answer, but suggested we light a fire to dry

the rags so that there would be something to wrap the baby in when he or she was born. I obliged, happy to be useful.

Rivka let out a wild shriek, and I winced, heart pounding. I stared at Masha, wondering if she was perhaps evil or mad or both, and the rest of us were enabling her heinous schemes. Masha didn't even look at me, busying herself assisting Chana.

"Where is Dov?" Anna asked, looking worried. "He should be back by now."

Tateh must have heard, for he rose from where he was awkwardly hovering at the far side of the room, embarrassed at Rivka's labor. His cheeks were hot.

"I'll go find him," he said, putting on his overcoat.

I glanced sideways at Masha, who made a face but didn't say anything.

Tateh left, and Anna glanced at the bottle of milk. "We should heat some. For the baby."

"Not yet," I said. This was something I had experience with. When Anna had been weaned by our aunt, I'd heated her milk and fed her from a little cup. "If we heat the milk now there will be nothing left by the time the baby arrives."

Anna looked at me, startled, as if to ask what I knew of heating milk for babies. I smiled at her, and her eyes went soft as she realized I was thinking of her.

Another hour passed. Rivka alternated between quiet moans and loud cries. The room stank of blood and worse, and I paced nervously back and forth. *Is the baby even alive?*

"I can feel it moving," announced Chana, as if reading my thoughts.

"How much longer?" Exhausted, my shoulders sagged. "Will it be soon?"

"It should be," said Chana, shrugging. "Babies are not an exact science."

I nodded, wiping my brow. I recalled Anna's birth, the stops and starts and screams. I tried not to think of how it ended.

"Crowning!" shouted Chana suddenly. "Lina, get the blanket ready."

Blanket? Desperately, I grabbed the largest two rags. Rivka screamed loudly as her entire body shuddered, her back arched high to the ceiling. Chana buried herself between Rivka's pale legs, groping and grasping.

"Here it is!" she shouted, and with one swift movement yanked the infant free. Predictably, it screamed, and Anna, Masha, and I heaved a simultaneous sigh of relief at its healthy lungs. I stared, shocked, at the umbilical cord, that alien-like tie between the mother and child. Anna's face glowed, enthralled at the miracle.

I held out the clean cloths, but first Chana shook her head and placed the baby on Rivka's bare chest. Rivka herself was only partially conscious, her face flushed with fever, but she seemed to be at least somewhat lucid.

"My baby," she rasped, her arms encircling it.

"A boy," whispered Chana.

"A boy!" I echoed. Tears sprang to my eyes. I watched, rapt, as Chana helped Rivka bring the baby to her breast.

Maybe she'll live, I thought, my heart full of hope. *Maybe she'll survive.*

My hope was short-lived, as Tateh chose that moment to return, the door slamming shut behind him. He was alone.

"Where's Dov?" asked Anna.

Tateh glanced over at Rivka, his face alighting with momentary joy as he noted the mewling newborn. Then he shook his head. My eyes widened.

"How?" I whispered.

"An accident," he said quietly. "A faulty ladder."

"Dov is dead?" Even stony Masha looked taken aback.

Masha looked over at the baby and the thankfully oblivious Rivka. "Dov," she said in a low voice. "The baby's name is Dov, after his father."

"Is—is there a body?" I turned to my father, my voice overcome with sorrow. This baby would never see his father.

Tateh shook his head. "They already took the body," he said, his voice barely audible. "The wagon…."

I nodded, resigned. Anna made a small noise and turned away.

Chapter 7

ANNA
Spring, 1940

RIVKA DIED the morning after the birth, the swaddled baby still on her chest. I had been watching them closely. Her slow, shallow breaths were like a swinging cradle, moving baby Dov up and down. When she stopped breathing, the baby stirred and cried softly, upset at the disruption.

Masha and Chana took turns sleeping. We'd all slept fitfully, with Tateh, Lina, and I taking turns to keep watch over Rivka and baby Dov, while either Masha or Chana helped latch the baby onto Rivka's breasts to feed when he cried. Chana explained that there was a bit of new milk before the main milk came in, and that the baby should drink as much of that as possible to conserve what little bottled milk we had. From time to time, Rivka would stir and mutter something incoherent, and one of us would place a cool hand or damp cloth on her fevered forehead.

I shook Lina, who'd dozed off. "Lina?"

Lina moaned softly, rolling slightly to the left on the floor.

"I think Rivka died."

Lina sat up. "Are you sure?"

"She's not breathing."

Lina scrambled to her feet, wincing as she rolled her head to one side and then the other, cracking it loudly. "Wake Chana."

I rushed to Chana, who was sleeping half slouched against the wall, crumbs of peeling paint dusting her gray wool shawl. I squeezed her arm gently, and her eyes fluttered open. She stared at me uncomprehendingly for a moment, then looked around and nodded. "Right," she said, remembering. "Does the baby need to feed?"

"I think Rivka is dead," I answered uncertainly. I looked over at mother and baby, now pulled apart. Lina had scooped up the baby and was swaying gently back and forth.

Chana nodded, resigned, and went over to where Rivka lay. She felt for a pulse first in Rivka's wrist and then her neck.

"She's gone." Chana's expression didn't change. She went over and roused Masha, who was curled in a ball like a cat. "Masha. She's dead."

Masha yawned and woke quickly, still feline-like as she sprang to her feet. "The baby?"

"Alive." Chana nodded over at Lina, who kissed the top of his tiny head. I felt a bond with the poor little thing, who now would never meet his mother, either.

"I'll go and speak to the wet-nurse," said Masha, grabbing her shawl. "Let her know the baby will be coming."

Tateh appeared. No one had thought to wake him, but he

was now at my side. "I'll get someone to take care of Rivka," he said quietly, and left.

I realized with a jolt what he meant: someone to take the body. I felt a wave of grief but quickly steeled myself.

"Chana," I said, calling her over. "My father is going to get someone for Rivka's body. We should prepare her."

Lina hung back with the baby as Chana and I gently washed Rivka's dead body, respectfully covering it with a sheet. She rocked the baby in a slow and continuous motion; a human rocking chair.

Masha returned, bursting through the door in a noisy panic.

"The wet-nurse is dead!" she said, breathing heavily. "The typhoid took her last night. We'll need to find someone else to feed the baby."

Chana said something under her breath and Lina huddled protectively over the baby. I stared from Masha to the baby and to Rivka's body beneath our last clean sheet.

"I'm going to find milk," I announced. I groped around the room for my school jacket.

Lina looked at me. "Anna, you've barely slept...."

"I'm going," I said firmly. I buttoned the jacket and tied the threadbare scarf around my neck. "I know someone who can help."

Masha looked over at me, interested, but said nothing. I knew she worked for the Judenrat. But there were rumors that she also worked for the Polish Resistance, something I'd overheard while bartering with Sam. He'd told me to mind my own business, but I'd managed to learn that there were apparently groups working against the Nazis both in and outside the ghetto. It made me feel there was still hope out there if you knew where to look. I had told none of this to Lina. Though I was younger, I had recently felt the urge to protect my dreamy sister.

"I'll be back with the milk." I tried to slip out the door, but it slammed loudly as if a wind had caught it. I had a vision of Rivka's spirit leaving the apartment and shivered as I clattered down the cement steps.

⁂

I hadn't been back to the butcher shop since the day I'd brought home the pork. I didn't like to frequent places or speak to people more than once if I could help it. If someone had the slightest suspicion, I'd be shot by the Germans. They wouldn't care how old I was.

I'd seen Jerzy again but I hadn't let him see me. I'd ducked behind a hedge until he'd passed. He was a kind person, and they asked the most questions.

Now I tried to remember the route, to retrace the steps from that evening. Surely a butcher would have some idea where to get milk. Butchers killed cows; cows made milk. I assured myself this wasn't a fool's errand as I hurried through the streets, distracting myself from the drizzling rain by jumping over the smaller puddles.

I must have made a wrong turn at some point, puddle-hopping, because I couldn't find the shop. Panicked, I hurried back to the last street corner I was sure was correct and shut my eyes briefly to reorient myself.

"Lost, girl?" I opened my eyes to find a drunken Pole towering over me, leering. As he leaned in closer, I could smell liquor on his breath.

"I'm fine." My entire body shook as I tried to turn away, squaring my trembling shoulders.

"There you are!" A younger voice, vaguely familiar. I opened my eyes to see Jerzy, waving frantically. "Anna!"

Jerzy smiled at the Pole. "She's my sister," he said. "She's been unwell. Flu."

At the word flu, the Pole recoiled. He muttered something and shuffled away.

"You need to be more careful," Jerzy scolded me, grabbing my elbow. "It's not safe on the streets."

"I'm not a child," I shot back, feeling stubborn and grateful at the same time. "I'm going to be thirteen in the summer."

Jerzy rolled his eyes but kept his hand firm on my elbow as we navigated a larger group of soldiers.

"What are you doing out here, anyway?" He turned to look at me with a small frown. "Shouldn't you be in school?"

I struggled to think of a good answer. In truth, I had completely forgotten about school.

"My cousin had her baby," I said instead. "She died. We need milk for the baby. I was—I thought maybe your cousin would know where we can get some."

Jerzy exhaled loudly, shaking his head. "I'm sorry." His voice softened. "These are terrible times." He scratched his head with his spare hand, thinking.

"Can he help?" I asked, uncertain now. "I thought…."

"My uncle lost his shop," Jerzy said flatly. "He's been sent to a labor camp somewhere."

Stunned, I nearly tripped. The shop was gone?

Jerzy steadied me. "Are you alright?"

"Yes." I straightened my uniform. "I'm just…surprised." Exhausted from the previous night, my resolve began to crumble. My throat felt thick with the urge to cry.

Jerzy kept walking, still clutching my elbow. He lowered his voice. "It was the man who had the shop near his. Remember I told you they didn't get along? He told the Germans."

"What did he tell them?" I kept my own voice quiet.

"He said my uncle was in the Polish Resistance." Jerzy shook his head and made a derisive noise. "He's a butcher with a bad leg!"

"I'm sorry," I said, feeling sorry for myself too. Where would I find milk now?

Jerzy sighed. "I may be able to get you some milk. I know someone who has a cow."

My heart leapt. "A cow?"

"Yes." We were clear of the soldiers now, and Jerzy paused, looking thoughtful. "It will be a bit tricky, though, with the curfew." He chewed his lip, frowning, then fumbled in his pocket and retrieved a crumpled piece of paper and a bit of chalk.

"Write your address for me, and I'll bring it to you." He thrust them at me. "There's no sense both of us risking being caught after curfew."

I held the paper in my hand, staring at it. I didn't move.

"Well?" He looked at me curiously. "What's wrong?"

"I—I can't." I thrust the paper back at him. "Thank you anyway."

He cocked his head to one side and stared at me, baffled. "But why?"

Now the tears came. "I can't tell you!"

I broke into a run, desperate to get home. Maybe they found another mother to take the baby. Surely someone could take in little Dov.

"Anna!" Jerzy caught up with me and grabbed my arm again. "What are you doing?"

"Jerzy, please." I was weeping openly now. It was frigid out, and I could feel the tears cool and freeze on my cheeks. "I need to go home now."

"I'll walk you, then."

"No!"

"Anna, I…." Suddenly, realization dawned on his face, and his expression changed from confusion to horror.

"That's why you were near the ghetto," he breathed. He looked stricken. "You live there. You're one of the children they talk about. That's why you're so thin."

"I'm not a child," I snapped. I breathed deeply, trying to clear my head. "Who talks? What do you mean?"

"The children that come in and out of the ghetto. For

81

food. Everyone knows." He shook his head. "You could be killed, Anna."

I felt as if I'd swallowed a knife. "Jerzy—please. Please don't turn me in."

Jerzy made a small noise, looking at first aghast and then offended. "You think I would turn you in? Do I look like a monster?"

Abashed, I shook my head. "I'm sorry. I just...."

"I'm not a snitch, either, like my uncle's neighbor, that rat." He spat on the ground and then looked at me, angry.

My heart was racing so fast I thought I might collapse right there on the pavement.

"I can get the milk," he said finally. "Can you meet me tomorrow?"

"Yes," I said. "Yes, tomorrow."

He wanted to walk me back to the ghetto, but I wouldn't let him. He didn't realize that he was in danger now, too.

"I couldn't get the milk today," I announced as I walked inside our flat. I didn't say hello, nor did I make eye contact with anyone in case they could tell I had put us all in more danger. "I can get some tomorrow."

"Anna?" My sister's voice made it clear she could tell something was wrong. Baby Dov was swaddled in a blanket and crying softly in Lina's arms. "Did something happen?"

"I just—I couldn't get it. I'm sorry." I sat down heavily. "I'm so sorry."

"Stop it," Lina said sharply. "This isn't your fault."

I ignored her and looked around. "Where is everyone?"

"Chana has gone to help others. Masha is looking for milk, or another mother to take the baby. Tateh is still trying to find someone to take Rivka's body."

A sob caught in my throat. "Has the baby had anything to eat?"

"Yes. We still had the bottle of milk, and he did nurse a bit from Rivka before she passed. Chana says his stomach is very tiny right now and doesn't need much."

As if on cue, Dov began to cry.

"How do we know for sure?" I watched as my sister rocked him back and forth, shushing him quietly. "How do you know he's not hungry?"

"I don't know." Lina's face was strained and tired. "I don't know anything."

"Can I hold him?" Tentatively, I put out my arms. "Have a rest, Lina. You look exhausted."

Lina looked relieved and grateful as she handed the little bundle to me. She sat down and rested her head on the table.

"I'm just going to close my eyes for a few minutes," she said, yawning.

"Go rest, Lina," I said kindly. "Please."

She didn't answer—she was already asleep.

I stood with Dov in my arms and mimicked my sister's movements, rocking and swaying and whispering softly. "Shush," I murmured as he stirred.

I began to sing. I hadn't sung since we'd come to the ghetto, and it felt strange. I sang a Yiddish lullaby to the little newborn:

Shlof mayn kind, mayn treyst, mayn sheyner,
Shlof zhe, lu-lu-lu.
Shlof mayn lebn, mayn kaddish eyner,
Shlof zhe, zunenyu....

Sleep my lovely child, my comfort,
Sleep, lu-lu-lu.
Sleep my life, my only kaddish,
Sleep, my little boy....

❦

"Milk," said Jerzy triumphantly the following day. He handed me a bag and I peered inside: four glass bottles. I gasped, my breath a small cloud of smoke in the morning air.

"Thank you," I managed to say, almost speechless. I hugged the bag tight to my chest.

"You should have some too," he said gruffly, blushing. "You look so thin." He shoved his hands in his jacket pockets, fidgeting with something.

I said nothing. I didn't like to think about how I looked. I could feel the uniform hanging off my bony frame, getting baggier each week.

"Anna," he said quietly. "I may be able to help you. And the baby."

"You've already helped," I said quickly. "I'm so grateful, Jerzy. I don't want you to put yourself in any danger."

He waved his hand. "Anna, listen." He leaned in closer,

nervously looking around even though we were the only two on the street. "There's a woman who can help you, a Polish social worker. She goes in and out of the ghetto as a nurse and she gets people out. Children."

"Out?" Confused, I frowned. "Out where?"

"She gets them false identification papers, Anna. Then she takes them to live with Polish families."

She gets people out. I imagined little Dov with a new family. Somewhere in the Polish countryside, maybe with lots of grass and trees. Maybe with a cow for milk.

I breathed deeply, again watching my breath. "Who is this woman?"

Jerzy took out the paper he'd been fiddling with in his pocket and pressed it into my hand. "Her name is Jolanta. She's at this address, a makeshift hospital of some kind."

I stared at the crumpled piece of paper in my hand. "How do you know all this?"

Jerzy grinned. "My uncle…it wasn't a total lie, you know. He may have a bad leg, but he was still running messages wrapped in butcher's paper. He's the one who got me involved."

I had a tough time picturing Jerzy as a courier or a smuggler, but then I wasn't a typical smuggler, either. War had a funny way of turning us into people we'd never imagined we'd be.

"Thank you." I folded the paper neatly and tucked it into my pocket. I wondered if Masha knew anything about this nurse who trafficked in false papers and smuggled children.

Jerzy hesitated, as if deciding to say more. "You should think about trying to get out, too," he said finally.

I stiffened. "I'm not leaving my sister and father."

He nodded. "I understand. But if you need more milk…."

"It's not safe," I shook my head. "You'll get caught and it will be my fault. If we keep meeting like this, someone is bound to notice."

He opened his mouth to argue but then closed it, resigned. I was right and he knew it.

"Thank you," I said. "For the milk and for…." I searched for the right word. I recalled how badly he felt about not being able to go fight. "For being brave."

He went red. "I'm not brave."

"Of course you are!" I smiled at him. "I'll remember your kindness, Jerzy. Be careful."

"You, too, Anna." He smiled back, and I clutched the bag of milk as I turned back toward the sewers.

Chapter 8

LINA
Spring, 1940

WE DIDN'T TELL Anna we were sending her out of the ghetto as well.

When Anna returned, breathless and full of stories, I was so grateful for the abundance of milk that, at first, I paid little attention to the slip of paper with the name "Jolanta" on it. Send Rivka's baby out of the ghetto? To a stranger? What if they were caught and the baby seized by Germans? I didn't put it past the Nazis to harm a baby. A week before, they'd shot a trio of five-year-old boys for sneaking through the fence.

I fretted over whether to tell Masha. Masha was a person who got things done and she might be a source for more information about food and medicine and hiding places. But since she was a member of the Judenrat, I worried that she might tell someone else on the board, and they would send us to be shot.

"They're not all bad," pointed out Tateh about the Judenrat after I confided my fears. "Some say many of them are also involved in resistance efforts."

"Really?" I was surprised. "They're not afraid to be caught by the Nazis they're working with?"

Tateh shrugged. "I guess they feel they have very little left to lose."

"You've changed your tune, Tateh," I observed. "A week ago, you wouldn't even speak to Masha."

"I'm not too old to admit I don't know everything," he said softly. "It was Masha who saved the baby and got a proper funeral for Rivka. I've learned a lot this past week."

The death of Rivka and Dov and the birth of the baby had changed us all in some way. When our little cousin David, Tante Rachel's boy, also died of typhoid, I no longer felt indecisive.

As we mourned this little boy, I sought out Masha and explained what I had learned from Anna.

"It's probably too dangerous," I said, resigned.

Masha made a derisive noise and took the scrap of paper. Instead of fretting, she immediately tracked down the mysterious Jolanta and made arrangements for baby Dov.

"It's done!" she said matter-of-factly a day later, untangling herself from her worn woolen shawl. It was a frigid spring, and she stomped the snow from her caked boots. "They can get the baby out. There's a family willing to take him."

"A family?" My heart twisted as I held him in the crook of arm.

"Gentiles," she said brusquely. "In the countryside. He'll have milk, and meat when he's ready."

"Giving him away to Gentiles. What would Rivka think?"

I held the baby tighter, and he made a small stirring noise. I felt overwhelmed with guilt.

"Hopefully, she would be happy he isn't dead." Masha's voice was sharp and devoid of sentiment. "He'll leave in two days."

"He hasn't been circumcised." Tateh, who rarely said a word these days, spoke up quietly. He was sitting in the corner holding a book he'd already read three times. "We should have his *bris*. So, he knows who he is later."

"Better he doesn't ever know," retorted Masha. "He'll be safer without one."

"No," I said firmly, surprising myself. I shushed the baby and rocked him gently; he had begun to cry. "We will have the bris. It's eight days tomorrow. Masha, I am sure you can find us a *mohel*."

Masha scowled, as if tracking down a mohel to carry out the baby's ritual circumcision was both beneath her and a waste of her time.

"Have you thought of how risky this is, to do this here? Now? We could all be shot just for holding the ceremony."

I took a quavering breath. I wasn't used to arguing with someone like Masha. "If he's never going to know his parents and he's going to live with Gentiles, he needs to have the bris. He needs to be made a Jew. The Germans may hate us, but if we start hating ourselves, who are we?"

Masha was quiet for a long moment.

"Fine," she said, finally. "But he would be better off

without it." Abruptly, she turned on her heel and headed back through the door, into the snow.

"Sending him to stay with a Polish family is the right thing to do," said Tateh.

"You're sure?" I felt anguished. "Poles? Strangers, Tateh."

"They'll keep him safe," said Tateh simply. "He'll die here, Lina."

Dov let out a sudden wail, as if he'd heard my father. It was true—everyone around us was dying of hunger or the typhoid fever.

"We're going to die, too," I said out loud. Dov cried harder, and I rocked him, tears welling in the corners of my tired eyes.

Tateh didn't argue. "Send Anna," he said instead. "Send her, too."

"Anna?" I stared at him stupidly. "Our Anna?"

"She'll be safe and well-fed and after the war we can find them both."

I continued staring. *Send Anna away?*

"She won't go," I said. "She won't agree."

"She won't know. Don't let her know."

I searched for something else to say, some other reason not to let her go, then felt myself crumpling. "But Tateh, our Anna?"

"The children are dying, Lina." Tateh closed the book and put it down at his feet. "Typhoid, rickets. There isn't enough food. Even without disease, they aren't growing."

I handed Tateh the baby and went to warm a pan of milk. I lit the stove, watching the milk bubble slowly. Anna wasn't growing. Her clothes from last year still fit and even hung loose on her skinny frame. Her chest was still flat, and she showed no signs of womanhood. At her age, I'd been taller and I had begun developing. I wracked my brain. Had I seen Anna drink the milk I'd tried to give her? Or had she discreetly put it back for baby Dov?

"Do you think they'll take her?" My voice was small. "The family who takes the baby. Do you think they'd take her, too?"

"We'll make them take her," said Tateh roughly. Dov had stopped crying, quiet now in Tateh's arms. "Masha said they're helping children. Anna is a child. They have to take her."

"She can't know," I said. I took Dov back and hugged him to my chest. Tateh came over and wordlessly took the wooden spoon, stirring gently. "She'd never go, if she knew."

"No," agreed Tateh. He dripped a bit of milk onto his wrist to test the temperature, then removed the pan from the stove. "We'll tell her she's going to help Masha bring the baby."

"Right," I said. I dipped a finger into the milk and into the baby's mouth. Even Masha had been unable to procure baby bottles. He sucked it greedily. I dripped more milk onto Dov's tiny pink lips.

"It's the right thing to do, Lina," Tateh said again. "If I could, I would send you, too."

"I'm a grown woman. Old enough to have babies of my own, really."

"Thank God you don't," said Tateh grimly. "With Anna safe, you can worry about yourself. Keep yourself alive."

"And you?" I asked pointedly, searching for a dry cloth to diaper Dov.

Tateh stared at me but said nothing, the look on his face sad. I wanted to be hopeful, but Tateh seemed resigned to a darker fate.

"You're a healthy young woman," he said, as if reading my mind. "You need to be strong so you will survive."

I pinned the diaper and pulled the blankets tightly around the baby. It didn't seem so long ago that I'd diapered and swaddled Anna. I breathed deeply, trying not to cry so as not to upset my father or Dov.

"I will find her," I said, scooping up Dov. "And you will, too." Dov squinted at me with his baby blue eyes, and I kissed the top of his soft head, feeling his heartbeat against my lips.

❧

The bris was a small, solemn affair, with all of the angst but none of the joy that usually marks the ceremony. Masha had found a mohel, an older man whose shoulders shook when he coughed. We all watched with apprehension as he bent over Dov, flinching in expectation of another wracking cough. A bit of wine had been offered by a neighbor, and a thimbleful kept the baby sleepy and unaware. We kept our voices hushed and our eyes trained on the door out of fear of discovery.

There was no grandfather to hold the baby, so Tateh did it. Anna, curious as ever, watched closely, asking polite questions and playing the helpful assistant. When it was over, it was Anna who swaddled and held the baby against her while the rest of us shared what remained in the bottle of wine and a bit of bread.

"What will they call him?" I watched as Anna swayed with Dov. "I mean the Polish family. Dov is a Hebrew name."

Masha nodded. "They'll give him a new name, but we won't know what it is. This woman, though, this nurse—they say she keeps all the names."

"What does that mean?"

"They say she writes down each child's name on a slip of paper. Their real name on one side, and the new name on the other. She puts them in a jar."

"A jar?" I looked over at Anna and Dov and had a sudden vision of them with a pair of smiling Polish farmers. Their new family.

"She buries the jars in her garden," said Masha. "When the war is over, the names will be there."

From the distance, I watched Anna laugh at something Tateh was saying to her.

I said to Masha, "Anna will have a new name, too."

Masha looked at me pityingly. "Yes."

"A new name," I whispered. I sank my teeth into my cheek in an effort not to cry. "A name in a jar."

"So you can find her later," said Masha. She put a hesitant hand on my shoulder, and I startled at her touch. Masha never touched us.

"She won't be the same," I said. "She'll be someone else."

Masha's eyes met mine, and I saw a flicker of sadness there, behind the look of steel. "None of us are the same as we were."

"And she'll be safe?" It was a half-statement, half-question. I wanted reassurance.

"She will be safe," she answered firmly. "She will live."

I watched as Anna tried Tateh's wine, making a face. *She will live*, I told myself. *She will live, and I will find her.*

I will find her name in the jar.

※

We left in the evening. Tateh stood in the doorway, his eyes heavy with sadness. He couldn't say good-bye to Anna without her figuring out our plan.

"Be safe," he said, hugging her to him tightly. "I love you. Be careful."

"I'm always careful, Tateh," she said smiling. "You worry too much."

He stared at her, as if trying to memorize every detail of her face. I looked away so I wouldn't cry.

"See you soon," said Anna over her shoulder.

He nodded but said nothing. Instead, he held up his hand in a wave.

Masha hurried us through the streets, refusing to tell us where we were headed. Anna held the baby. I made a show of "hurting" my arm on the door and needing her help.

"I can take him, Lina," Anna offered quickly, as I feigned discomfort. "Let me help."

I felt a stab of guilt at the deception, momentarily tempted to blurt out the truth. Sensing this, Masha gave me both a warning look and a hard pinch on my arm that really hurt.

"This way," said Masha now, motioning. "Hurry."

It was snowing, the thick sort of snowflakes like little torn bits of paper. I could feel the worn soles in my boots give way to tiny holes and cracks, the cold and wet seeping in.

"Here," said Masha. "Through here."

"The courthouse?" I asked surprised. It was an old building, straddling the border between the ghetto and the outside world. Denied proper upkeep, the outer façade was weathered and peeling. Masha said nothing but led us inside, the building as dank inside as out. I looked around anxiously, as if Nazi soldiers might jump out from behind a door or desk and grab my sister and the baby. But the building was quiet. Here and there, people shuffled quietly through the halls, avoiding eye contact.

We followed Masha to the basement. A woman was waiting there, a woman not much older than myself with a kind smile.

"I am Jolanta," she said, crouching down to peer at Dov. "And who is this?"

"This is Dov," Anna smiled, tenderly kissing his forehead before holding him out to this stranger like an offering. "Masha promises you'll take good care of him."

I noticed then that she, like the rest of us, wore the yellow star on her arm. She must have seen me looking because she turned to me as she scooped up Dov.

"I wear it when I'm in the ghetto," she explained. "When

we go through the gates, though, I will take it off. The child should remove hers as well." She nodded at Anna. "Anna, isn't it?"

Anna frowned, taking a slow step back. "How do you know my name?"

Jolanta looked puzzled, her eyebrows raised at Masha and me.

"She doesn't know," I blurted out. "We haven't told Anna."

"Haven't told me what?" Anna's eyes widened, like a mouse being cornered by a hungry cat. "Lina, no!"

"You have to," I said. I rushed at her, grabbing her shoulders hard. "You have to go."

"I will not!" She writhed frantically. "I won't, Lina!"

"We need you to take care of the baby," said Masha quietly, intervening. She took Dov back from Jolanta and handed him to Anna. "We need someone we can trust to make sure he's protected."

Visibly struggling, Anna clutched at the swaddled mass. "I don't want to leave."

"Of course you do," I said bravely. "You'll have food, where you're going. And milk for Dov."

"Lina." Anna sobbed openly. "Lina, no."

"Yes," I said firmly. I knelt before her and loosened her armband. I removed it and tucked it inside my boot. Later, I would burn it.

"Be strong," I whispered. "And be brave."

"No tears now," said Masha, though I could see even she was struggling with emotion. "You're going to follow Jolanta.

On the other side of this building is a church. You've been at prayer there. Do you understand?"

"Yes," whispered Anna. "I understand."

"Does she know the paternoster?" Jolanta looked at me, and I felt a surge of panic. But Anna replied in perfect Polish, "Yes, I know it."

"How?" I stared at my sister, who shifted the baby to one arm so she could swat away her tears.

"They made me learn," she said. "When they gave me the school uniform. In case anyone ever suspected."

"Well, thank goodness!" I said, my knees weak. "Anna, I love you."

"I love you, Lina." We stared at each other, and I tried to memorize her face.

"Tateh!" she cried. "I didn't get to say good-bye!"

"But he did," I said softly. "He loves you so much. It was his idea. To keep you safe."

"We must go now," said Jolanta gently. "Come, Anna."

Anna remained frozen.

"Go," I said. My heart felt as if it had cracked clean in half, but I turned to Masha. "Let's go now," I said. "It will be easier if we leave first."

"Stay well and strong, Anna," I said. I turned my back to her. "I will find you."

I hurried toward the stairs before I could change my mind.

Part II

Chapter 9

ANNA
Summer, 1941

IT TOOK ME six months to answer to the name Maria, but after a year I started to forget I had ever been Anna. Once I learned to respond to a new name, it felt a bit like the old me began to disappear. Jolanta had promised me before she smuggled me out of Warsaw that she would keep my name in a jar in her garden, and sometimes I pictured myself and the baby trapped inside it, faces pressed against the glass.

Baby Dov was now Patryk, as if he had never been Dov at the start of his life. It was strange to think of him as anything other than Patryk, and of the Nowaks as anyone other than his parents. The difference between our endangered old life and our current safe one was so huge that I sometimes felt confused. Had any of it really happened? Was this life my "real" life and the old one with Lina and Tateh only a dream?

Jolanta had delivered us that day to a former soldier called Szymon, a scruffy, stocky young man who had escaped a German prisoner of war camp. Szymon was mostly silent, keeping words for when they were only totally necessary. He led us for three days, navigating the forests and a network of abandoned barns and farm cellars. The Resistance, it turned out, had safe houses dotting the Polish countryside.

"Don't trust anyone," Szymon hissed at me as I asked about the Resistance one late night in a damp hayloft. "Most people would happily turn you in for a bit of sugar."

I remembered Jerzy's uncle, whose neighbor had turned him in.

"I know," I said curtly.

Szymon rarely spoke above a whisper, when he spoke at all. It made me anxious that he would not speak to me, even if there was no one around for miles. When he did speak, it was in one-word replies, as if speech were being rationed like eggs or milk.

"Where are we going?" I would hike along beside him, panting as I struggled to keep up. "How do you know it's safe?"

"I know," he'd answer abruptly. "Quiet!"

"But where...?"

"Someplace safe."

"But...."

"Quiet!" The last was accompanied by a frozen stare. Frustrated, I fell silent and resigned myself to kicking rocks and stomping on leaves, until he shushed me for that, too. He wore the baby wrapped up on his chest beneath his coat so you couldn't even see Dov. When he cried, Szymon would stick a finger in his mouth and pray in Polish.

"If we are stopped," he said repeatedly, "we say that I am

delivering you to your father's cousin because your mother died and your father cannot take care of you."

"I know!" We were resting beneath a tree so I could eat a bit of bread. Szymon, as usual, did not eat. "I understand. I used to go through the ghetto tunnels, you know, and…."

"Too much talking." He shook his head, exasperated. "Do you want to get caught?"

"You spoke to me first!"

"Who am I?" he asked, ignoring me. "What's my name?"

I sighed. "Szymon Bielski. You are my mother's cousin's son. You are taking me and my baby brother to our father's cousin in the country because they have no children of their own."

"And their names?"

"Elsbietta and Marek Nowak." I tried not to roll my eyes. Szymon didn't seem to care that I was perfectly capable of remembering this story. I had excelled in school and memorized most of an anatomy textbook, never mind that I'd run my own secret operations in the ghetto.

"Feed him." Szymon thrust the baby at me, and I clambered to grab the tiny bundle and drip some milk into his gaping mouth before he started to wail and attract attention. I checked to make sure he was dry. We'd stopped an hour before to change his diaper, which annoyed Szymon.

"A baby," he muttered to himself, shaking his head. "A baby."

I ignored this, though I was sorely tempted to remind him that it was me who was feeding and changing the baby. As far as I could tell, Szymon's role was mostly to complain quietly and glare at me.

When he finally delivered us to the Nowaks' farm, however, I hung back, feeling surprisingly attached to him despite days of him scowling in my direction.

"Go on," he said gruffly, nodding at the couple standing in the doorway. I noticed the woman had reddish-gold hair not unlike my own. "They won't bite you."

I said nothing, staring at the ground.

"You're a good girl." He reached out and ruffled my hair. "Very good."

"I thought you hated me." I looked up at him. "You wouldn't speak to me!"

"I was afraid you would get killed." He shook his head, looking exhausted. "You and the baby. I could never forgive myself."

"Oh." It was my turn to fall silent, now that I understood.

"Come," he said, taking my hand. "Let's go meet your new family."

I swallowed. They couldn't be my family. I already had a family.

The Nowaks stood together on their porch, watching us approach. He—Marek, I reminded myself—was large and beefy with jovial brown eyes and a balding head; she—Elsbietta—was small and slender, her hair tied into a neat braid. Elsbietta hung back, looking shy and toying awkwardly with her apron strings, while her husband, red-faced, scooped me into a bear-hug.

"Maria!" he cried out, winking exaggeratedly. "So good to see you again, though we were so sorry to hear about your poor mother."

I stared at him blankly, momentarily forgetting the narrative. After all, my mother had been dead for twelve years.

"Marek." Elsbietta put a hand on his arm and smiled tentatively at me, her cheeks rosy and bashful. "Give her some space. She must be terrified, not to mention exhausted."

"I'm fine, ma'am," I said automatically.

"You must come in and have something to eat." Elsbietta guided me in gently, Szymon close at our heels. He still had Dov—Patryk—tucked into his coat. He undid it and carefully removed the sleeping infant.

"Oh!" Elsbietta and Marek both gasped, looking briefly at each other and then at the baby.

"May I…?" Elsbietta looked at Szymon hopefully, then at me.

"Of course." A relieved-looking Szymon dropped baby Patryk into Elsbietta's outstretched arms.

"He is your brother?" Marek patted me on the shoulder as we watched Elsbietta tenderly adjust the worn blue blanket.

"No," I said quietly. "He is…was a friend's baby. The parents both died."

Elsbietta looked up at me with fierce eyes. "We will not let anything happen to either of you."

"We always wanted children," added Marek. He watched his wife affectionately. "God never chose to bless us with any."

I took a closer look at Elsbietta and Marek and realized they were considerably older than I'd originally thought. About forty, maybe. Likely past the age where they would ever have children of their own.

Szymon cleared his throat. "The baby needs more milk." He gestured at his rucksack, now nearly empty. "We've run out."

"Of course!" Elsbietta perked up. "We have milk ready. And baby bottles."

I sighed with relief. Proper baby bottles—thank goodness. Finger-feeding an infant was a struggle when he was wailing to be fed.

"Come." Marek motioned for us to follow him into the farmhouse kitchen. I gaped at the size of the room. It was the size of our entire apartment before the war.

"My goodness!" I said. "Your house is huge." I wondered if Lina had ever seen a kitchen this size, and what she would make of the oversized wood-burning stove or the sink that looked as big as a bathtub.

Lina. I swallowed, feeling the familiar lump in my throat. Was she getting enough to eat? Was she well?

Was she still alive?

And if she wasn't, would I know somehow, in my soul? Or would I be going about my life here with the Nowaks while she died from typhoid fever?

"Sit," said Marek, motioning to a long wooden bench. Szymon and I sat obediently while he fetched some milk, bread, and cheese. "Eat."

I didn't reach for the food immediately, even though my stomach growled. I thought of Lina chiding me for my manners and didn't want to appear rude and greedy.

"Eat," urged Marek, pouring me some milk. "You are too skinny." He heaped a plate full of sliced bread and cheese and placed it before me.

"Thank you," I said, overwhelmed. I had not seen such an abundance of food in months. It didn't feel real. I poked at the earth-toned innards of the bread, marveling at their softness. In the ghetto, all the bread had been tough and stale.

I took a bite with a thick slab of hard cheese and chewed slowly, savoring it.

"We make the cheese here," Elsbietta said. She slid in next to me on the bench, cradling a sleeping Patryk in the crook of her arm. "We still have three sheep, and one cow."

"The Germans haven't noticed the cow yet," added Marek grimly. "We've hidden her in the barn behind a fake door."

"Do they take cows?" I asked. I imagined a ghetto of mournful cows, closely packed and underfed. Ribs prominent beneath spotted coats. Yellow stars around their necks in lieu of bells.

"Yes, for their own milk and meat," answered Elsbietta sourly. "Many of our neighbors have lost their livestock to the Germans."

"They took three of our sheep." Marek spat angrily on the ground. "Bastards."

"Marek!" Elsbietta looked scandalized. "Not in front of Maria."

She cast me a shy glance. "I hope you don't mind being called Maria. We don't know your real name."

Szymon looked up sharply. "To you it is Maria." He gave me a warning glance. "So long as you are only Maria, you are safe. You understand? All of you?" He looked meaningfully at Marek and Elsbietta before turning his angry gaze back to me.

"Yes. Yes, of course." Elsbietta looked abashed. She stood again, ostensibly to shush a waking baby Patryk, but I could see Szymon had unnerved her.

"You'll call us aunt and uncle," declared Marek. "Uncle Marek and Aunt Elsbietta."

I thought of my Tante Rachel, my favorite aunt, who'd so recently died.

"Thank you," I said instead, and then added shyly, "Uncle Marek."

Marek beamed at me, and I was grateful that I had been blessed with kind hosts. I watched Elsbietta with the baby, crooning softly to him in Polish. I didn't recognize the song, but she had a beautiful singing voice.

The baby stirred then, crying out, and for the first time in days I didn't panic at the sound. Szymon straightened involuntarily, looking alert and anxious, then relaxed. As Elsbietta handed over the infant to Marek and rushed to prepare a bottle, I reached for my own glass of milk, grateful the baby was safe.

This is how Lina must feel, I realized, and I felt less angry with her for sending me away.

❧

The days turned into weeks and then months, the seasons passing as I changed from Anna to Maria, and my adopted baby "brother" became a laughing toddler.

"Ria!" This was the name little Patryk called me. He took two unsteady steps toward me and then fell flat on his bottom. I laughed and clapped encouragingly so that he wouldn't cry, the bed sheets I was hanging to dry flapping in the wind in time to the applause. Patryk had begun walking in short bursts a few months ago, several days before his first birthday. His real first birthday, that is—the day he'd been born in the ghetto. The date on his fake identification papers was earlier and was the one we celebrated with songs and a real cake. We'd managed to trade some of our butter for eggs with our neighbors. The Nowaks' last chicken had disappeared months before, the victim of either Germans or wolves.

"Ria!" Patryk struggled to get back on his feet, grasping at patches of grass. "Ria!"

I clipped the last sheet corner to the clothesline and rushed over.

"Brilliant, Patryk!" I cried out, kissing the top of his head. At a year, he still had only wisps of hair, something that relieved me greatly. What if it grew in dark and curly like his father's? What if people suspected he had Jewish parents?

I tried to hold his hand, but he shook me away.

"No." He shook his head firmly, and I smiled at his resolve to do it himself.

"Maria?" The faraway voice was Elsbietta's, but it wasn't coming from the house. I frowned, looking around toward the vegetable garden.

"In the field," she called. "Can you come quick?"

"Yes!" I shouted back.

I bent to pick up Patryk, but he shook his head again, this time with scrunched up eyes and nose.

"No!"

"We have to go see Mama." The word felt natural now, no longer stinging. It no longer brought to mind memories of his birth mother, Rivka, dead from childbirth. Elsbietta was his mother now. The Nowaks loved Patryk, had parented him since he was weeks old. It was only natural he called them mama and papa—and easier to explain to neighbors or raiding Germans.

"Mama!" Patryk brightened. "Mama, Mama!"

"Yes! Let's go see her, shall we?" I put my arms out again, and this time he agreed to be foisted onto my hip.

It seemed I'd grown hips overnight. One day, I looked no different than Piotr from the neighboring farm, a boy my age who never spoke, and the next I'd had hips on which to rest Patryk. They had taken me by complete surprise, these odd new appendages. I'd grown much taller, too. It felt strange as though I was trying out a new body. My legs especially felt long and ungainly. Then, of course, there were the breasts.

"You're becoming a woman," explained Elsbietta. She blushed deeply as she provided me with a soft, white silk undergarment, exactly my size.

"Auntie, where did you get this?" I took it, turning it over in my hands. It was delicate and silky and, from my days of mending with Lina, I could tell it was well-made. I felt guilty at the thought of the Nowaks spending money on me.

"Never mind that," she said brusquely. "Do you know how to put it on?"

I didn't, but she helped me, even though it was awkward for both of us. It felt like my entire body was aflame as she showed me how to put it on and take it off.

"Thank you," I impulsively had thrown my arms around her neck. "Thank you for everything."

"Of course," she had said, and hugged me back. When we pulled away, I could see she was crying.

"Are you…are you okay, Auntie?"

"Yes." She dabbed at her eyes with a handkerchief. "Don't mind me. I just—I never thought I'd ever have a daughter to do this with. It's what I've always wanted, to have children. But we could never have any of our own."

She took a deep breath. "I feel guilty, Maria. This is the happiest I've ever been, but it's so wrong. There's a war going on, and you and Patryk have lost so much. I am so selfish."

"You're anything but selfish!" I grabbed her hand. "You are so wonderful to us!"

"You're so grown up, for your age." She shook her head. "Let me take care of you a bit. It's okay to just be a girl sometimes, you know."

I felt overcome with emotion. "I don't want to be a burden."

"A burden!" She pulled me to her, and I allowed myself to

111

rest my head against her slim shoulders. "You're anything but a burden. You are a blessing."

"Mama," demanded Patryk now. I nodded and kissed his head again as we made our way to the field. Elsbietta was there with the sheep, kneeling in the grass. I hurried over to join her.

"What's happened?" I asked, putting Patryk down. There was a sheep in the grass lying on its side. It moaned loudly, an unearthly sort of sound.

"Baa!" exclaimed Patryk.

"Yes, darling," I laughed, crouching down next to Elsbietta. "Sheep."

"Baa," he agreed.

"Something is wrong with Cilla," she said, nodding at the sheep. "I'm worried. She isn't eating and she seems like she's in pain."

The sheep were, technically, the property of the Germans—all farm animals had been confiscated by decree—but as no one had arrived to slaughter Cilla, Paulina, or Nadia, we had paid our dues to the Reich in sheep's milk and wool, stashing some of the supply for our own use and trade.

I put a hand on Cilla's belly, then another. Palpating gently with both hands, I frowned. "Auntie," I said. "Can you please get me the book?"

The Nowaks were not great readers. They had only five books in their home. One was a Christian Bible, but they also owned an illustrated veterinary text that I'd taken to reading and rereading. Every day I silently thanked my Tateh for owning a bookshop and teaching me to read not just Yiddish, but also Polish and German. Slowly, I'd built up a reserve of knowledge on animal health that first the Nowaks, and then our neighbors, were happy to make use of. The local veterinarian had been killed during the invasion, and there had been no one to replace him. In his absence, I filled a void. At first, Elsbietta was reluctant—she didn't want me to feel I somehow had to earn my keep—but as we grew closer, she realized how much I enjoyed it.

"A little Madame Curie," she said admiringly when I confessed my passion for science, and I felt a pang of homesickness, thinking of Lina and her tales of our own Mama.

"She's a remarkable girl," Marek said, tugging at my braid. "But too skinny."

It was our little joke. He constantly chased me with whatever extra food he could find. Elsbietta would roll her eyes and playfully whack him with whatever kitchen implement she happened to be holding.

Now, Elsbietta dashed away. Patryk frowned, glaring at me with hands on his hips.

"Mama," he said mournfully.

"She'll be back," I said easily. I turned back to the sheep, frowning. I stroked her between the ears, trying to calm her as she writhed in pain.

"Baa," said Patryk solemnly.

"Indeed," I murmured. I put my head on her belly and tried to listen for her heart. There it was, steady but rapid, like someone knocking hurriedly at the door to be let in from the rain.

"Here." Elsbietta returned, breathlessly clutching the book. I spread it open, studying the drawings of sheep innards intently.

"Her belly is swollen," I commented, noting the difference between Cilla and the drawings. I turned the pages, worried. Was it some sort of growth? It would be sad to lose Cilla, but also a serious hardship. The milk, cheese, and wool she produced were our main source of trade. Without them, finding things like new shoes for Patryk would be tough.

I put my ear back to Cilla's belly and felt a jolt as something moved inside. I frowned, but then flipped quickly through the book.

Could it be? Possibly. There was only one way to find out. I rolled up my sleeves and stared grimly at Cilla and Elsbietta.

"Stand back," I announced, moving between the sheep's back legs. "I need to check something."

Elsbietta scooped up Patryk and moved out of the way. I bent in toward the groaning sheep and with a deep breath, inserted a hand deep within her private regions. Grimacing, I felt around, trying to ignore the kicks and noise of Cilla as I tried to find what I suspected was there.

"There it is." I felt a small hoof and beamed with the satisfaction of being right. "She's pregnant."

"Pregnant!" Elsbietta's eyes grew wide with shock, then narrowed with suspicion. "That ram of the Kowalskis!"

"Yes," I agreed. "Remember he was lost? Ran away?"

"Broke out of his pen, more like," said Elsbietta. "Impossible beast."

"Well," I said, nodding at Cilla. "I guess this is where he went." I blushed, not being used to discussing such things aloud, but this was a farm. Even children understood the facts of life.

Elsbietta and I both stared at Cilla, contemplating her delicate condition, and then I frowned again, looking at the book.

"I shouldn't feel a hoof," I said slowly, studying the diagram. "I should feel a head."

"Oh!" said Elsbietta, nodding. She looked worried again. "The lamb is breech."

"Breech," I said, trying out the word aloud. It could happen with people, too, I knew—babies who tried to come out feet first. I remembered Dov's birth, recalled how his smooth head had entered the world before the rest of his body. "She'll need help getting it out. The lamb, I mean."

"I'll get Marek." Elsbietta sat Patryk down on the grass. "Patryk, you be a good boy. Don't pester your sister."

Breathing deeply again, I reached inside Cilla and once again found a hoof. Gritting my teeth at the smell, I grappled around. Where was the other leg?

"Ria," sang Patryk. "Ria, baa, baa."

"There it is!" Delighted, I grabbed at a second hoof and tugged gently. Cilla bleated loudly and I stopped, unsure how to proceed.

Marek and Elsbietta appeared beside me. "Do you have it?" Marek asked urgently. "The lamb?"

"Yes!" I said. "I have both legs. But Cilla...."

"You need to pull," said Marek, cutting me off. "And fast. I've seen this before."

"Got it." Wincing, I reached and grabbed both legs and pulled hard. It was more difficult than I would have thought, and I nearly tumbled backwards down the hill.

"Steady, now." Marek grabbed me at the waist as I pulled at the breeched lamb. "Pull!"

There was a loud sound like a balloon popping and then I was on my back on the grass with an alien-looking creature splayed on top of me. Slick with afterbirth, it looked nothing like the fluffy lambs of my imagination.

"Oh, my goodness!" Elsbietta clapped a hand over her mouth. "Look at that!"

Patryk pointed at the slimy sheep resting on my chest, the weight of it pinning me flat to the earth. "Baa," he said triumphantly.

Marek burst out laughing. He scrambled to his feet and swept up the newborn lamb. "Maria, are you alright?"

"Yes," I said, dazed. I stared at my hands. Had I really just done that?

"Come look." Marek helped me up and, putting an arm around me, guided me to where Cilla was recovering, licking her new baby between the ears. "It's wonderful."

"What shall we call her?" asked Elsbietta. "Your choice, Maria."

I stared at the little creature, shaky on her feet but up and on them, nonetheless. It was nothing like when Dov—Patryk— had arrived in this world, mewling and helpless. The baby lamb was already independent. She teetered over to nurse from her mother, unflappable. I started to laugh, amazed.

"Lina," I said, smiling. "Her name is Lina."

"Lina!" echoed Patryk. "Baa."

"Yes," I said, picking him up, laughing. He made a face at my slimy hands and pulled away, but I grabbed him and kissed his cheek. "Lina. Baa."

Chapter 10

LINA
Fall, 1941

TATEH DIED unexpectedly—as much as death in the ghetto could be unexpected. Unlike the others, it was not typhoid that took him, but what he confessed in the end was probably cancer. "Cancer of the bladder," he admitted, nodding at Anna's book. "I diagnosed myself."

I ignored the stab of pain I felt whenever I thought of my sister.

"Tateh," I said, my voice filled with sadness. "Why didn't you tell me?"

"I couldn't," he said, shaking his head. "Better this way. Fast."

"But we could have…," my voice trailed off. There was nothing to say, because we could not have done anything. In the ghetto, whoever went into the hospital usually didn't come out.

"Does Masha know?" I asked suddenly. It seemed Masha knew everything these days. She was the opposite of my willful blindness. I drifted along in a fog, existing only moment to moment. Masha on the other hand—Masha made plans.

Tateh hesitated. "She guessed, and I saw no reason to lie."

"She guessed?" I echoed. My stomach twisted. How could Masha have seen it, when I did not?

"Lina." My father grasped my hand. "Lina, you have to… wake up."

"What…?" I began, then lapsed again into silence. I knew what he meant without having to hear it. I had always been one to live in my own head, but this year without Anna had made me withdraw almost entirely. There were days I went without saying more than ten words to Tateh or Masha or the new couple that shared our space. Mutely, I cooked and I cleaned, trying to imagine my sister in her new life. Did they treat her well? Was she happy?

Eyes downcast, I squeezed Tateh's hand. "Why?" I whispered. "It's easier to stay asleep."

"No, Lina." He shook his head, and I could tell it took all his energy to do so. "You have to stay alive. For Anna. Anna is out there, waiting for you to come for her when the war is over."

"The war is never going to end," I said bitterly. I took my hand back. "It will go on until we're all dead."

"No." Again, he mustered the effort to shake his head. "There are always survivors. You need to survive for your sister."

He was right, and I knew it. I wished I had the natural strength of Masha or Anna. Anna didn't get lost in her own head. She had navigated the sewers and brought back milk and eggs.

"Okay," I said, swallowing. The permanent lump in my throat grew as I realized both the gravity of my promise and the reality that if my father had forced me to make it, he wasn't long for this world. "I will do everything I can."

Tateh closed his eyes, his facial muscles relaxing. "Thank you."

"I love you, Tateh." A tear rolled down my cheek into the corner of my mouth, hot and salty. "Don't leave me here alone."

"You're not alone," he said firmly. He reached again for my hand. "Your sister is alive. And she is waiting for you."

The next morning, he died. I smoothed his hair and removed his glasses, gently shutting his eyes for the last time. I wanted to throw myself across his skeletal frame and scream at him for leaving me. Remembering my promise, however, I steeled myself, breathing deeply. I found my father's old, worn overcoat and spread it out over his lifeless form. I reached into his pocket and took out the pipe, cradling it briefly. Taking another long breath, I went to tell Masha.

⁂

"I want to help," I said to Masha. It was several days after my father's death and I rose from my brief shiva, resolved.

"You?" Masha regarded me skeptically. We ate alone, our dinner bowls of thin, tasteless soup. The couple that now shared our apartment had not yet returned for the night. I couldn't remember what it was they did during the days. The hospital? Factory? I could barely remember their names—and why

120

bother? The mother and daughter who had preceded them had both died of typhoid in under a month.

"I promised Tateh," I said. My stomach growled, responding as it still did to the bits of food I occasionally received.

My belly cried for food and I gritted my teeth, admonishing it for its weakness. *There is no more food coming,* I told it sternly. *Only this thin soup and that stale bread.* But still it groaned, hoping for more. Surges of nausea that accompanied starvation and dizzying waves struck at random, leaving me breathless.

Masha stared at me for a long moment. "You're too weak," she said finally. "You're better here, keeping house. We need you to make these rations last. You're good at that."

My hand trembled as I brought the spoon to my lips, both disgusted by and savoring the metallic taste. "I'm more than just a homemaker," I said firmly. "I can do more."

She regarded me dubiously. "Such as?"

I wracked my brain. "Children," I said suddenly. "I raised Anna. I could help with the children. Help get them out of the ghetto. Like Anna and the baby."

Masha shook her head. "It's dangerous work. You might not have the stomach for it."

The word "stomach" brought on another growl and I cursed my lack of strength.

"I'm no longer like that," I said. I resisted the urge to look down at my lap and instead held Masha's gaze. "I've woken up. I promised Tateh. For Anna's sake."

Masha frowned and then sighed. "Fine, then," she said. "Tomorrow, you'll come with me. But you only get one chance, Lina. There are lives at stake."

I said nothing, my eyes lowered. I had promised my father and I owed it to my sister. I would not let them down.

⚹

"Jolanta comes in three times a week," Masha explained. I hurried alongside her, struggling to keep pace. The streets were filthy, and the smell almost unbearable. I kept my eyes on Masha, trying hard to ignore the bodies that littered the streets—some alive, some not.

"Keep moving," said Masha sharply, noticing my expression. I had rarely left the apartment in the year since Anna left, and the despair of the people lying in the streets was difficult to see.

"I am," I said quickly, then hesitated. "I suppose there's nothing we can do for them?" I gestured widely to the bodies on the sidewalks.

Masha shook her head tightly. "Even the ones who are still alive—we can't help them. They're too far gone, Lina."

I swallowed. "Right."

She regarded me with a dubious expression. "Do you want to go back?"

"No!" I grabbed her arm. "Let's keep going."

"She works with the infectious disease offices," explained Masha, resuming her brisk pace. "That's where we'll start."

"Jolanta?" I recalled the kind face of the stranger who'd gently pulled Anna from my embrace.

"Yes. She's a Polish social worker. It's not her real name, of course."

"No?" Surprised, I looked up. "Why?"

"Because if people knew who she really was, she'd be in great danger." Masha explained this slowly to me, as if I were a child. "Everyone who smuggles the children out uses a fake name."

"Of course!" I said again, embarrassed. Of course, they didn't use their real names. Everyone had false names—even the children.

I wondered what Anna's new name was.

※

We arrived at a shabby building. Inside, it smelled like a mix of iodine and peroxide.

"Through here," instructed Masha. She held a heavy yellow door ajar, and I slipped past her, noting the peeling paint on the walls and the cracks in the windowpanes.

"Jolanta." Masha stopped in front of an ancient desk and nodded at the woman sitting at it. My heart flip-flopped at the sight of her. I longed to lunge at her, to demand where my sister was.

"Masha." Jolanta looked up and gave us a tired smile. "How are you?" She motioned at the papers before her. "I have another few sets of documents here, ready to go. We can take at least four children today."

"This is Lina." Masha nudged my lower back, pushing me forward. "She'll be helping you from now on."

"Welcome, Lina." Jolanta's eyes crinkled in the corners. She had the sort of eyes that always appeared to be smiling. Recognition flickered briefly across her face as she studied me.

"Anna," she said finally, putting a comforting hand on my arm. "Your sister was Anna."

"Was?" It came out as a half-scream, half-whisper, a monstrous sort of sound. "She's not...."

"Goodness, no." Jolanta shook her head hard. "I just meant she *was* Anna, and for now she is someone else."

"Someone else," I echoed dully.

"For now," said Jolanta gently, correcting herself. "Someone else for now."

"Is she well? Do you know if...?" My voice trailed off as I noted the frown on Masha's face.

"I don't have any information, I'm afraid," said Jolanta apologetically. "I do know she made it safely to her host family."

Safe. I breathed a sigh of relief. I hadn't known I had been holding so much back these past many months. I wanted to ask more but I restrained myself, knowing she was unlikely to pass anything along for safety reasons.

Masha cleared her throat, making it clear what she thought of my questioning.

"We should explain to Lina what needs to be done," Masha interjected. "Four today, you said?"

"Yes." Jolanta nodded. She was a pretty woman, about thirty or so. Her brown hair was neatly pinned behind her delicate ears, and besides her merry eyes her expression was serious. She dressed simply but neatly, in a white blouse and navy skirt. I eyed the clean, pressed blouse with some envy, feeling shame at my own worn attire.

Jolanta lowered her voice and leaned in toward me and Masha. "I have four sets of false identification papers for the children we discussed. The boy, the two girls, and the baby."

Masha nodded. "Lina," she said, retrieving a small paper from the inside of her sleeve. "These are the four children at the orphanage."

I stared at the paper, confused. There were no names on it, only a string of numbers. I wracked my brain, not wanting to appear ignorant in front of Masha and Jolanta.

"It's coded," explained Masha. "In reverse alphabetical order."

I frowned, then brightened, understanding. "So, the last letter of the alphabet is one, and so on?"

"Yes." Masha looked relieved. I resisted the urge to retort I wasn't stupid, only consumed with grief.

"Bring the children here. If anyone asks, they're showing signs of typhoid, or worse. The Germans are terrified of disease, they won't bother you." Jolanta brushed something invisible off the cuff of her blouse. "Once you're back, you can help me finish these papers. I assume you can read and write?"

"Yes," I stammered. "My father owned a bookshop. I helped him run it."

"A bookshop!" She looked pleased. "That's wonderful. Then you'll have a neat hand?"

I nodded. I had lovely penmanship. I used to spend hours writing, cataloguing, and preparing invoices and receipts. And writing stories, of course, though those days seemed very long ago.

Masha left me, vaguely citing other work to do. I wondered where she was off to. Part of me was glad I didn't know. I didn't want to feel guilt over the occasional extra bit of bread or sugar she brought home.

I left the building and walked to the orphanage with my numbered list, clutching a pencil I'd borrowed from Jolanta. It felt wonderful to have one in my hand again after so long. Would she need it back? I contemplated keeping it and finding some paper.

Chaya Cohen, I translated. *Adam Czernowitz. Bluma Adler. Malka Guttman.*

I reached the orphanage and pushed tentatively against the doors. They were locked. I knocked once, quietly, and then louder a second time when no one came.

"Yes?" A worn-looking nurse stared at me expectantly. She had dark circles beneath her eyes, as if she hadn't been sleeping. "Can I help you?"

"I'm looking for some children," I said, parroting the lines I'd been fed by Jolanta and Masha. "They're needed at the Infectious Disease Office."

"Come in, then." The nurse opened the door wider, ushering me inside. "Have they got medicine there?" She looked back hopefully over her shoulder. "Vaccinations?"

"I—I'm not sure," I said. I cursed myself for not asking more questions earlier to better prepare myself. "I'm just a clerk."

She seemed to accept this response, sighing. I gave her the names of the children, and she frowned, giving me an odd look.

"What?" I asked, feeling anxious.

"None of these children are ill," she said, perplexed. "Or one was, I suppose, but she—she's passed." The nurse lowered her eyes. "Chaya died two days ago."

I felt a pang of sadness for Chaya.

"Of course, the infants rarely survive." She yawned involuntarily, and I could see how exhausted she was. "Especially if the mother dies. I'll take you to the others," she said. "Come through here."

The orphanage was a sorry place. There were holes in the walls and windows covered with bits of cloth to keep out the wind and rain. Everything was gray—the walls, the floors, the metal beds with insufficient bedding. Here and there were bedpans—used ones—and it stank. Children stared at me as we passed through, their eyes dark and hollow with starvation and disease. Some beds appeared to host two or three children, packed in tightly, like pencils in a box.

"There are many more children than beds," I commented, shocked.

"It's about three to a bed at this point," said the nurse, looking grim. "It just spreads the infection, but there's nothing to be done."

I followed her to an office where she consulted various long lists of names. *So many children.* I looked around. *How to tell them all apart?*

"This way," she said, straightening. "Adam and Bluma are in Room Two."

I trailed behind her. She seemed unbothered by the terrible smell, and I aimed to emulate her admirable indifference.

"Adam," she said, coming up behind a lanky boy somewhere around eight years old. "This is…." She paused and stared at me. "I'm sorry, I don't know your name."

I stared at her. Did I give my real name? Jolanta didn't use hers. "Rivka," I lied.

"Rivka," she said. "She works with the infection control office. She's here to bring you somewhere."

Adam nodded listlessly and rose from where he sat staring at the wall. He didn't say anything as he moved to my side.

"Bluma Adler!" she called out then. She turned to me. "Bluma hides."

"Hides?"

"We found her hiding after her family had died. It's how she copes, I suppose." She looked around for evidence of Bluma. "Bluma!"

A tiny girl of about five emerged from under a metal cot. She had her thumb in her mouth and huge blue eyes.

"Bluma, this is Rivka. You're to go with her and Adam to see the doctor."

Bluma said nothing. Adam moved to take her small hand and I felt a sharp tug at my heartstrings.

"Malka," she mused. "Malka will be with the infants in Room Three. She likes to help."

"How old is she?"

"Eleven? Twelve, maybe?" The nurse shook her head. "It's hard to keep them all straight."

We found Malka cradling an infant, singing quietly. She looked startled at our appearance beside her.

"This is Rivka," explained the nurse once again. "You're to go with her and the other children to the disease control office."

"But why?" Malka looked concerned. "I'm not ill."

"We don't ask questions," the nurse answered brusquely.

"The baby should go." She looked over at me. "She has a bad rash."

"She's not on the list," said the nurse patiently.

I watched Malka's face fall and looked over at the flushed face of the baby. *Four spaces*, I thought to myself. Would one infant not be as suitable as another? Who would know?

"You can bring the baby," I said suddenly. "If it's show-ing the...signs of infection." I said the last part with feigned confidence. I hadn't the slightest idea what I was talking about.

"You're certain?"

"Yes. Yes, that's fine." I nodded at Malka, who now held the baby.

I led the children outside through the door. From the nurse's actions, she didn't seem to know the plan. How would I explain the children's failure to return? Would anyone come looking for them?

"The children may be gone for a while," I improvised,

trying to sound authoritative. "They will be…isolated to see if they show symptoms. Then taken to hospital."

"Of course," said the nurse. Her eyes briefly met mine, and in that moment I realized I was wrong. She did know. I felt a wave of admiration for her terrific acting skills.

"Miss?" We were outside, and the children had said their good-byes to the nurse and followed me obediently through the ghetto streets like a row of little ducks. Malka continued to hold the baby and walked hesitantly with her. I had offered to take her, but Malka had refused, insisting the baby was more familiar with her.

"Yes, Malka?"

"We aren't sick, none of us, except maybe the baby. Why are we going to see a doctor?"

"We are going to see a…a specialist," I said finally, choosing the word carefully. "I don't have much information, I'm afraid."

Bluma took her thumb out of her mouth and spoke up. "My mama and papa died," she announced. "And Daniel. They wouldn't wake up."

"Oh, darling." I stopped and knelt before her. "My mama and papa died, too."

This seemed to interest her greatly. "You had parents?"

"Why, yes," I said. "Everyone has parents. Or had them," I corrected myself, feeling stupid.

"Can you carry me?" She lifted her tiny arms up toward me the way Anna had done as a little girl. "My feet hurt."

"Of course," I said, and scooped her up. Momentarily

breathless, I shifted her to my hip and inhaled and exhaled deeply.

I looked over at Adam, the only one who hadn't said a word. He stared back at me, eyes solemn and unblinking.

"Let's go," I said finally, turning away. "Time to see Jolanta."

❧

"Jolanta?" I peeked through the crack in the doorway, tentatively pushing the heavy wooden door open with my free arm. There was no one there, but I decided we would wait inside. It was safer that way, in case someone came by asking questions I couldn't answer. I deposited Bluma on a chair, groaning with relief at being freed from her weight. Once, I'd toted Anna around Warsaw easily on my hip. I'd been strong then, with a full belly. Without food, everything was harder. I rubbed my upper arms, wincing at how bony they felt. I imagined myself as a tree in winter: all skinny bare limbs, ready to snap.

"Come, children," I said quietly, ushering them inside. "We'll wait here."

Malka entered the room, the baby sleeping soundly in the crook of her arm. She had a natural poise and a curious, fearless gaze. Adam trailed behind her, still not speaking. He stared at me expectantly, and I motioned for him to sit in the chair next to Bluma. He climbed up on it silently and folded his hands in his lap, eyes fixed on the floor.

"Where is the doctor?" Malka looked around, frowning. "This doesn't look like a hospital."

"Well," I said, stammering. I wracked my brain for an appropriate response. "This is…the office."

I struggled for something else to say, but thankfully Jolanta appeared, brightening as she spotted me and the children. She shut the door carefully behind her.

"Well done," she said to me, looking at the children. She smiled at Malka, noting the baby in her arms.

"Are you Malka?"

"Yes." Malka still looked wary. "Are you a nurse?"

"Something like that. My name is Jolanta. And that must be Chaya?" She nodded at the baby, a tender expression on her face.

"No, Chaya…Chaya is no longer with us," I said carefully. I didn't want to upset the little ones. "This baby has a rash, so we brought her with us."

"Ah." Jolanta's face changed quickly. She reached for the baby, taking her from a skeptical-looking Malka.

"What's her name?" Jolanta mimicked my earlier gesture, checking the baby's forehead temperature against her hand.

"It's…," I faltered. What was the baby's name? I realized I had never asked. I looked over at Malka, who stared back at me, horrified.

"I don't know," she said, sounding equally puzzled. "I forgot to check when I picked her up." She looked upset now, her voice rising. "I don't know who she is!"

"It's alright," I said feebly. I wanted to tell her they'd all have new names soon, new lives. That it didn't matter. But that wasn't true. It mattered who you were and where you were from. The baby had once had parents, and those parents had given their daughter a name.

"I can go back and find out," said Malka, eyeing the door. "The nurse at the orphanage would know."

"I'm afraid that isn't possible." Jolanta switched the baby to her other arm and rested her hand on Malka's shoulder. "We need you to stay here."

"But why?" Angry now, Malka's cheeks flushed and she clenched and unclenched her fists. "Why do we need to stay here? I'm not even sick." She looked over at Bluma and Adam. "They aren't sick, either."

"You'll be leaving the ghetto today," replied Jolanta calmly. "From here, you'll go to a safe house in Warsaw, and from there, to families in the countryside."

Malka looked shocked. "How?"

Jolanta shook her head. "We won't know until the last minute. It's a tricky business, getting children out of the ghetto."

"No!" Adam was on his feet now, eyes wild. "No!"

"Adam?" I crouched down to his level and grasped his hands tightly. "What is it?"

"I'm not going in the sewers again." His eyes rolled with terror. "Please, let me go back to the orphanage."

"You've been in the sewers?" I thought of Anna. "Getting food?"

"Yes." He began to shake violently. "It's so scary down there. I felt like I was trapped and never going to get out."

Jolanta handed me the baby and bent down to talk to Adam.

"I understand," she said seriously.

"I don't want to go in the sewers." Adam stared hard at his hands and I could tell he was trying not to cry.

"We'll try to find another way out for you," said Jolanta. "There are a few ways. Some involve small spaces. Others don't."

"I like small spaces." Bluma took her thumb out of her mouth and looked over at Jolanta. "I slept in a cupboard until they took me away."

Jolanta reached over to tuck a stray hair behind Bluma's ear. "And why were you sleeping in a cupboard, my dear girl?"

"I felt better in there," said Bluma matter-of-factly. "We had one bed, but Mama and Papa and Daniel were in it and they wouldn't wake up."

"I'm sorry to hear that, Bluma." Jolanta did indeed look sorry. Her eyes filled with a genuine sadness.

"What if we're caught?" Malka looked anxiously from me to Jolanta and back again. "We'll be shot for sure."

"What's the difference?" Adam spoke up again. "At the orphanage, we'll get sick or starve and die anyway." His eyes were hard now, and he seemed like a different boy.

The baby chose that moment to wake and let out a loud wail. Instinctively, I brought her to my chest, whispering to her like I had with Anna, only Anna had smelled sweet. This poor infant smelled of sour milk and unwashed linens.

Malka's voice rose again, panicked. "She has no name. How can we help her if we don't know her name?"

"I have a solution for that." Jolanta smiled at Malka. "We will give her a new one. I have new ones for the rest of you, too!" Her voice was upbeat, trying to model enthusiasm as the children's faces betrayed a mix of confusion and fear.

Little Bluma spoke first. "Why?"

Malka looked at her sadly. "Because we have Jewish names and we're going to families in the countryside. And those families aren't Jewish."

"How do you know?" Adam glared at her. "You don't know everything just because you're the oldest."

I leaned in to intervene, but Malka beat me to it.

"Because if they were Jewish, they'd probably be here, in the ghetto," she snapped. "I am from a small village. My family was sent to the ghetto."

Adam fell silent again. "Sorry," he mumbled.

"Malka is correct. You all need new names, names to match your new families in the country." Jolanta went over to her desk to shuffle some papers.

"Malka, you will be Monika. Adam, your new name is Andrzej. Bluma, from now on you're Kasza."

"That's pretty," said Bluma dreamily. "I like that name." Then her forehead creased with worry. "What if I forget?"

"Best not to talk at all, if you can help it," said Jolanta grimly. "You'll be with an adult. Let the adult speak. You'll stay quiet."

All the children nodded, already taking this advice to heart. Children living in an orphanage knew how to be quiet.

"And the baby?" Malka came over and retrieved her from me, cradling her. "What will her name be?"

"Her name is Katarzyna," said Jolanta.

"That's very pretty, too," said Bluma. "It sounds like a princess in a story."

"Does it?" I smiled at her. "Do you like stories?"

"Oh, yes," she said seriously. "My father was a teacher and he knew lots of stories."

"My father knew lots of stories, too," I said softly in reply. I thought of the mountains of books still buried beneath our old apartment building. "We owned a bookshop."

Malka's eyes widened. "A whole shop of books?"

"Yes," I said wistfully. I had taken it for granted. The books, the paper, the pencils.

"We didn't have many books in our village," said Malka.

"How about you, Adam?" Jolanta looked at him kindly. "Do you like to read?"

Adam nodded, his face crumpling. Impulsively, I pulled him into a hug.

"You read with your mother?" I whispered it into his ear. "Your father?"

"My mama," he choked.

"Did she get the typhoid?" I asked.

He shook his head. "She wasn't eating. She gave us all her food—to me and my sister. We didn't notice until it was too late. My sister, she caught the typhoid after that. My father too."

He wept openly now and I hugged him tighter, fighting back my own tears.

"Lina," Jolanta broke in gently. "I need your help."

I pulled back, wiping my eyes quickly with the fraying sleeve of my shirt. "What do you need me to do?"

She spread the documents out over the desk.

"They need to look like this," she explained, showing me a set of Polish identity documents. "And here is the list of their new names."

She handed me a sheaf of paper, precious paper. My hands trembled as I fingered the edges, leaning in to breathe in the pulpy smell.

"We haven't got enough supplies for mistakes," she said apologetically. She fished around and found some scraps of paper from old newsprint and torn books. "Practice on these, but please, Lina, be careful."

"I will," I said, determined. I may not have had Masha's physical strength or steely resolve, but I did have a good, steady hand.

I worked in silence, my tongue twisted between my teeth in concentration. Around me, the children chatted with Jolanta and each other, Jolanta gently explaining what would happen next. Malka and the baby would go through the sewers. Adam would go to the church as Anna had. And little Bluma, who liked small spaces, was to be smuggled out in a coffin.

Malka gasped at this, but Bluma seemed nonplussed. "What's a coffin?"

"It's a box that people are buried in," said Adam, looking horrified. "Dead people."

"Oh." Bluma contemplated this. "Is it very small?"

"It is a grown-up size," Jolanta assured her. "So, it will not be too small for you."

Bluma nodded. "I like small spaces," she said again. "It will be like my cupboard."

Adam, who showed his relief at not being chosen for the coffin route, spoke up then in a small voice.

"My mama said I have an uncle in Chicago, America." He sounded uncertain. "What if he tries to find me?"

"I'm glad you asked that." Jolanta crouched again to his level. "I am keeping all your real names with your new names in a jar. That way, after the war, your family will be able to find you."

Adam looked relieved, nodding. Malka leapt up.

"The baby."

"She's fine." Jolanta gestured to a basket where little Katarzyna was curled up, asleep.

"She doesn't have a real name." Malka looked stricken. "No one will ever be able to find her."

I put my pencil down. "I will find her name," I said. "I will go back and get the baby's name and make sure it goes into the jar."

"Do you promise?" Malka gave me a fierce stare, and I felt a pang at how much she reminded me of Anna, the girl who'd snuck in and out of the sewers to find milk.

I looked her straight in the eye.

"I promise," I said solemnly.

Chapter 11

ANNA
Winter, 1941

"MARIA," whispered Elsbietta. "Maria, wake up."

"Hmmm?" Groggily, I rolled over onto my stomach. It couldn't be time to wake up already.

"It's the Kowalskis' cow." Elsbietta shook me gently. "Something is wrong."

"Cow!" I blinked. "The dairy cow?"

Elsbietta nodded. "Yes. The one the Germans come collect the milk from. They're worried."

"Of course." I yawned widely, trying to shake myself awake. The Kowalskis relied on bartering the milk for medicine for their youngest daughter, six-year-old Eva. A charming child with golden braids, even the Nazis had softened at her cherubic smile and agreed to find her some epilepsy medication in exchange for fresh milk, cheese, and butter.

"What time is it?"

"It is past midnight, but before dawn," said Elsbietta, her voice low so as not to wake Patryk.

I yawned but was awake now, adrenaline pumping through my veins.

"I'm coming," I said, tossing the sheet aside.

"I'll get your coat and boots. It's snowing." Elsbietta rose quickly, leaving me to dress. Groping blindly in the dark, I found some clothing and tied my hair back into a tight braid.

Marek was waiting at the door for me with Piotr Kowalski, a boy two years my senior who rarely spoke. He nodded at me, then looked away.

"Piotr will walk you there and back," said Marek.

I looked at Piotr, who was staring at his dirty boots. Irritated, I picked up the bag with my book and the few implements I'd collected from the old veterinarian's widow.

"Let's go," I said pointedly. "If it's an emergency, we need to move fast."

"Be careful," said Marek, glancing sharply at Piotr. Piotr looked up from his intense study of his boots and turned red.

"I'll keep her safe," he said gruffly. I tried my best not to roll my eyes. I was perfectly capable of keeping myself safe. I had slipped in and out of the Warsaw ghetto undetected. What could Piotr even offer if we found ourselves in danger? All he did was stare at his boots.

Elsbietta and Marek rushed to hug me before I left, and I hugged them back. I let Elsbietta help me into my coat. Being motherly soothed her, and I secretly enjoyed it too.

I followed Piotr out of the house holding my book. The door slammed behind us despite my effort to close it gently. I hoped Patryk wouldn't wake. He could be tricky to settle back to sleep, and I knew Elsbietta was exhausted.

"This way," said Piotr, and this time I did roll my eyes. It was dark and he was several steps ahead of me with the lantern, so he didn't see as I cast my eyes all the way up to the gibbous moon, silently cursing being stuck with him.

We hurried in silence after that, Piotr sneaking occasional glances in my direction.

"I'm fine," I snapped under my breath after the tenth time he turned around. "I know the way."

He didn't answer, only quickly looked away and walked faster, the lantern swaying precariously.

"Careful," I hissed. "You don't want to set the entire countryside on fire."

"I am careful," he snapped. He lifted the lantern and shone it directly at me. "Why are you so mean?"

I flinched at both the light and his words. "Me?" I was incredulous. I was a nice, cheerful person—he was the misery. "I am not!"

"You are." He looked eerie in the light. "You never even speak to me."

"You don't speak to me! You just stare at your boots." Hands on my hips, I scowled at him.

He moved the lantern slightly and it caught my eye again. I sneezed loudly.

"Damn," he whispered, glaring at me and looking around nervously. "That was loud."

"Well, you shouldn't have shone the light in my face," I retorted.

He looked baffled. "What does one have to do with the other?"

I stared at him, incredulous. He really was an idiot.

"The light," I said. "It made me sneeze."

He gave me a funny look and shook his head. "I've never heard of that before."

I frowned. I had always sneezed from light. So had Lina, and so had Tateh. I wracked my brain, trying to think if anyone else did. Was it only my family?

Worse, was it some sort of Jewish trait? Had I exposed myself?

My fear must have shown, as Piotr's expression suddenly softened. "I can do this," he said, holding up his left hand. His fingers hyperextended, so that they looked like a series of wavy lines.

"Everyone has something strange about them," he offered, when I said nothing. My heart still beat fast, fear of exposure driving each rapid thud against my chest.

"Yes," I managed. "I suppose so."

He gave me a small smile, and I gave him one back.

"Let's hurry," I said. "We have a cow to save."

He nodded and held up the lantern as we picked up our pace through the field.

❧

The cow was in clear distress when I arrived, Mr. Kowalski was crouched down beside her whispering soothing words and patting her softly between her ears. He looked up at me, anxious.

"She got into the clover, we think," he said grimly.

Clover. From my textbook, that would likely make it bloat, a dangerous condition for cattle. If left free to roam the pasture, they would occasionally gorge on clover, filling their bellies until the pressure from gas made it impossible for them to breathe.

"Can she pass urine?" I asked. I sat down beside Mr. Kowalski on the pile of hay and reached for my book.

"Yes," he answered, looking worried. He scratched the poor cow's ears as she moaned loudly, her eyes bulging.

"That's good," I said automatically. In my book, I found the section on bloat and scanned it rapidly before visually examining the cow.

"What's her name?" I asked, leaning forward. I could feel Piotr hovering some distance behind me, watching.

"Anna," said Piotr.

"Yes?" I answered automatically. I turned to him.

His eyebrows were knit together in confusion. "Anna," he said again, pointing at the distressed cow. "You asked the cow's name. It's Anna."

"Right," I said quickly, my heart hammering again. How had I let that happen? Twice, I'd nearly exposed myself to

Piotr. I shook my head quickly, as if to clear whatever fog had descended to cloud my thoughts. "Sorry, I didn't hear."

I breathed deeply and crouched over my namesake, examining her more closely. Her tongue protruded from her mouth, her breathing rapid and labored. Gently, I placed a hand on her vast stomach.

"It's bloat," I confirmed, gesturing. "See? The stomach is distended here on the left side."

Mr. Kowalski exhaled loudly. "The clover. We should have been more careful." He shook his head reproachfully. "She's our last cow. We can't afford to lose her."

I reached for my textbook again to avoid the beseeching look he was giving me. I was an amateur, a self-taught girl who had a book and a bag of tools I had mostly never used.

The trocar—a sort of lance—was in my bag, as well as a cannula, a little tube. If it was bad enough, I'd have to make an incision into the cow's belly and let the air out of the poor creature. I had never done it before, only read about it. I swallowed, fearful, but squared my shoulders.

"Let's try something," I said. The book said that if the case wasn't too severe, a thin tube could be inserted through the cow's mouth to her stomach, and I could give her mineral oil to relieve the gas. If this worked, there'd be no need to lance the cow.

"I need a thin rubber tube," I announced. "And some mineral oil."

Mr. Kowalski stood quickly, wiping his hands on his trousers. "I have a tube we can use," he said, already moving toward the barn door. "Piotr! Go find your mother and get some mineral oil."

"Yes, Father," said Piotr quickly. We exchanged a brief look before he, too, dashed from the barn and toward the house. The cow moaned softly, her ears twitching.

"Poor girl," I said, stroking her brown head. "Poor Anna."

It felt strange, saying my name aloud.

The cow looked at me pleadingly and I felt a thrill of fear. *It would be bad luck to lose a cow with my name*, I thought.

The cow stared at me. Unnerved, I felt for my bag and took out the trocar, staring at it. Could I do it, if I had to?

Piotr came back with the mineral oil. "Here," he said, winded. He thrust it at me. His father appeared behind him, clutching a thin, bright red rubber tube.

"Thank you." I set it down next to me and regarded this other Anna with a determined expression. "I'm going to help you," I told the cow.

"What can we do?" Mr. Kowalski was at my side, fidgeting anxiously with the tube.

"We need to get that tube into her stomach," I explained. "So, I need your help holding her mouth open and getting it down."

"Piotr," barked Mr. Kowalski. "Come help."

A reluctant Piotr sidled up beside his father, his shoulders slumped.

"Hold her mouth open," I instructed, bravely brandishing the tube. "As wide as you can."

"Have you done this before?" Piotr looked mildly repulsed

as his father wrenched the beast's mouth open, her tongue hanging limply.

"No," I said simply. "I'm just a girl with a book."

"We're grateful to have you." Mr. Kowalski gave his son a look and nudged him hard with his elbow.

"That's not what I meant." Piotr kneeled down and, wincing, grasped the cow's jaw. "Aren't you afraid?"

He regarded me with frank curiosity, and I realized that his quiet demeanor was not a sign he lacked intelligence. He was a sensitive, deep thinker who kept to himself. Suddenly, he reminded me of Lina.

"Let's go," I said bravely, leaning forward. "Now."

Anna the cow put up a feeble struggle as I fed the tube down her throat, praying it was traveling down the right pipe. She continued to breathe, reassurance that I hadn't accidently shoved the tube into her windpipe. I led the tube in slowly, realizing with a rising panic that I wasn't sure when to stop. I would have no choice but to guess, measuring the cow's body compared to how much tube was still available. I closed my eyes briefly, trying to picture the tube traveling through the lumen and into the cow's second stomach.

"Let's try now," I said, opening my eyes. I saw Piotr watching me but no longer felt irritated. "Mineral oil, please."

With tremendous care, I poured the mineral oil into the tube. The cow moaned loudly, and I steeled myself, avoiding her mournful eyes.

"What happens now?" Piotr's voice was quiet.

"Hopefully," I said grimly, "the air will come out."

"The air?" He frowned, then his eyes widened. "Anna has…gas?"

Our eyes met and he smirked. I could see he was trying not to laugh, and something in his expression made me smirk, too.

"It's not like that in cows, though," I said, trying to sound dignified. "It can kill them."

"It nearly killed my mother last week, too," said Piotr, now laughing openly.

Mr. Kowalski scowled at his son, but I started to laugh, too.

Anna was visibly improved from the treatment. Having loudly expelled a large amount of gas, she looked immediately more animated. Biting my cheek hard to try to stifle my laughter, I began to pull back the rubber tubing.

"She'll need to move around," I said, avoiding looking at Piotr. "To let out the rest of the gas."

"We'd better clear out," he said, snorting.

"Really, Piotr." Mr. Kowalski's face matched the color of the tubing. "You're nearly sixteen."

"I'm sorry," said Piotr, but then our eyes met and we both began laughing all over again. I turned away, determined not to laugh again until it was clear Anna the cow was out of danger.

I removed the tube, and Mr. Kowalski and Piotr helped me encourage the cow to stand. She was doing better. Her breathing had returned to normal and the doleful mooing had ceased.

"You saved her," said Mr. Kowalski, grasping my hands with both of his. "How can we ever repay you?"

"Don't be silly," I said, embarrassed. "I didn't even know what I was doing."

"You're a brilliant girl," said Mr. Kowalski, admiringly. He looked at Piotr. "Piotr, you could learn a thing or two from Maria."

That stopped his laughter. Now it was Piotr's turn to flush red.

"Piotr doesn't want to farm," continued his father. "He wants to be a schoolteacher."

"That's very interesting," I said quickly, sensing Piotr's mortification. "I love to read."

"We have a farm. He's going to be a farmer." Mr. Kowalski's eyes met his son's. "He should spend more time with the cow and less time with his books."

"Mr. Kowalski," I interjected, glancing outside. The sun was rising. "Anna should get some exercise." I nodded at the creature that shared my name. Relieved for both the cow and myself, I gave out a satisfying yawn.

"You're tired," said Mr. Kowalski. "Piotr should walk you back. But have something to eat first."

"No, no," I protested. I knew they couldn't have enough for themselves, let alone enough for me to share.

"But you must." His tone was firm. "You are our guest and we owe you for saving Anna."

Saving Anna. The words made me shiver.

"Thank you," I said finally.

"Piotr, please show Maria where she can wash up."

Piotr was staring hard at his boots again, his face scarlet from his father's criticism. "This way," he mumbled.

Feeling sorry for him, I said nothing, following several steps behind him to give him space.

We entered the house, the door creaking slightly as Piotr pulled it open. Inside, it was still dark. It wasn't quite time to rise, even on a farm. His mother and sister were still asleep.

"It's over there," he muttered, gesturing at a heavy wooden door painted a buttery yellow color. "There are towels in the cupboard."

"Thank you," I said formally, easing past him.

"That was so…impressive. What you did with Anna." Piotr looked at me. "I could never do that."

"You could if you had to," I said, thinking of all the things I'd never thought I could do.

"No." He shook his head. "My father's right. I'm not good at anything useful."

"Books are useful," I countered. "I couldn't have done any of that without a book."

"That's not the kind of books I like," Piotr said ruefully. "I like stories."

"All books are important." I thought of the books we had buried beneath our old apartment building in Warsaw. "Books are…proof."

"Proof?" He looked at me quizzically.

"History. Stories. Proof that things happened, that people lived." I struggled to explain myself. "One day people will read about this war and that will be the proof it happened."

Piotr's face changed. "That's…I've never thought of it like that."

"My family had a bookshop," I said. "I loved our books."

Piotr looked surprised. "Elsbietta's cousin owns a bookshop? In Warsaw?"

My stomach dropped. *What have I done?*

"Yes," I said. It was too late to change the story. I would have to stick with it. I made a mental note to let Elsbietta and Marek know, and prayed that the fictional cousin was not a baker.

Piotr looked wistful. "What's it like in the city?"

I recalled the crowded misery of the ghetto. "Dirty," I said. "Crowded. Noisy. People hungry everywhere, people dying of tuberculosis and typhoid. The war has been hard on the city, Piotr. It's much better here."

His shoulders slumped. "I'm stuck here forever. If I had only been of age to enlist…."

"Then you'd be dead or in a prison somewhere," I pointed out. Half the men and boys from the village who had become Polish soldiers were killed or disappeared when the Nazis invaded. It was how I'd ended up as a makeshift veterinarian.

Piotr said nothing, his cheeks coloring again. "There's soap in there," he said, and I nodded, understanding the conversation was over.

When I was done washing up, Mrs. Kowalski was awake, cutting some bread and cheese at the kitchen counter.

"Maria," she said, beaming at me. "Piotr just told me what you did. Come have something to eat after all that hard work."

"Thank you," I said, and it was now my turn to blush. "It wasn't so difficult. And Piotr and Mr. Kowalski helped."

I sat down next to Piotr at the table, feeling guilty for sharing their few rations. It would mean less for them. "I'm really not that hungry," I lied.

Mrs. Kowalski raised her eyebrows at me. "Eat," she said simply, placing a plate in front of me. My stomach growled loudly, betraying me. Sheepishly, I took a bite of bread.

"Hi, Maria!" Eva appeared, her blonde curls flying behind her as she raced into the kitchen.

Eva skidded to a halt and sidled up next to me. "How come you're here for breakfast, Maria?"

Mrs. Kowalski placed a plate in front of Eva and motioned for her to sit. "Maria saved the cow last night."

"Anna!" Eva looked worried. "Is she alright, then?"

"I think she'll be fine," I answered, smiling at the little girl. I paused to swallow a mouthful of cheese. "She had bloat from getting into the clover."

"Like the time you ate a whole cake, Eva," chided her mother. "Remember how sick you were?"

Eva looked wistful. "I'm not sorry, now that I know there will never be cake again."

I couldn't help but agree. "I love cake, too, Eva," I said with a sigh. "Poppy seed cake."

"There will be cake again," said Mrs. Kowalski peaceably. "The war won't go on forever."

"Feels like it," grumbled Eva, her mouth full of crumbly black bread.

"Eva," scolded her mother. "No speaking with your mouth full."

Eva rolled her eyes at me, and I winked back.

"Piotr, why so quiet?" Mrs. Kowalski looked at her son, picking halfheartedly at his breakfast. "It's not like you."

"Just worried about the cow," he mumbled. "Hope she'll be alright."

"Maria saved her!" sang out Eva. "She's like a doctor."

I shook my head quickly. "I'm not a doctor. I'm a girl with a book."

Eva perked up. "Piotr reads a lot of books, too," she informed me. "He borrowed a bunch from a traveler who used to come selling things. But then the war came, and he never came back and so Piotr ended up stealing them."

"It's not stealing!" Piotr's face was flushed again. "When he returns, he can have his books back."

"He's probably dead," reasoned Eva matter-of-factly. "Probably the Nazis shot him."

"Eva!" Mrs. Kowalski looked scandalized. "Stop making up stories!"

"It's true," she insisted. "You know that traveling salesman? The one who sold string? I heard he's dead."

"They were Jews," spoke up Piotr. "They weren't allowed to work anymore."

They were Jews. The words stung. The bread, so tasty a moment ago, felt suddenly like sawdust on my tongue.

"My friend says all the Jews are dead," said Eva. "She used to go to Krakow with her father and she says they're all gone now."

Piotr said nothing. I stared hard at my plate, my appetite gone.

When it was time for Piotr to walk me back, I waited until the others were out of earshot to turn to Piotr, hesitant.

"Piotr," I said. "Could I borrow a book?"

His expression changed. Worried he wouldn't want to share, I continued hurriedly.

"I'll take excellent care of it, I promise, and I'll return it to you as soon as I'm done. It's just I'm a bit tired of the veterinary book, and I…."

"Of course you can have a book," he said, staring at me. "I have six."

I heard the pride in his voice and thought of my father's bookshop, the hundreds of tomes on the shelves.

"I will take a novel, if you have one," I said shyly. "I could use an escape into a story."

"An escape into a story," he echoed. "That's…beautiful."

I blushed furiously. "It's just an expression."

"I have the perfect thing," he informed me. "Wait here."

I waited near the front of the house. One of the barn cats that roamed the property, a paunchy creature with a black and white masked face, approached and rubbed its head against my shins. I bent to scratch between its ears and it promptly tipped over at my feet, purring loudly.

Piotr reappeared clutching a large hardback. "I see you've met Ursula, the cat," he said, nodding at the buzzing feline. "She's a bit of a flirt."

"She's very friendly," I said, smiling. "We have several cats, but only some like to be petted by people. The others hiss and swat at you for even looking at them."

"That's the best part about cats," said Piotr, grinning. "You have to work for their affection. Dogs are nice to everyone."

"I hadn't thought of it that way," I said, laughing. "I like that."

We stood facing each other, grinning stupidly. Piotr cleared his throat and held up the book.

"It's Henryk Sienkiewicz," he said. "Have you read him before? He's quite famous, I think."

I thought immediately of Lina, who would have known.

"No," I admitted. "My sister would have. She loved reading novels. She—she's gone," I added.

His expression changed. "I'm so sorry. Was it the typhoid? Like your parents?"

I pictured Lina and Tateh and my heart twisted. I struggled to maintain my composure. "Yes," I said. It was my turn to stare at my boots. I dared not lift my head, lest my eyes betray me. Maybe it was true by now. Maybe Lina and Tateh were dead.

"I'm sorry, Maria," said Piotr again. He put a tentative hand on my arm, looking embarrassed. "I can get another book. Poetry?"

"No," I said quickly. "Thank you. I would love to read this."

"It's part of a series," he said. "The peddler, he said he would bring me the rest, but then...."

"Do you really think they're all dead?" I blurted out. "The Jews?"

He looked taken aback, but then shook his head slowly. "My sister has a wild imagination. How could they all be dead? You can't kill that many people."

We fell silent, but this time it wasn't the unpleasant kind.

"I'll walk you back now," said Piotr finally. "You must be tired."

"Yes," I admitted, grateful. "Yes, thank you."

This time, he didn't walk ahead of me.

Chapter 12

LINA
Summer, 1942

I WAS AN EXPERIENCED counterfeiter now, and good at it.

The years of maintaining neat ledgers and drafting legible receipts had paid off. My unique skills proved useful to Jolanta and her team. We operated in the shadows, none of us knowing who the others were. Sometimes, while I shaded my letters or mixed my ink, I daydreamed about who else was working with her. The old rabbi from our synagogue? The Polish shop owner who used to give Anna free sweets? Was Masha involved, or was she simply a go-between? We lived side by side in our cramped apartment, but she never said a word about her work.

I worked quietly in the first aid office as an "administrator," overlooked and ignored as my mind wandered and I improved my forgery skills. For the first time since I'd left school, I felt useful and proud of myself. In forging documents for Jewish children, I was saving lives. One painstakingly drafted and forged life at a time. Hundreds of little Annas and Dovs, tucked safely away with Polish families throughout the country. It made the days easier to endure.

The evenings, though, were harder. They were cold and filled with filth and hunger. Masha and I shared our apartment with three women now, all older widows. Mrs. Levy's husband had died in the first round of typhoid; Mrs. Goldblatt's in the second. Mrs. Einarsson's husband had died of a heart attack when they packed up their home to move into the ghetto.

At night there was little to do but listen to the irritable banter between these older women. Unable to relate to their stories of husbands and babies and mothers-in-law, I busied myself with housework. On Fridays, we let the candles burn a bit longer to mark the Sabbath before I finally snuffed the flames to conserve the precious wax.

When the candles went out, the women never failed to complain.

"No light now," said grumpy Mrs. Levy one humid evening in July. "I can't talk in the dark. It hurts my head."

"That doesn't make any sense, Eva. You realize that doesn't make any sense?" Even in the blackness, I could feel Mrs. Goldblatt rolling her eyes.

"I don't care," retorted Mrs. Levy. "I know what I feel."

Masha, who had been silent until now, spoke up. "I don't like the dark, either."

Everyone fell silent. Masha rarely spoke.

"I understand," said Mrs. Einarsson. Her voice changed. "In the dark, you can feel the baby. His spirit. I know, Mashale.

I lost three babies. It was a long time ago, but still they come in the dark."

I held my breath. No one ever spoke to Masha about her lost baby. I didn't even know how Mrs. Einarsson knew. I certainly hadn't told her.

"Yes," said Masha finally, in a whisper. "Yes. He comes in the dark."

I said nothing, feeling like the outsider. No husband or babies to mourn. Uncomfortable, I stared at my lap, even though I could not see it in the darkness. Should I reach for Masha's hand? What was the right thing to do?

Masha shifted next to me, and as my eyes adjusted I could see Mrs. Levy held Masha's hand in her own.

"I'm sorry," I said in a low voice, looking at Masha. "I'm so sorry about your baby."

"Perhaps it is best," she said quietly. "He would have died here, surely. The typhoid would have taken him."

I didn't know what to say to that. I thought of the children I was saving.

Masha rose abruptly. In the dark, she found her shoes and excused herself, the front door inadvertently slamming behind her. The sudden, brief influx of cool air felt good against my skin, and I lifted my face toward it.

"Don't feel badly, dear," said Mrs. Goldblatt, patting my arm. "You're just a girl. No one expects you to understand."

I scratched at the melted candlewax on the table, enjoying the sensation as it molded to the shape of my palm.

"When the war is over, you'll find a husband," Mrs. Levy chimed in. "Pretty, capable girl like you."

I nodded mutely, though I wasn't sure the war would ever end.

I pinched hard at the wax, angry. Pretending it was the universe, I bent it to the will of my fingertips.

❧

It was Sunday and I was at work, at peace with my pencils. I felt more at home in that office than I did in our dank, overcrowded apartment.

"Something is going on…." Benjamin, who had been training to be a doctor before the war, was the only other person in the office. He leaned toward me, looking anxious.

I didn't look up right away. I was working on the new Polish name for a five-year-old girl, a girl I fantasized had shiny black braids and feathery eyelashes. I lavished extra time on the names, imagining I was infusing the child's new identity with extra love.

I finally looked up at him, temporarily pausing and trying not to sigh. I hated being interrupted.

"Something bad is about to happen," he said meaningfully. He seemed breathless. He leaned in further, and I caught a hint of sour breath. The smell of starvation.

"There are rumors everywhere. They say the Judenrat is helping the Germans plan deportations."

"Deportations?" My hands felt suddenly numb.

Benjamin shook his head. "My brother-in-law says Jews are being sent to work camps in the east. Resettlement. But no one knows for sure."

"Resettlement," I echoed. "What sort of work camps?"

"I don't know," he said honestly, "but I figure working for the Germans. For the war. Lifting, hauling. That sort of thing."

"Just men, then?" I couldn't be deported. Anna wouldn't know where to find me if I was resettled in the east.

"Well, no. But there could be factory work, too."

I swallowed audibly. "Where did you hear this?"

"My brother-in-law knows someone who heard it from someone on the Judenrat," said Benjamin. "Masha hasn't mentioned anything? I know you share an apartment."

"Masha doesn't talk much," I said flatly. "I wouldn't know."

"Oh." He looked as if he might say something else but thought better of it. "There's been six cases of dysentery this past week," he said instead. "Four were children. I'm concerned."

"Is that higher than usual?" I looked down at the papers I was working on and thought of the imagined Veronika of the black braids and solemn eyes. Would she catch it and perish before she had the chance to escape?

"Yes. I'm worried about an outbreak." His voice seemed especially agitated.

I sighed, running my hands through my hair, agitated. "Have you told Jolanta and the others?"

"Not yet." He paused, still hovering. He had a pained look on his pale face, as if he was struggling with whether or not to speak.

"I know what you're doing here," he blurted suddenly. "I need you to get my daughter out."

I deliberately avoided eye contact. "I don't know what you mean."

"Please." He put a hand down on mine, his expression urgent now. "My wife has been unwell since the first round of typhoid. If I'm deported—who would look after Shayndl? My parents are dead, we have no one left. You need to get her out. She'll die here."

"I don't know what you mean," I said again, more firmly this time.

"Please!" he was shouting now, and I shrunk against the back of my chair. "Please, Lina. I know you get the children out. Take Shayndl. She's only five. Please."

I looked down at the papers I was painstakingly drafting, and didn't speak for a moment. How could I let Shayndl languish in the ghetto when I had the means to get her out? I took a deep breath, then leafed through the list of names and ages I'd been given by Jolanta for the week.

"Veronika," I said quietly.

"Pardon?" His eyebrows furrowed in confusion.

"Your daughter. Her name is now Veronika. She's five and recently orphaned. She's going to stay with her Aunt Emilia outside of Lodz." I tapped the paper with the back of my pencil, gesturing.

He blinked and sank to his knees. "Thank you, Lina. Thank—"

"Get up," I hissed, thankful no one else was in the office. "Benjamin, if you ever say anything…."

"I would never…." He clasped his hands together.

"Just go. Someone will be in touch with details."

"How can I ever repay you?"

"Shush." I motioned for him to go, but then grabbed his arm.

"Benjamin."

"Yes?"

"Shayndl. What does she look like?"

His expression softened and he reached into his pocket to retrieve a tiny, crumpled photo.

"She's beautiful," he said, voice catching.

I stared at the photograph, at the little girl with two dark braids and soulful brown eyes.

"Yes," I said, handing it back to him. I looked away so he couldn't see I was crying. "Yes, she is."

❧

"The east," I said to Masha. My tone was sharp.

"What about it?"

I could tell she wanted to change the subject. She took a step back, as if by increasing the physical space between us she could avoid my question.

"People are saying there are going to be deportations. Resettlement somewhere. Is this true?"

Masha hesitated.

"Labor camps," she said finally. "The Germans are demanding workers. That's all. Some people may be asked to resettle. In the east, somewhere."

"The women, too?" I stared hard at Masha.

She stared back, unblinking. "Probably." It came out barely above a whisper.

We stood near the sink where I clutched an egg, a precious egg that Masha had brought home for us wrapped in a faded blue cloth. I raised it now like a fist at her.

"What work are the women going to do, Masha?"

Masha looked uncomfortable. "There are factories," she said vaguely.

"Factories?" I tried and failed to imagine myself as a factory worker. "What kind? And how do you know all this?"

"Lina, for a smart girl, you ask a lot of stupid questions." Her voice was harsh now. "Sometimes it is better to be quiet."

Shocked, I lost my grasp on the egg. I watched it fall to the ground.

"No!" I cried as the shell shattered, giving way to oozing innards. I dropped to my knees, brushing frantically at the white and yellow, grabbing a bowl to try to scrape it into. Flecked with dirt and dust, it should have been thrown out, but we could not reject an egg for the sake of a little dirt. I would salvage it. Miraculously, the yolk, round and shiny, was still intact.

"This is where questions get you," said Masha. "Don't ask any more."

"But, Masha...."

I broke off as the yolk ruptured. I gave a small cry of despair and frustration, watching as the viscous insides slipped through my fingers like water.

⁊⁘

Once, before Mama died, before Anna was born, we took a trip to the countryside. We packed a picnic and ate on the grass. Fruit and cheese and boiled eggs still in their shells, which I loved to peel.

There was a couple nearby having a similar afternoon, enjoying the pleasant weather with their dog. It was a large dog, a German shepherd, and frightening looking, even though Tateh assured me these dogs could be friendly.

"Its teeth look sharp," I recall whimpering, and I remember Mama patting my arm reassuringly.

"That's because it's a carnivore," she explained. "It eats meat. It needs sharp teeth to hunt and tear at its prey."

Tear. The word had filled me with acute fear. I imagined the jaws of the fierce-looking animal around my leg, tearing.

I shrank into my mother, hiding in her armpit.

The dog danced around its owners as I watched out of the corner of my eye. It dug its nose into the bushes, burying its snout deep in the greenery.

That's when it happened.

There was a loud cry. The dog lifted its head, screaming in agony. It turned itself in several circles before trying to run. In frozen horror, I watched as a nest of wasps pursued and attacked the poor beast while the couple tried to chase the swarm away.

The woman eventually turned and ran in the opposite direction, screaming loudly, and never even pausing to look back. The dog continued to howl as the wasps mercilessly attacked him. They turned on the man as well, and he cried out as he was repeatedly stung.

When they rounded up Jews for the first deportation from the Warsaw ghetto in July, I remembered the swarming wasps.

I was leaving work when I heard the shouting. I hadn't made it past the front steps, and like the child I'd been at the picnic, I froze as the shouting soldiers grabbed people, pushing and herding them like cattle. Frightened, people tried to escape only to be chased by the swarming officers angrily waving batons and shouting as they steered the bewildered mass of humanity toward the train station at Umschlagplatz. In the distance, I saw a hazy figure I recognized as Benjamin being hit by a Nazi soldier while he was forced to move into the station.

I fled.

Like the woman who'd abandoned her husband and dog, I turned and raced back up the concrete steps, taking them two at a time. I didn't stop running until I was back in my office.

"They're rounding people up," I said breathlessly. I didn't pause to see who was still there. "Hide!"

There was a confused silence, followed by panic. Under desks and into cupboards we went, overturning boxes and scattering supplies. I stuffed myself into a shallow cupboard formerly filled with supplies. The air was hot and thick, and I dozed off. When I finally woke up and left, it was night.

"Where are the others?" I asked when I returned to our

flat. Only Masha was there. My clothes were damp from hours of sweating in the stifling closet, and I stank. Masha's nose wrinkled as I came near.

"Gone," she said quietly. She didn't look at me.

I sucked in my breath. "All of them?"

"Yes."

"What if I hadn't come back?"

She wordlessly handed me a small loaf of bread and said nothing.

❦

"Benjamin was deported," I told Jolanta dully the following day. I wiped my brow, heavy with sweat. "I saw it."

Jolanta's face softened. "I know."

"His daughter, Shayndl, I…."

"I know, Lina. He told me, before. We've got her."

"Veronika," I said softly. The hot, damp hair on the back of my neck felt cool as I thought of the little girl and her new name. "Her name is Veronika now."

"Yes."

"Jolanta…those trains…." I fidgeted nervously with the pencil in my hands. "Do you know…? Where were they going?"

Jolanta looked grim. "Work camps. Or so we've been told by the Resistance."

I nodded uneasily.

"We want to get more children out," said Jolanta. "Not just orphans anymore. As many children as possible."

I thought of little Shayndl, now Veronika.

"Children with parents, you mean."

"Yes. Parents are desperate."

"Because the children will be left behind?"

Jolanta gave me a strange look. "Weren't you outside yesterday? Didn't you witness it?"

"The roundup?" I flinched. "I—I saw some of it." My cheeks felt hot as I remembered hiding in the supply cupboard.

"They took the children, too," she said softly.

I stared, confused. "But—children can't work?"

"That's why we think they may not be work camps." Her voice was small.

"Not work camps?" I repeated stupidly.

"No," she whispered. "Not work camps."

Chapter 13

ANNA
Fall, 1942

"GOING TO SEE Piotr?" Elsbietta winked, and I blushed furiously.

"Yes, but I'm just going to return this book," I protested. I waved it as proof.

"Sure," said Elsbietta slyly.

"Ria." Patryk rushed and grabbed me around my knees. "Up!"

"Patryk, come now. Your sister needs some time to herself." Elsbietta moved to pull him back, but he clung tighter.

"You know what? You can come." I scooped him up and rested him on my hip. Patryk beamed and threw his arms around my neck. I inhaled the sweet baby smell of his head and kissed it.

"Oh, Maria, no." Elsbietta looked distressed. "You rarely have any time to yourself."

"It's no problem," I said cheerfully. "Patryk can come. He can play with Eva and Ursula."

"Meow!" Patryk looked excited. He loved Ursula, who was much friendlier than our aloof barn cats.

"If you're sure." She looked dubious.

"Of course! It will be fine." I set Patryk down. "Ready? You can walk like a big boy. You can run! It'll be a race."

"Run!" He clapped his hands together excitedly. Elsbietta and I exchanged a smile.

Patryk and I made our way through the field between our farm and the Kowalskis', avoiding the main roads so Patryk could run and tumble. He ran ahead of me, his little bowlegged frame toddling and pointing.

"Ria!" Patryk pointed excitedly. "Woof!"

He ran toward a moving speck in the distance. I squinted. There was a dog, and close behind it was a man in a pale brown uniform.

"Nazi," I whispered to myself, freezing. Patryk continued to run, arms waving in excitement at the four-legged creature trotting toward us. My heart quickened as the soldier came closer.

"*Heil Hitler!*" he declared. He grabbed the dog's collar. "Careful, Shatzi," he said to it. "You'll knock him down."

He flashed me a toothy grin, and I forced a weak smile. He was young, near Lina's age. I scooped Patryk up into my arms despite his wriggles and protests.

"Your son?" The soldier nodded at Patryk and stared at me, his gaze lingering on my face before dropping lower.

My *son*? I shook my head. "My brother," I whispered.

The Nazi shrugged. "You look a bit young, but you never

169

know with Polish peasants." He flashed another grin, but this time I didn't smile back.

"What's your name?" he said, turning to Patryk.

"Patryk," I answered for him.

"And you?" His eyes traveled up and down my body. "What's your name, *Mädchen*?"

"Maria," I whispered, my eyes on my battered shoes. I clutched my bag with the book against my chest with one hand.

"My mother's name!" He nodded approvingly. "She's not a redhead like you, though."

I said nothing, fidgeting anxiously.

"I've always liked redheads." He caught my eye. "Your brother doesn't have red hair."

"Maybe not," I agreed, my voice trembling. "It looks as if it may be blonde, like my father's was."

"Blonde?" He frowned, inspecting. "Perhaps."

"Dog?" Patryk had stopped squirming, still staring longingly at the German Shepherd, now seated. Grateful for the distraction, I forced a beseeching smile.

"May he pet your dog, sir?"

"But of course," he said, putting out his arms for Patryk. "And you can call me Hans, pretty Maria."

"Thank you…Hans." His name felt repulsive on my tongue.

"You live over there?" He gestured toward our farm, and I nodded.

"I'll make sure to call on you."

Warily, I watched him take Patryk and set him down

next to the giant dog. Delighted, Patryk pet the animal gently between the ears, making small barking sounds.

"Adorable," said the soldier. "Shatzi is very friendly."

"Patryk loves animals," I said, becoming more uncomfortable. "Okay, Patryk," I said after a few moments. "Time to go."

"Bye, dog!" Patryk gleefully pet the animal's head one final time.

"Say thank you, please," I reminded him.

"Thank you, please," he echoed brightly. Hans gave a loud laugh and reached down to ruffle Patryk's downy hair.

"Have a good day, pretty Maria," he said, winking. "I'm sure we'll see each other again soon."

I nodded uneasily, glad to leave him behind. I grabbed Patryk's hand and we moved quicker through the field. I didn't look back. I had a feeling if I did, Hans would still be watching.

❧

"Is the German who brings Eva her medicine named Hans?"

I had dropped off Patryk with Eva, who was thrilled to babysit. Piotr and I were in the hayloft, our legs dangling over the side.

Piotr made a face. "The young one is Hans. The older one is Joseph; he's a good sort of person, for a German. He has a daughter with epilepsy, like Eva. Hans is different."

"How?" I thought of his cold grin.

Piotr frowned. "He's the kind of man who seems like he would pull legs off spiders, tails off mice."

I winced. "Patryk and I met him in the field."

Piotr sat up straighter. "He didn't hurt you, did he?"

"No." I shook my head. "But he made me feel…." I struggled to find the right word. "Unsafe," I said finally.

Piotr kicked a bunch of hay and we watched it float to the ground below like yellow snow.

"I wish I was old enough to fight," he said. "I hate the Nazis. I hate that they're here."

I put a tentative hand on his arm. "Me too."

He shook his head. "I'm so insensitive. Your parents are dead because of them, and I'm complaining."

I thought of Tateh and Lina, who may very well be dead by now. I wondered what Piotr would think if he knew the truth.

"Let's talk about something else," I suggested, and retrieved the book.

"Oh!" Our fingers touched briefly as he took it. I felt a small jolt that made me want to touch him again, while at the same time I wanted pull away. Our eyes met. Flustered, we both looked away.

"What did you think of the book?"

I stole a glance at him. His cheeks were quite red. My face flushed in response, and I stared at my lap. My mind had gone blank.

"Umm," I said. "It was very good."

I stared at my dangling feet, at the too-small shoes that pinched my toes. I noticed that Piotr's leg was closer to mine than it had been previously. Our knees were almost touching.

"What about you?" I asked. I inched my leg even closer to his, my calf momentarily brushing against his.

"What about me?" His voice sounded slightly hoarse.

"What did you think?"

"Good," he croaked.

I found I couldn't look at him. Instead, my gaze fixed downward on our legs, now touching. I wondered if he knew they were touching, or if it didn't mean the same thing to him.

"Maria!" Eva came rushing into the barn, and Piotr pulled away quickly, twisting away from me. I didn't know whether I felt disappointed or relieved.

"Is everything alright?" I jumped up. "Patryk?"

"He's asking for you. He says he has a stomachache."

"Oh, no." I clambered down the ladder.

"What's wrong, sweetheart?" I found Patryk curled up on the grass.

Patryk pointed to his belly. "Hurt." He rolled over and began to cry.

"Is he alright?" Piotr looked anxious. "What's wrong with him?"

"Probably just needs to…you know. Go to the toilet." I blushed. What was wrong with me? Piotr had grown up on a farm. He wasn't unfamiliar with bodily functions.

"Right." Piotr was blushing too. "It's this way."

"Piotr." Eva rolled her eyes. "He's too little! He wears diapers."

"Oh." Piotr flushed an even deeper red. "What do we do, then?"

"I think he's going right now," announced Eva cheerfully. She gestured at Patryk, whose own face had gone purple, his eyebrows furrowed in a look of deep concentration.

"I'll fetch some cloth and pins," she added. "Piotr, go get Maria a towel."

Piotr rushed off.

"Feeling better?" I asked Patryk tenderly.

"All done," he agreed, beaming at me.

I laughed. "You stink," I informed him, grinning.

He laughed too. "Stink!"

"Yes," I agreed. I waved my hand in front of my nose dramatically. "Stinky!"

He laughed harder, and I bent next to him to tickle his chubby belly, poking out from beneath his small shirt.

"Here," Piotr appeared beside me, sounding breathless. He was brandishing a large bucket and a stack of towels. Eva was at his heels with the promised cloth and pins, and also some talcum powder.

"Goodness," she said appraisingly, settling the supplies down beside me on the grass. She stared at the bucket. "He's a small baby, Piotr, not a cow."

Piotr looked mortified. "I wasn't sure."

Eva crouched beside me. "I can help," she said proudly. "I've helped with my cousins."

"Thank you," I said gravely, recognizing this was important to her. "Can you get a damp towel ready?"

Eva busied herself with the towel. Piotr sat on the grass next to me, wincing at the smell as I pulled off Patryk's short pants and the dirty diaper.

I wiped Patryk's tiny bottom. He giggled and tried to grab and eat fistfuls of grass. Eva kept him distracted, grabbing at his hands and making faces as I cleaned him up.

Next to me, Piotr was very quiet. I stole a glance at him and noticed him staring between Patryk's legs. His eyes met mine and I frowned quizzically at the expression on his face. What was he looking at? For a boy who lived on a farm, he was acting quite strange.

Eva didn't notice. She expertly handed me cloths and pins, and together we got Patryk clean and dry.

"There you go," I said to him, standing him back up.

"Happy," he said, clapping his hands together, and Eva clapped her own, delighted.

"Can I give him a biscuit?" she asked me in a whisper. "Mama found a beehive out behind the barn. We made some biscuits with real honey."

"Of course!" I said warmly. "He would love that."

Eva took Patryk by the hand, and he toddled alongside her.

I turned to look at Piotr, who was staring at me with an odd expression.

"Piotr?" Uncertain, I took a step toward him. "Is something wrong?"

"No," he said hurriedly, but he wouldn't meet my gaze. "No, why would it be?"

"You're acting strangely," I said carefully.

"I just—I'm tired, that's all." He yawned exaggeratedly.

"Okay," I said dubiously, a slight twinge in my belly.

"And I said I'd help my father with the cow, so I should probably get going."

"Alright." I felt a sudden cramp in my abdomen and my breath caught. I bit down on the inside of my cheek. "I'm actually not feeling that well myself, so I should probably get going, too."

For a moment, he was the old Piotr again. "Are you alright?" His eyes flickered with genuine concern.

The pain passed. "No," I said quickly. "No, I'll just get Patryk and head back."

"Probably best," he agreed, not looking at me again. I felt another pain, this one very different from a belly ache.

I found Patryk, who was not happy to leave Eva. Wailing loudly, he pounded at my shoulder with tiny fists as I carried him off.

"No!" he cried, squirming. "Play! Play Eva!"

"Another time," I told him. I shifted him to my other hip as I felt another cramp.

Eva rushed over with another biscuit. "Here you go, Patryk," she said kindly.

Greedily, he grabbed for it, but she pulled it back.

"Only if you stop crying and are a good boy for Maria," she said firmly.

The crying stopped as suddenly as it had started. Patryk graciously accepted his treat and sucked happily on it. I smiled wanly at Eva and deliberately did not look over at Piotr, who turned away. He was trying not to look at me.

"Ow," I gasped, pausing. It felt like I'd been stabbed with a hot poker beneath my navel.

Patryk pulled back to look at me, worried.

"Ria hurt?" He looked sad.

"Yes," I agreed, wincing at the pain. "Ria hurt."

"Patryk walk," he announced, wriggling out of my arms. "Run."

Patryk broke into a run ahead of me, giving me some time to think about Piotr's sudden strange reaction. I thought of his face, the stricken expression. Patryk's diaper, his exposed bottom and wriggling legs. Could a dirty diaper really make someone that uncomfortable?

"Race, Ria?" Patryk waved his arms. "Run?"

I nodded and picked up my pace, but the cramps continued. I wondered whether I was getting sick like those in the ghetto, people dying of typhoid, like Rivka. Then I thought about Rivka and Dov, both dead before the baby's bris.

The baby's bris.

I stopped in my tracks as the realization hit me. Polish boys didn't look like that, between the legs. What had I done? Piotr had seen Patryk naked, had seen he wasn't like the Polish boys. Patryk had been circumcised. I remembered when Lina had explained to me that it was an important Jewish tradition.

Piotr was smart. He must have noticed immediately.

How could I explain my carelessness to Elsbietta, after all her kindness? Frantic, I scooped up Patryk. Maybe I could run off with him. There were partisan groups in the forest, I knew. Maybe we could hide with them.

As I stumbled home, Elsbietta was in the field, her hair matted with sweat as she planted row after row of potatoes and carrots. The Nazis would take most of it, she had explained, but there would be some left for us. *I should have been here helping,* I thought, furious with myself. *If I hadn't run off to see a boy, this would never have happened.*

Elsbietta could see something was wrong.

"Maria," she said, putting an arm around my shoulder. "What is it?"

I couldn't hold back the tears. I crumbled, sobbing as I pulled away from her. I held my stomach.

"Maria!" She sounded baffled, and Patryk chimed in, wailing loudly.

Breathless, I doubled over.

"Oh, Maria." Elsbietta's voice softened. "I understand. Let's get you inside and clean you up."

I stared at her confused. I followed her gaze downward and stared at my dress. A small red stain had appeared between my legs.

"Did the boy see? It's part of life, my dear girl, but I know how you must feel. Especially without your mother."

"He didn't notice," I managed to say.

"Are you in much pain?" she hugged me to her, and I gave in, overcome with shock. "I have a hot water bottle that can help."

"I only know the science," I admitted helplessly. Nothing in my books had prepared me for the practical side of becoming a woman, the reality of the blood and pain.

"That's what I'm here for," said Elsbietta with a kind smile, and I dissolved again into tears. How could I tell her what my tears were really about? I wondered what the penalty was for hiding Jews. I buried my head in her shoulder.

Tucked into bed, I wondered if Piotr had already told anyone. How much longer did we have?

Drifting off, I dreamed of Piotr grabbing me by the hand and leading me into the forest.

"A beehive," he said, pointing. "See?"

"Yes," I answered. "But what is that?"

I pointed to a small lump on the ground, covered by a sheet.

"That is Patryk," he said, pulling it back. Covering Patryk's body were hundreds of bees. When I looked up again, Piotr's shape had shifted. In his place stood Hans, the Nazi, smiling malevolently down at me.

Chapter 14

LINA
Fall, 1942

THERE WAS POUNDING on the door of our flat before dawn, and shouting in German and Polish.

"Everyone out!" The voice barked loudly. "Everyone out, now!"

I grabbed my dress and wrestled it over my head.

"Schnell!" The German word for "fast" rang in my ears as I tied my shoes. I turned to see two soldiers—one old, one young—brandishing guns.

I stood quickly, head bowed, and said nothing.

"Let's go," the older one snapped. "Now."

"Am I coming back?" I asked quietly; a simple question. I avoided eye contact with the older soldier, who was doing all the barking, and cast a sideways glance at the younger. He was about my age and looked uncomfortable.

The older man laughed. "Not likely. Let's go." He waved a gun at me and turned from the doorway.

The younger man looked at me helplessly. I gave him a

soft smile and stood. I crouched beneath the bed to grab my photos of Mama, Tateh, and Anna as a baby.

"What the hell is going on in there?" I heard the older man's voice. "Franz?"

"We're coming," Franz shouted, then lowered his voice. "Do you have everything you want to take?"

I thought of everything I wanted to take with me: my lost sister, my dead father and mother, the books we'd left behind.

"Yes," I said instead. And then, "Thank you."

Franz reddened and averted his eyes. I wondered if he carried photos of his loved ones, too.

Masha was at the door, trembling. She held papers in her hand.

"I'm an essential worker," she said, trying to square her shoulders. She gestured at the papers and launched into a stream of German.

The older Nazi waved away the papers, dismissive. *"Schweig!"*

"But…."

"Quiet!" He repeated, and hit Masha in the ribs with the butt of his rifle. I saw the younger man flinch and turn away.

"Everyone out and no goddamn talking." He looked at Masha. "Do you hear me, Jew?"

Masha's face was neutral, a blank mask, though she was in pain. She nodded, a slight motion of her head that managed to convey defiance.

We marched out quietly, joining the throngs of our neighbors in the street.

"Mama, where are we going?" a little boy nearby whined loudly.

"Shush," his mother said anxiously, looking around.

"But Mama…."

"We're going on a journey," the woman interrupted, her voice shaking.

"To where Papa went?"

"Yes, so be brave if you want to see him again."

I glanced sideways at Masha, whose stony gaze was fixed on some unknown point in the distance. Our Nazis had joined up with their compatriots and were no longer identifiable.

"Masha," I said softly.

She looked at me, her eyes alight with a mixture of anger and despair. "There's nothing I can do." Her voice was toneless.

"What about…?" I struggled to remember the name of the head of the Judenrat. "Czernikow?"

"Adam Czernikow is dead."

"Dead?" I was shocked. Men in charge didn't die, I thought, even if they were Jews.

"He killed himself," she said curtly. "Cyanide capsule. He couldn't bring himself to deal with the deportations. He couldn't live with the guilt."

"Where are they taking us, Masha?" I grabbed her arm.

She was silent for a long moment, her eyes on the pavement. "To a place called Treblinka," she said finally.

I searched my memory. "The mining town?"

"Quarry. But most won't be working."

I thought of what Jolanta had said.

"But, Masha," I said practically, trying to ignore my pounding heart. "Why not just shoot us all here?"

"I'm not sure," she said, shaking her head. "But I know it's something terrible. That's all I've heard, Lina, I swear it."

I fell silent. The crowds shuffled in, wearily attempting to pick up the pace as the soldiers shouted and prodded them on with batons and rifles. I closed my eyes and withdrew into myself, focusing on images of the past to motivate me to move forward, rather than simply sink to my knees on the high street and be trampled or shot.

Anna as a rosy-cheeked infant. Anna as a jovial toddler. Anna as a clever student. Anna brave in the tunnels, risking her life for our food.

My feet moved of their own accord, detached from the rest of me. It was hot and the collective sweat of the marching bodies began to stink. I breathed through my mouth, and my throat went dry and scratchy.

"How much further?" a woman nearby carrying a baby cried out in obvious exhaustion.

"I can help carry her," I said quietly, nodding at the baby. "If your arms are tired."

"Thank you," she said, grateful. She held the baby out to me, and I tucked her against my hip.

"Do you know where we're going?"

I chose my words carefully. There was no need to frighten this young mother. She would learn the truth soon enough.

"Treblinka. It's a quarry. I suppose we'll be forced to work."

She looked worried. "Who will look after my baby?"

"I don't know," I mumbled.

The baby began to cry. I jiggled her in my arms, shushing her. Her mother did not move to reclaim her, instead looking frightened.

"She needs to eat," she whispered urgently. "I need to feed her."

I looked around nervously. "She'll have to wait," I said. "We need to keep going. There is nowhere to feed her here." The woman swallowed, nodding. Her hair was matted with sweat, and she pawed at the loose strands that touched her neck with a frantic urgency.

I jiggled the baby and stuck a finger in her mouth, something I'd done with Anna when I didn't have a bottle ready. The baby stared at me, shocked, but stopped crying before I handed her back to her mother.

We walked and walked. I don't know when I lost Masha, but when I realized she was gone I felt even more anxious.

"Those are cattle cars," I blurted out to the woman with the baby.

"They're putting us in those?" She stared in disbelief as we approached. She looked down at her baby daughter sorrowfully. "Sometimes I wish the typhoid would have taken me like it did my husband. What is the point of living if this is living?"

She waved at the cattle cars and at the broken people around us.

"I understand," I said simply. I put a hand on her shoulder and squeezed gently before she was forced into a separate line.

She stared desperately at me before she turned away, no longer visible in the crowd.

Lines were formed as we filed into the cattle cars. Those who had brought luggage were forced to leave it in a growing pile.

"Your belongings will be brought separately," we were told repeatedly. "They will come on a separate train."

"But how will we find them?" one man called out, worried. His eyes were on his suitcase, one of many in a sea of baggage.

"Into the train!" the soldier barked. The man's shoulders sagged, staring longingly at his bag as he was forced inside a train.

I wondered what was inside the suitcase. *Photographs? Love letters?*

"Name?" someone barked at me. He was younger than me, but old enough to shave. He looked at me with determined brown eyes, even while his hands trembled.

"Lina Krawitz," I said calmly.

"Papers?"

I handed them over.

"Into the train." He jerked a shaking thumb, and I felt inexplicably sorry for him. Did he have any more choice about being here than I did?

I stepped inside. It was already full, with women seated on the floor around the perimeter and men standing closer to the center. Many of the women had children in their laps or held against their chests. The smell was unbearable.

I scanned the car for someone I might know. My eyes

found Masha, and I realized our fates were obviously inter-twined. She stood close to the perimeter, away from the men but not entirely with the women, either.

"Lina," she said, looking relieved. "Thank goodness."

"Thank goodness?" I echoed. "What is there to be thank-ful for?"

"I saw two people shot," she said flatly. "An old woman who couldn't walk, and the young man who talked back to the soldiers about it."

I thought of the mother and baby. Would they shoot an infant?

A man who clearly knew Masha came over, keeping his voice low. "No matter how you feel, when we get there, you must act like you're strong and healthy."

"And if we're not?" I challenged. I wondered how long we'd be crammed in here. There was a bucket in the corner that would serve as a toilet for all the prisoners inside the car. I didn't see any food.

"I've heard they kill everyone who can't work," he said quietly. He was deliberately avoiding looking around him; at the mothers with small children. At the old men who held their caps in hand, twisting them nervously.

"How do you kill so many people?" I whispered. "Why not just kill everyone here and now?"

"They must have more space for bodies there." Masha kept her voice low too. "That's what people are saying, anyway."

The man swallowed, his Adam's apple visible in his emaci-ated neck. "I've heard something worse."

"Worse?" I said sharply. "What is worse than death?"

"There are reports of poisonous gas," he said uneasily.

"So, it's true," Masha breathed, and I gave her an angry look.

"You said you didn't know anything more," I said accusingly. "You swore it."

"I didn't know for certain. What would be the point of spreading such a rumor?"

I didn't answer. I looked around the car at the poor souls who believed their luggage would meet them. I thought of the Nazi with the shaking hands. Would he get his pick of the spoils?

There was a loud whistle outside and the rumbling of an engine. I tripped slightly, knocking Masha off-balance. We clutched each other and, when I saw the terrified expression in her eyes, I shut my own.

I didn't imagine the journey would be pleasant, but I could never have dreamed the misery of the journey to Treblinka. The waste bucket soon overflowed and, with the movement of the train, it sloshed over our feet, I wondered if it would be easier to give in to sleep. The train had a rhythm to it, the slow sound of the engine, the grind of the wheels. I rocked in time to the sound, my body swaying. I slept in minute-long fits as I stood, my knees buckling from exhaustion. Around me, mothers tried to calm frightened children who cried for food and water. The crowd, civil at first, turned on each other as the hours passed.

"Can you shut that thing up?" a man snarled in the direction of a wailing baby.

"She's hungry and wet and sitting in her own shit," the mother snapped back. "What can I do?"

"Feed the stupid thing," someone else called.

"She's two! She eats food! If you have some, I'll gladly take it."

"Put a goddamn hand over her mouth," another muttered.

"Shut up, all of you!" It was Masha, next to me, and I jumped.

The car fell silent. An elderly woman with a bit of bread divided it between a group of hungry toddlers. Their chewing sounds made my stomach growl and twist like metal screws scraping one another.

The hours passed and I needed to relieve myself. I ignored it at first. Weaving in and out of consciousness, my half-awake dreams were of water: puddles in the ghetto, running faucets, a leaking pipe in our old apartment.

I jerked awake for a third time and realized, mortified, I had wet myself. Tears stung my eyes at the discomfort and the indignity.

"We've all done it by now. You were the last, I think," Masha said, still beside me.

"How did you know…?"

"I'm standing next to you, Lina. My shoes are wet, and you smell."

I had a sudden urge to laugh. "I smell?"

I could hear the smile in Masha's voice. "You smell like a dirty diaper."

I sniffed, a half-laugh, half-cry. "Well, your breath smells like rotten eggs, Masha."

Masha barked with laughter, then groaned. "I would eat rotten eggs now. You're making me hungry."

My stomach growled at the word "hungry."

"Apparently, I would too," I said. Wiping the tears from my cheek, I impulsively licked my hands. The salt tasted wonderful, the moisture soothing.

The train continued, and Masha and I took turns sleeping while the other held the sleeper upright.

Finally, abruptly, the train stopped. Those near the door cracks and windows pressed their faces against the walls to try to see outside.

"What do you see?" a man called out.

Another, tall enough to peer out, shook his head. "Not much. There's nothing, really."

"Nothing?" a woman's voice echoed his skeptically. "How can there be nothing?"

The doors were flung open suddenly, knocking down an elderly man and a heavily pregnant woman.

"Out!" The soldiers waiting on the outside looked even more cruel than the ones in the ghetto. *"Raus! Raus!"*

People scrambled, driven by hunger and fear.

"Women and children, this way!" one soldier shouted out, gesturing. "Men, this way."

"No!" someone called out. "I'm not leaving my wife."

"You'll be reunited soon," another soldier said reassuringly. "After."

"After what?" someone demanded.

"After the delousing and cleaning," the soldier said. "Men and women separate for the showers."

We dutifully exited. Four had not survived the journey: an elderly woman, a middle-aged man, and a woman and her new-born infant curled in a corner, blue from lack of air. I looked away quickly, the image seared in my brain.

"Women this way!" a soldier barked at me and Masha, jerking his rifle to the left.

"Where are we going?" I asked in German. "What is going on?"

He stopped, studying me appraisingly. "You speak German?"

"Yes," I said warily.

"You too?" He looked at Masha.

"Of course she does," I said quickly. I tried to remember if Masha spoke German or not—my mind befuddled from hours on the train. I gave silent thanks to Tateh for teaching me to read and speak Polish, German, and even a smattering of Russian and English.

"Come with me," he said.

We followed him, our hands laced tightly together. We bypassed the long line of women and crying children, past a large brick building where those in line were filing inside. Faint screams could be heard even through the thick stone walls. Masha and I exchanged a fearful glance.

"*Was gibts dort?*" Masha asked in German, and I felt relieved. She could speak German after all.

The soldier looked uneasy. "Showers. They scream because it's crowded, and the water is very cold."

Something about this did not ring true, and I squeezed Masha's hand tighter.

We followed the German along gravel roads. There were few buildings. The prisoners so thin and haggard that we seemed robust and healthy in comparison. With heads shaved or close to it, it was hard to tell their sex or age. They could have been eighteen or eighty, men or women.

"Where are all the workers?" Masha said innocently.

"Oh, they're around." The soldier gestured vaguely. "This is quite a big camp, you know."

I didn't know anything, but I nodded. The soldier saw someone he knew and waved. The man waved back and yelled something in rapid German, slang I couldn't quite make out, but I knew it was lewd about me and Masha. I flushed and stared at my feet, now covered with a thick gray coat of gravelly dust.

"This way," the soldier said, nodding toward a cavernous building. It looked like a barn that had been converted to a more solid structure. My heart pounded as we followed him inside.

"Laundry," he said, gesturing to the open door of a large room. "We need more women to do the laundry. Ones who can speak German."

"Hannelore!" he shouted to a woman in a Nazi soldier's uniform at the front of the room. "I found two healthy, German-speaking women for you. They stink, but they're not too ugly. I know you hate ugly Jews."

Hannelore turned to stare at us, starting at our feet and working up to our faces. She walked over, swinging her baton in time to her step.

"This one is a bit skinny," she said, nodding at me. She poked me hard in the ribs, and I tried not to cry out. "Shouldn't you have breasts by now, Jew?"

"Passable face, though," the soldier protested. "Look at her blue eyes."

Hannelore snorted, and proceeded to reach out and squeeze one of Masha's breasts. "This one at least has some meat. I hate all these starving people, Heinrich. It's depressing."

"This one seems more difficult," Heinrich warned her. "I don't like the way she looks me right in the eye."

"Is that right, Jew?" Hannelore took her baton and whacked it, hard, against Masha's behind. Masha blinked hard, but said nothing.

"Well, they'll do, I suppose." Hannelore sighed loudly. She snapped and hailed another woman, who hurried over, looking frightened.

"Take these two to get cleaned up. Get them uniforms. They smell foul and it is making me unhappy. I am thinking I might blame you for it, Magda."

Magda murmured something incomprehensible and signaled to us. We followed her, relieved to leave Heinrich and Hannelore behind.

"This way," she mumbled. "Hurry."

"How long have you been here, Magda?" asked Masha. "And how did you end up here?"

The woman gave her a pained look. "You ask a lot of questions. And my name isn't Magda. She calls all the Polish girls 'Magda' and all the Jews 'Sarah.' My name is Halina."

"I'm Masha and this is Lina," Masha nodded at me. "How did you end up here?"

Halina motioned for us to go through a door. "There was a bakery bombing in Warsaw. I delivered a message."

"From the Resistance?" Masha looked impressed.

Halina shrugged, tired. "Yes, but look where it got me. It would have been better to die in the bombing."

"Did any of *them* die?" Masha's voice dripped venom at the word "them."

Halina's lip curled into a half-grin. "Three."

There was a shower through the door, and a stack of uniforms. Halina pointed to each in turn. "Get cleaned up and put those on. Hurry, too, or she'll beat you. She enjoys it. She's much worse than any of the men."

"What is this place, exactly?" asked Masha, disrobing. Halina moved away as the pungent odor from Masha's clothing dissipated once it hit the tiled floor. "What happens here?"

I followed suit. It felt better to be free of the stinking, damp clothing.

Halina gave us a pitiful smile.

"This is Treblinka," she said sadly. "People are sent here to die."

Chapter 15

ANNA
Fall, 1942

"DID YOU AND Piotr have a falling out?" Elsbietta gave me a sidelong glance from where she squatted in the garden, planting potatoes. "He hasn't been by in over a week."

I stared at the ground, hitting the earth hard with my small shovel.

"He's probably busy with the cow," I muttered.

"You haven't gone there, either," she said pointedly. I nodded but said nothing, focusing instead on scooping out soil into a neat little pile.

"I'm sorry," she said after a moment, head bowed. "I remember being your age. You want your privacy, not some nosy old lady bothering you with questions."

I startled, biting my lip. How could I tell her it wasn't that at all, but rather that I was waiting for the Germans to knock on the door at any moment? That I lay awake all night worrying? That I had behaved carelessly so I could be with a boy?

I opened my mouth to try to say something reassuring, but was saved by Patryk who ran to us waving something clutched in his tiny fist.

"Look!" He ran over to me and Elsbietta. "Pretty. For Ria." He pressed it at me, and I put out my palms curiously.

"Ah," I said. It was a string of rosary beads. I smiled at Patryk and handed the beads back to him. "This is Mama's."

"Mama," he agreed, beaming. He walked over to Elsbietta and handed her the string of beads. "For Mama."

Elsbietta smiled and accepted them, and Patryk sat down beside her.

"Pretty," he said again, nodding at the beads.

"These are for praying," Elsbietta explained. She ran her fingers along the beads, showing him.

"We say our prayers," she said. "Like this."

She pronounced the words of the Hail Mary carefully. "*Zdrowaś Maryjo, łaski pełna.*"

Patryk repeated after her, mangling the words slightly. Elsbietta laughed and looked over at me as if to share the humor.

I tried to recover quickly, but I couldn't help thinking of Patryk's bris, back when he was still Dov. His birth parents were gone; Elsbietta was now his mother. Was Patryk now a Catholic child?

Noting my stricken expression, Elsbietta's hand flew to her mouth. "Maria, I'm sorry. I didn't think, I…."

"No, no." Hastily, I shook my head. It was obviously best to assimilate Patryk—not that it would matter once

Piotr reported us. "It's safest. You're doing the right thing. But Elsbietta, I…."

I struggled to find the right words. I wanted to tell her about what had happened, but how to let this kind woman know I'd put us all in terrible danger?

"It's okay, Maria." Elsbietta put a hand on my shoulder and squeezed gently. "I understand how it must feel."

Just then, I heard a familiar voice behind me. "Maria?"

It was Piotr. I froze and took a deep breath as Elsbietta caught my eye, winking encouragingly.

"Piotr! Hello. Maria and I were just discussing your cow." Elsbietta winked again at me, and my heart sank. Slowly, I turned around, reluctant to meet his gaze.

"Hello," I whispered.

"Hello," he said tentatively. "May I take a walk with you?"

"Of course," said Elsbietta, enthusiastically. Poor Elsbietta really had no idea the trouble I had gotten us into. I wondered why Piotr was here alone. Perhaps to warn us the Germans would soon arrive? I thought of Hans and the way he'd stared at me and my insides clenched.

"Piotr!" Patryk jumped up, waving, the rosary beads flying in his hand like a kite string. "Look, pretty!"

Piotr saw the beads and reddened, but quickly recovered. "Very pretty, Patryk." He smiled warmly. "Are you helping your Mama and your sister?"

"Yes." Patryk jumped up. "Play?"

"I'll tell you what." Piotr crouched down until he was at

eye level with Patryk. "Let me have a walk with Maria, and then we can play kick-the-ball."

Patryk brightened. He loved to kick the ball around with Piotr.

"Ball," agreed Patryk happily.

"Excellent." Piotr reached out to ruffle Patryk's hair, and Patryk laughed and ran back to Elsbietta, who gently retrieved the rosary beads and tucked them into her shirtsleeve.

"Maria?" Piotr gave me a sideways glance, looking awkward. "Shall we take a walk toward the forest?"

"If you'd like," I said carefully. I brushed the crumbs of soil from my skirt and followed him, my head still bowed.

I followed Piotr through the field, silent and several steps behind him. When we were out of Elsbietta's earshot, Piotr grabbed my hand. "Why won't you look at me?"

I wrenched my hand away.

"I think you know why." My heart raced. What if he had told? What would I do?

"I know what you're thinking, Maria, because of what I saw but you can't think that I would ever tell, I—"

I cut him off, pulling away. "How do I know you haven't already?"

"How can you even say that?" He sounded wounded. "How could you think I would do that to you? To Patryk?"

I looked up, finally, into his eyes. I saw nothing there but honesty and hurt. My shoulders slumped with relief as I realized he was telling the truth. I exhaled loudly and sat down hard on a nearby rock.

"I've been so scared," I admitted, and I realized I was crying.

"I can't believe you would think I would ever tell." He shook his head and crouched beside me. "That I would let them hurt you."

"I don't know you, Piotr," I said bluntly. It was true. I only knew the Piotr who thought Maria was a good Catholic girl who'd come to live with her relatives. I didn't know how he felt about Jews. I thought of my former Christian friends and the Polish shopkeepers back in Warsaw who'd closed their doors to us once the Germans had arrived. All that hatred lurking under the surface. Who knew what was in anyone's heart?

"That isn't true." He frowned. "I'm still the same person I was before I saw…before I knew."

"Are you?" I stared hard at him.

"Yes!" He glared at me now. "I'm offended, Maria. I just can't believe you would think that of me. That I would tell… *them*." He spat the last word.

"What if it was to save Eva?" I countered. "You let them into your home for Eva's medicine."

His cheeks colored. "That's different."

"Is it?" My voice was bitter, cutting. "I'm not so sure."

"I didn't say anything. I will never betray you." He puffed out his chest bravely. "Please. Maria, you must believe me."

For the first time, I felt rankled at being addressed as Maria and had a sudden yearning to be called by my real name. "My name is not Maria," I blurted.

Piotr stiffened, surprised, then nodded. "Of course, it isn't," he said softly. "Please. Tell me your name."

I felt a rush of different feelings. I was putting myself in even greater danger, hovering recklessly between truth and safety, needing to keep secrets but desperately wanting to break them.

"I can't." I shook my head, my braids whipping the sides of my face, stinging.

"Please." He crept closer, taking my hand. "Please, tell me."

"It's too dangerous."

He brought his face close to mine.

"Tell me." I could feel his breath, hot and damp against my ear. He smelled of earth and salt and milk.

"You can't use it," I said, weakening. "You can never say it. One slip and I'm dead."

"I know that…."

"Dead!" I said harshly. My lips brushed his ear. "Dead against the barn wall, shot…."

"Stop it!" He pulled me gently down onto the grass. Our eyes met and locked, and I felt a wave of something powerful from something deep inside me.

"Anna," I whispered. "My name is Anna."

"Anna," he whispered softly. He brought his lips to mine. I closed my eyes, my body thrilling even as the reasonable girl inside my head admonished me for being a fool.

I ignored her.

❧

Later, Piotr and I walked hand in hand following a path through the forest.

"Anna," he breathed, stepping on a pile of twigs.

"Shush!" I thought of Lina and the promises I'd made. "I told you, you can't use it. Please, Piotr. Think of Patryk."

"No one's here." He waved his arms around, looking relaxed. "I love it out here just for that reason."

"You never know who else loves it out here," I pointed out.

That quieted him.

"Sorry," he whispered.

"It's alright." I reached up and pulled a loose branch, snapping it from its tree trunk. I'm used to secrets and lies, but you're new to it."

"What happened to your parents?" he looked at me, curious and sad. "Was it all just a story?"

"Sort of." I held the branch between my palms, feeling the edges. "My mother died in childbirth. My father and older sister were alive when I left Warsaw. Patryk is an orphan, the baby of our friends. His mother died after his birth."

"So, he's not really your…," Piotr began to speak and then stopped, shaking his head. "No, that's not true."

"What's not?" I furrowed my eyebrows, frowning.

"I was going to say he's not really your brother, but that's not true. He's just as much your brother as Eva is my sister. It's not about who you're born to."

"No," I agreed, and I realized I was squeezing his hand. He glanced over at me and smiled shyly as he squeezed back. I wanted him to kiss me again, but I didn't know how to initiate it. Instead, I changed the subject.

"What will you do, you think? After the war?"

Piotr brightened. "I'm going to America," he informed me. "New York. I will miss my family, but I don't want to farm. I want to live in a big city."

"Why not Warsaw?" I thought of my father and sister. Were they even still there, still alive?

Piotr shook his head. "I'm afraid the Germans will win the war. There won't be a Warsaw. Not like there once was."

"Don't say that!" I pulled my hand away. "They can't win."

"I'm sorry." He looked abashed. "But Anna—Maria. It doesn't matter in America. There are all kinds of people there. Your father, your sister—they can come with us. Patryk, too."

"Patryk is Elsbietta and Marek's son now," I said ruefully. "He's learning how to pray the rosary."

Piotr reached for my hand again, tentatively. I let him take it.

"I'm sorry." His voice was quieter now. "It must be very hard."

"I don't know," I said honestly. "Maybe it's for the best."

We continued to follow the path, crunching twigs and leaves beneath our feet. The noise startled a gray bird in the tree overhead, its flapping wings rustling the branches as it took sudden flight.

Piotr watched it fly off. "A cuckoo," he commented.

"How appropriate," I said dryly, and he frowned quizzically.

"They leave their eggs to hatch in other birds' nests," I explained. "Like me and Patryk."

Piotr looked sad. "It's not like that at all," he said. "Elsbietta and Marek love you and Patryk."

"They love Patryk," I agreed. "I'm just part of the package."

"Don't ever say that," said Piotr sharply. "You know it's not true. You should see how they look at you, how they speak of you. Marek told my father you're both the daughter *and* son of his dreams. They love you."

"I love them too," I said, tearing up. "I do. But sometimes I feel like a stranger everywhere, here and even in the ghetto. For me, there is no home anymore."

"That's why you'll come with me to America," Piotr said confidently. "After the war."

But even in a game of make-believe, it felt disloyal to imagine a new life without Tateh and Lina.

"Let's go this way," Piotr suggested, gesturing left. Here, the path was less defined, more overgrown.

Suddenly, Piotr pointed excitedly, moving quicker.

"Wild berries!" He grinned broadly. "Look how many!"

Berries! I eyed them hungrily.

"You're sure these are safe to eat?" I picked one off the bush and eyed it suspiciously. "How do you know these berries aren't poisonous?"

Piotr laughed. "Spoken like a city girl. Everyone here knows which plants you can eat."

I popped a berry into my mouth, delighted at its sweetness.

"See?" Piotr looked pleased. "I told you. Delicious!"

We picked furiously at the berries, popping as many into our mouths as we could. Since the war, no one was ever really full.

"We're going to get sick," I said, giggling. Even as I said it, I reached to pick another.

"It's worth it," said Piotr, and I agreed, stuffing another several into my mouth, savoring the flavor.

Suddenly, we heard barking from nearby, then a rustling of footsteps. They were heavy, solid against the floor of the forest. I looked over at Piotr. They were the steps of boots, and our eyes locked.

"Hans," I whispered.

"Maybe not," he said unconvincingly.

I held my breath, waiting. Had he heard any of what we'd said? What if he'd been hiding all this time, listening in on us?

Hans revealed himself, the dog at his side as before. His eyes lingered on the two of us.

"How charming," he laughed. "Young love."

I shifted uncomfortably, moving slightly away from Piotr.

"You're a lucky boy," he said to Piotr. "Pretty girl like that, in the woods alone with you."

Shame burned my cheeks, traveling through my body like hot soup in an empty stomach. Next to me, Piotr bristled, lunging forward. I grabbed the back of his shirt.

"Piotr," I warned. "No."

The Nazi chuckled. "Listen to your little girlfriend, boy," he said. "I would hate to have to shoot you. My superior is fond of your family, for some reason."

The dog whined, yanking hard on the leash in the opposite direction. He looked beseechingly at his master, trying to pull him back into the woods. Hans reached down to scratch his ears.

"If you're looking for berries," added Hans, still pulling hard on the animal's leash, "you might want to try back that way. I might have seen wild strawberries." He jerked his thumb behind him, and I frowned, wondering what else might be lurking in the woods. Certainly not wild strawberries. Hans stared at us both a moment longer, then turned. He seemed ready to move on, whistling for the dog to follow him as he yanked harder on the leash.

"See you soon, pretty Maria," Hans called out over his shoulder. I shuddered as he winked at me, and I grabbed Piotr again as he clenched his fists.

"He's leaving," I whispered under my breath.

Piotr relaxed slightly. When he finally disappeared, I collapsed into Piotr.

"Shush," Piotr whispered, stroking my hair. "He's gone. We're alright."

"But Piotr, he's so horrid." I felt a mixture of anguish and anger. "If he knew…."

"He'll never know." Piotr's voice was harsh. "Never."

"What do you think is back there?" I nodded warily in the direction the soldier had pointed.

"Not strawberries," said Piotr grimly. "Probably something dangerous. Let's go back to the farm now." He took my hand.

I started to follow, then hesitated.

"What's wrong?" He turned to me, concerned. "Are you okay?"

"I just...." I looked again over my shoulder, toward the woods. "Maybe we should go look."

Piotr frowned. "That Nazi wanted us to go back there. It can't be good, Maria." He caught himself using my alias again and bit his lip, looking abashed.

"You're probably right. But Piotr, did you see the dog? The dog wanted to go back there. And dogs don't chase after berries, I don't think."

Piotr drew me in close and squeezed my hands. "Please, can we head back now?"

"Yes," I said, nodding. "Let's go now."

Part III

Chapter 16

LINA
Winter, 1943

ONE-HUNDRED AND fifty-six days. That was how long we'd been at Treblinka. I kept a tally on the walls of the barracks where we slept, scratching it in the decaying wood with my fingernails. Evidence that I'd been here, that I still existed. I didn't have a lot of hope that I would be here much longer. If I didn't die of starvation, I expected to meet my end like so many of my Jewish sisters and brothers. The camp chimney stack and its ominous black cloud were a constant reminder of what was really happening here. Because Treblinka was not a work camp. Treblinka was, as Halina educated us that first day, where people died. Treblinka was an extermination camp, designed for the exclusive purpose of putting people to death.

"What happens in there?" The first week, I'd worked up the nerve to ask Janina, the silent girl I had been paired to work the laundry vats with. Sweating, we bent over the steaming steel drums in the sweltering heat, stirring the brown uniforms inside like a giant Nazi stew.

"Where?" She didn't look up.

"The showers," I said quietly. "Are they all shot?"

"Gas," she said abruptly, and I recalled my conversation with Masha on the train. "Poisonous gas."

An efficient killer, and clean. No messy bloodstains to scrub away.

"How did you end up here?" I whispered.

Janina sighed and finally turned to look at me. I flinched as I saw, for the first time, the angry scar on the side of her face.

"They took my daughter. I fought them for her. It took two of them to hold me down." She had a satisfied expression at those last words.

"Where did they take her?"

"She was blonde and blue-eyed," said Janina, reaching up to touch her own cropped head of hair, also fair. "They said she looked Aryan. That she'd be given to a German family. She was three."

I thought of my Anna. "Do you know where they took her?"

Janina shook her head. "No. But if I get out of here, I'll never stop looking."

I wanted to tell her about Anna but bit my tongue. Better to keep the secret safe, buried deep inside a glass jar in Jolanta's garden.

Janina was moved to another work detail sometime around day 50, the office where they printed the daily exit passes for temporary workers. Halina told me about it late one night when neither of us could sleep.

"Maybe she could take one for herself and sneak out," I said dreamily. I imagined Janina bursting forth from the camp gates like one of the dogs they kept on patrol. "Maybe she could get a pass for each of us."

"Every day, the passes are a different color," Halina said grimly. "It makes it almost impossible."

I propped myself up on one arm and studied Halina, impressed. "You've thought of it?" I said.

"Of course," she said. "Haven't you thought of escaping?"

"Sometimes."

I'd had escape fantasies, but mine mostly involved the Allies raining down bombs on the officers' housing.

"It's make-believe," said Halina, rolling over. "We'll all die here."

I didn't answer. I scratched angrily at the lice in my short hair. It should have been shaved—Jewish girls had their heads shaved, Polish girls sheared short—but that first day, Hannelore had decided I should keep mine.

"Just cut it," Hannelore had commented, fingering my long brown hair. "If you shave it, she'll be ugly and I will have to look at yet another ugly Jew."

I'd shivered, trying not to recoil. Next to me, Masha's head was being shaved, hair falling to the ground in clumps.

"That one needs to learn a lesson," Hannelore had said, her eyes hardening at the stoic expression on Masha's face. "Shave it as close to the head as you can."

Masha never reacted, not once. I admired her strength, as I sorrowfully watched my hair fall to the ground. My vanity had died in the ghetto, but I felt the final pieces of the person I had been were being cut away.

Later, when I'd caught a glimpse of my reflection in the steel vat, I hadn't recognized myself. If I were to find Anna, would she even recognize me?

"You look like your sister," Masha had said quietly.

"I do?" I asked, startled.

"Yes. It's the eyes. You have the same expression in your eyes."

Surprised, I snuck opportunities to study my face, looking for Anna. Whatever Masha saw, I couldn't. All I saw was a hollowed-out face and close-cropped hair.

I cut the latest day, 157, in with my thumbnail. In the distance, I heard the rumble of engines, new truckloads of prisoners.

"Hurry," breathed Masha next to me, retying her shoes. "New ones. She'll be in a state."

"She" was Hannelore, who hated any disruptions to routine. New prisoners made her irritable and violent. I scrambled to find my shoes.

"My shoes are missing," I said, panicked.

Masha swore loudly. It wasn't uncommon to have things stolen. There simply was not enough of anything to go around.

"I told you not to take them off at night."

I squirmed, feeling like a disobedient child. "I just—I couldn't sleep. I must have kicked them off."

It was true. Masha may have been blessed with the ability to nod off at a moment's notice, but I struggled to escape into sleep, even at the brink of physical exhaustion. My body may have begged for rest, but my mind was in constant motion. At night, I thought about Anna. Over and over, I tried to visualize her safe and happy, tucked away in the countryside with a family of redheaded farmers.

"Well, now you'll have to make do with wooden clogs," snapped Masha, referring to the uncomfortable prisoner-issued footwear. Proper leather shoes were hard to come by. Masha had shown up about a month ago with two pairs.

"How did you get these?" I'd marveled, sliding my hands over the real leather. "These are real shoes, Masha!"

"Traded," she'd replied gruffly.

I'd frowned, puzzled. "But what do you have to…?"

She'd cut me off. "Put them on, Lina, before they're stolen. And never take them off."

Now, I stared at my bare feet, abashed. How could I have lost something so precious? I withered under Masha's disappointed gaze, searching valiantly for clogs before settling on a pair several sizes too big.

"You need to be more careful," she hissed, dragging me alongside her. "Do you want to freeze to death? Then who will find Anna after this is over?"

My shoulders sagged. I tried to keep up with Masha in the oversized clogs. "We're going to die anyway."

"Don't say that." She grabbed me by my thin prisoner's shirt and shook me. "Never say that."

I didn't answer. I was sick of her optimism and being treated like a disappointing child. I was sick of her pretending we weren't going to die here. We were, after all, in a death camp.

❧

I met Jerzy on day 162. He was new, assigned to emptying the vats. He had a natural cheeriness that irritated me. It felt out of place, like wearing a party dress at a funeral.

"Jerzy," he introduced himself to me. He stuck his hand out. "Are you from Warsaw?"

"Yes," I said shortly. I didn't offer my hand or my name.

He flashed his smile at Halina and Zofia, who had joined us in the laundry last month. Tiny and frail, Zofia had grown close with Masha, who was protective of her. "What are your names?"

Halina sighed. "Halina," she answered. "I'm Halina and this is Lina. And that's Zofia."

"Rhyming names!" Jerzy looked delighted. "Well, almost. I certainly won't forget that, Zofia and Halina. And Lina." He caught my eye and winked.

"You need to quiet down," I told him, annoyed. "You're going to get us all in trouble."

"Aren't we already in trouble?" he pointed out. "That's why we're here, isn't it?"

"Good lord, a comedian," muttered Halina. "He's going to get killed."

Zofia gave a small laugh. It was unlike her, and Halina and I both looked over, surprised. Her laughter was like the tinkling of a music box.

"I promise not to get myself or anyone else killed," Jerzy said solemnly. He studied me. "You look familiar."

I sighed. I didn't know this Polish young man.

"She's coming!" Zofia nudged me. "Shush!"

"You!" shouted Hannelore, hearing our conversation. I winced and turned back to my work, annoyed that we would all now pay the price for his mindless chatter.

"Apologies, I was just checking if this vat needed moving or emptying." Jerzy hastily backed away.

"Over there," said Hannelore, jerking her thumb to the left. She narrowed her eyes, staring at me, Halina, and Zofia.

"This isn't a nightclub," she spat. She reached over and pinched me, hard, on my breast. "Back to work. I don't want to hear your disgusting voices."

I worked in silence, my breast stinging from the vicious pinch. Across the room, Jerzy frantically tried to catch my eye, mouthing silent apologies. I ignored him, focusing on the swastika-laden stew of Nazi laundry.

"Are you alright?" When Hannelore had left the laundry, Halina shot me a concerned glance.

"Fine," I said, not looking up.

"You're bleeding."

I glanced down, startled. Sure enough, spots of red had appeared through my thin shirt.

"It doesn't hurt much," I muttered, trying not to move my lips. I looked up to find Jerzy's stricken eyes on my blood-stained shirt. Annoyed, I glared at him until he looked away, abashed.

Later, at night, when we were all piled into our crowded beds, Zofia gasped at the sight of my blood-stained shirt.

"She's a monster." She gave me a hug. "I'm so sorry."

"I'm fine." I hugged her back. "It doesn't hurt, really."

Halina leaned in toward us, conspiratorially. "You know she likes girls?"

Confused, I frowned. "What do you mean? She hates us."

Halina rolled her eyes. "She *likes girls*, Lina." She lowered her voice even further. "She's a pink triangle."

"Oh!" I put a hand over my mouth. "Pink triangles" were those who favored their own sex for intimacy. They were forced to wear an armband with a pink triangle, just like Jews were forced to wear a yellow star. I looked at Zofia, whose face reddened. She said nothing.

"How do you know?"

"She has her favorites," said Halina meaningfully. "Girls who agree to sleep with her. She gives them things."

"You don't know that's true." Zofia's voice was small.

Halina shrugged. "That's what I've heard."

"Sleep with her?" I felt stupid, but I had to ask. "What do…what do girls do with her?"

I felt foolish. I knew what happened between a man and a woman, and I had heard of two men sleeping together. But I had never heard of two women together before.

"I'm not sure," admitted Halina. "I think they are naked and they touch each other."

My cheeks colored. I shuddered at the thought of evil Hannelore's hands on me.

Again, Zofia protested. "You really don't know anything about it," she said, her tone harsher now.

"Why are you so defensive?" Halina raised her eyebrows at her. "You're defending Hannelore?"

"No," said Zofia quietly. "I just don't think it's right to talk about things you know nothing about."

Halina shrugged and continued, "I'm just saying what I hear. And I hear she gives them things," she said again.

I felt guilty participating in the conversation. Zofia looked both hurt and angry.

"Gives them what?" I asked.

"Food," Halina said, then paused. "And shoes."

Shoes. Suddenly, I felt winded, like I couldn't breathe. I looked around for Masha, whom I saw nearby, asleep. Had she slept with Hannelore, let her touch her, for the price of a pair of shoes?

And I had lost the shoes. I was overcome with regret.

"I'm tired," I said suddenly, turning away from Halina. "I'm going to sleep."

Halina gave me a knowing look, though she said nothing.

Zofia said nothing to either of us, climbing over to join Masha in her bunk. Did Zofia know?

But sleep eluded me. I tossed and turned fitfully, trying not to disturb the others who shared my bed. I imagined Hannelore pinching Masha's naked body for a pair of shoes. I relived losing the shoes over and over again.

"You look terrible," Masha pronounced in the morning. She studied me critically. "Are you ill?"

I yawned. "No," I said. "Just…couldn't sleep." My eyes wandered to her shoes, and my cheeks reddened.

"You need to learn to clear your mind," Masha said impatiently. "If you don't get your rest, you'll catch the typhoid and then who will find your sister?"

I glared at her. *I'm not like you,* I wanted to shout. *I'm not calculating, willing to let a monster like Hannelore touch me for a pair of shoes.*

Instead, I said nothing, obediently nodding and following close at her heels to the laundry. Zofia walked alongside us singing softly, it was a Polish song I didn't know. Masha smiled at her, complimenting her voice.

That morning, I watched closely as Masha interacted with Hannelore, though she gave nothing away. Hannelore didn't treat Masha differently than any of the other girls.

"Zofia!" she barked before our midday break, snapping her fingers at her. "Come with me."

Masha's head snapped up. "I can do it," she said.

Hannelore's eyebrows narrowed. "Did I ask for you?"

Masha bit her lip. "No, ma'am."

Hannelore fumbled with her belt and retrieved the nightstick that swung ominously at her hip.

"Bend over."

Masha breathed deeply and complied, folding herself forward.

"Drop your trousers!" yelled Hannelore, and I winced and shut my eyes.

"You! Pretty Jew." My eyes snapped open. Was she talking to me?

"Yes, you." She stared hard at me. "You open those eyes and watch." She looked out at us. "Anyone caught with their eyes closed will get the same treatment."

There was a murmur of frightened assent. A flushed and trembling Masha pulled down her pants and bent forward again, like a child about to receive a spanking. Hannelore smiled, satisfied, and got out the baton, raising it high and bringing it down hard again. Beating her over and over until Masha's skin was raw and bloodied.

"Now that we've all learned our lesson," said Hannelore calmly, "Zofia, you come with me!"

Zofia, who looked even tinier than usual, stumbled toward her. A shaking Masha brought her trousers back up and walked silently back to her vat. She had not made a sound, and I marveled at her strength.

I tried to seek Masha out across the room, but she didn't look up. Always the survivor, she focused intently now on the laundry before her.

❧

I saw Jerzy hovering, trying once again to catch my eye. I sighed, pointedly walking in the opposite direction.

"Lina," he called, hastening to my side. "I want to apologize for yesterday."

"It's fine," I said, watching for Hannelore. "But you see why we told you to be quiet."

"Yes," he said, abashed. "I'm so sorry. Are you alright?"

"I'll live," I said, shrugging.

"You do look familiar," he said again, frowning. "Could we have lived in the same neighborhood in Warsaw?"

"I doubt it," I said. "You know, I'm Jewish."

His eyes widened. "That's it!" he whispered excitedly. "It's your eyes. She had the same ones, only grayer. But shaped like yours, like almonds. She had red hair."

There was only person who shared my eyes who had red hair. I grabbed Jerzy by the sleeve.

"Who?" I said, my heart thudding hard against my ribs. "Who did?"

"The little girl from the ghetto," he said. "Anna."

Blood rushed from my head. I stumbled backwards, and Jerzy reached to steady me.

"You know Anna? Tell me." Greedily, I pulled him closer. "How?"

Anna. He knew Anna! "The little girl from the ghetto." He was someone Anna had met on the other end of the tunnels. Maybe the one who had supplied us with milk or eggs. I stared back at him, and he smiled slightly. He was quite nice-looking. Warm hazel eyes and a hint of golden fluff where his hair had been before being shaved.

"I helped her find food," he told me. We both glanced around, uneasy at the possibility of lurking guards. "Milk. She said there was a baby."

"There was!"

Jerzy's face fell. "He didn't live, then?"

"No!" I shook my head. "I mean, yes. Yes, he lived. He's

with Anna. They're—someone is hiding them in the country. I don't know where. They have new names, now."

Jerzy beamed. "So she went!"

I blinked. "It was you!"

"What was me?"

"The one who gave us Jolanta's name. To help get them out."

He grinned. "Yes, that was me. See? I'm not so bad."

Jerzy reached for my hand, but I pretended I didn't notice and turned slightly to one side. "She was such a resourceful girl," he said, now tucking his hands inside his pockets. "Brave and strong. I would bet everything I have she's alive and safe."

I grinned ruefully at him. "You don't have very much to bet."

He smiled back and reached to ruffle his hair before remembering he didn't have any.

"I do that, too," I told him. "I always fiddled with my hair when I was nervous. I still look for it."

"We need to get out of here, Lina," Jerzy shook his head.

"Get out of where?" I looked around anxiously.

"Here," he answered, impatient. "Treblinka. We need to escape."

I gave an unhappy laugh. "No one escapes from Treblinka. There's only one way out."

We both gazed at the smokestack where the ovens were and where the dead met their fate.

"We'll think of something," said Jerzy, unfazed.

"We will?"

"Yes. Your sister inspired me, you know. I got involved with the Resistance because of her."

"How come you're not dead?" It was a fair question. Those who were found to be part of the Resistance didn't usually make it to the laundry detail. They were shot on sight.

"They think I was just a messenger." He shrugged.

"And my sister inspired you?"

"Yes." He nodded. "I thought, if a little girl can be that brave, I can be brave too."

"She *was* brave," I agreed, feeling a pang of loss.

"Is brave," he corrected me gently. He reached again for my hand, and this time I didn't pull away.

❦

Back in the barracks, I couldn't find Masha anywhere. I squeezed into a space next to Halina. "Where's Masha?" I asked.

"Infirmary," she said grimly. "She collapsed as soon as she left the laundry."

I sucked in my breath. The infirmary was a place from where people didn't return. I wasn't ready to say good-bye to Masha. She was all I had left from my old life.

"Zofia is still with Hannelore," added Halina seriously. "What do you think she's done with her?"

"I'm going to go see if I can find Masha," I said. "I'm going to the infirmary."

Halina made a face. "Don't touch anyone there," she said. "I hear there's typhoid again."

I sighed. "There's always typhoid, Halina."

Halina said nothing, but looked at me with sympathy. Everyone knew I leaned heavily on Masha. As I flew down the path to the infirmary, I chided myself for always being the weak one. The weaker sister, even if I was the elder, and now the weaker friend.

Inside the infirmary, I found Masha face down on a cot in the corner. Her swollen, broken skin was exposed and covered in some kind of ointment. A nurse unspooling bandages glared at me.

"I'm here to visit Masha," I explained.

"I don't know why they bother with you people," said the nurse, gazing at me with contempt.

"Bother?" I said politely.

"Wasting bandages." She waved her hand. "Easier to put you down. I had a cat growing up. When he lost his hind legs, we put him out of his misery."

I bristled, furious at the comparison of Masha to a housecat. The nurse finished bandaging Masha and left, shooting me a contemptuous look.

"Is she gone?" Masha turned her head on the pillow, so that her face was visible.

"Yes." I crouched by the bed. "Masha, how bad is it? I'm so sorry."

"Don't be." Masha breathed noisily. "I'll be fine. Has Zofia returned?"

"Zofia? No. Halina said Hannelore still had her."

"Zofia is too fragile for Hannelore. I know from experience…." Masha writhed in pain.

My eyes widened. "Masha, what are you talking about?"

"Hannelore," she whispered. "She knows about me."

Bewildered, I took Masha's hand and patted it gently. "Masha, you should get some rest. You're confused."

"No." Masha shook her head, wincing at the effort. "No, listen to me, Lina. Hannelore…she knows something about me. Something that could have gotten me killed."

"Worse than being a Jew?" I frowned.

"I'm a pink triangle, too." Masha averted her gaze. "Hannelore found out. She found me with Zofia."

"Zofia?" I was confused. "But Masha, your husband—"

Masha waved her hand. "It was an arranged marriage. I could hardly tell my parents I preferred the other girls at school. And my husband was a good man. I loved him in a different way."

Shocked, I fell silent.

"I had always known but I had never…I had never met anyone like me, not that I was sure of anyway. But then Zofia and I…and Hannelore found out."

"I heard…." I paused. "Halina told me Hannelore is…like that. That she made you…well…." I couldn't say the words. My face felt as if it had been lit on fire.

"It's called rape," said Masha calmly. "And I know the others think I do it for boots or extra food, but I do it to protect you and Zofia. If I can keep her occupied, she'll leave you and whoever else alone." She added, "You must be horrified…."

"Masha...." I could barely speak, enveloped in a torrent of emotions: embarrassment, curiosity, disgust, admiration.

"You're horrified."

"No." I shook my head furiously. "No, I'm grateful. You know I've always thought you were so brave. I'm just—I didn't even know about—*this*."

Masha raised her eyebrows skeptically. "Really? You never heard the rumors about the Rabbi's son? And what did you think all the pink triangles referred to?"

I blushed again. I thought of Smulik, the Rabbi's son, who everyone had whispered was a little too fond of his classmates at the *yeshiva*.

"I didn't know there were women," I said honestly.

Masha laughed. "Everyone thinks women and men are so different, but I've never agreed. Both seem equally capable of love and violence, and strength and weakness."

I sat in contemplative quiet with Masha. I wondered what else I didn't know. What other secrets was I ignorant about?

"Zofia?" I said, tentatively. "Hannelore...took her to sleep with her?"

Masha stiffened. "I don't know what she's done with her. Lina, you must find her."

"I'll find her," I said, anxious, not knowing how I would keep my promise. "I'll ask around."

Masha was such a survivor. I thought about what it would take to survive the death camp of Treblinka and remembered Jerzy's earlier words about escape. "Masha?"

"Yes?"

"Has anyone ever escaped from here?"

She looked at me sharply, turning her swollen face.

"Why? What have you heard?"

I blinked, taken aback. "Nothing. I was just wondering. That young man, Jerzy, he was talking about it."

"Talking about it, how?" Masha gripped at my arm. "Did he mention Irka?"

"Who?" Bewildered, I wondered if perhaps Masha was feverish. Her face seemed flushed.

"Irka," she said impatiently. "The Polish girl who works in the other sick bay. She's a friend of Zofia."

"Oh," I said. "No, why would he?"

She sank back into the hard pillow. "No reason."

"Tell me," I said sharply. "Why do you never trust me with your secrets?"

"I trust you with my life, Lina."

"Then why am I always on the outside of your plans? Do you think I'm stupid? A coward?"

Masha looked shocked. "Oh, Lina, is that what you think?"

My shoulders sagged with shame and resentment. "It's the truth, isn't it?"

"Of course not." Masha struggled to sit up further, but I pressed her gently back down.

"I'm protecting you," said Masha simply. "If I'm caught, I'll be killed. No one is waiting for me. But you need to live."

"So, you don't think I'm a coward?" I whispered.

"I think you are very brave," she said. Her voice was barely audible. "And if you want to be part of this, I shouldn't stop you. Find Irka and tell her you want to help."

I swallowed. Was I brave enough for this?

Masha's eyes closed. I could see the pain was getting to her. Her face was shiny with sweat and the close-cropped locks at her hairline were matted. She seemed feverish, and I worried she might get the typhoid in the infirmary. "Lina, I need to rest now."

"Yes." I jumped up. "I'll be back tomorrow."

She didn't answer. Her eyes had already fluttered shut. Tearfully, I rose from the end of the cot, my legs trembling. It would be the last time I saw Masha.

Chapter 17

ANNA
Summer, 1943

I HAD GROWN lazy. Though I continued to help with the crops, the animals, and Patryk, my mind was elsewhere. It had gone soft on account of Piotr. While I resented the silly girl I'd become, kissing and flirting while Tateh and Lina were suffering in the ghetto, a part of me was happy and didn't care. I was fifteen now, and in the throes of first love.

"They're coming," whispered Eva. I was in the barn with Piotr and Eva, tending to the undernourished cow, which was failing to produce enough much-needed milk. Eva watched for signs of the Germans who came to trade for medicine. The older one brought the tablets for Eva, clandestinely wrapped in a handkerchief. He seemed like a kind man, and I wrestled with this contradiction. It was easier to believe all Germans were bad, that they were all ruthless killers.

"Is *he* there?" Piotr peered over Eva's head, looking worried. "He" was Hans, who roamed the village, bullying us all. Piotr couldn't stand the way he looked at me. I tried to reassure him by saying he looked at every female under fifty years of age that way. But I was secretly afraid, too. There was something about the way he stared that made me feel as if I were being consumed.

"Yes," said Eva.

"I'm going back to my place," I said quickly. I had no desire to see Hans, and there was no need for him to know I was here. If I slipped out quietly now, I could sneak home without him seeing me.

Piotr frowned. "I don't want you going yourself."

"I'm fine, silly." I rolled my eyes and brushed the hay from my skirt. "I've done the walk thousands of times."

"But what if they take the same path as you?" Piotr didn't look reassured.

"Then I'll go through the forest. There's no one there. Okay?" I nudged him playfully. "You're acting like Elsbietta."

Piotr exhaled, still looking unhappy. "I'll come by tonight, after supper."

"You'll miss curfew," I said, shaking my head. "It's too dangerous."

"I'll make it back on time," he said stubbornly. "I need to make sure you got home safe."

I was tempted to roll my eyes again, but instead I leaned in and let him kiss me quickly, on the lips. Eva squealed in delight at this, and Piotr gave her a good-natured elbow in the ribs.

I waited for their signal that it was safe to sneak out the back. I slipped out, nearly tripping over the cat.

She rubbed her head against my ankles.

"Shush," I told her as I bent to scratch her between the ears. "They'll know I'm here and then what?"

I could hear Hans' voice from out front and shuddered inwardly. Taking small steps so as to not make any extra noise, I quickened my pace.

Cautiously, I ducked into the woods, wincing as my upper arm caught briefly on a branch. I rubbed at it, discovering blood. I would need to be more careful. There were wild boars in these woods that would be drawn to its scent. I licked my finger and traced the line of my wound.

My stomach rumbled as I walked on, and I recalled the berry patch. It was slightly off the path, but on the way. I hesitated, torn between hurrying home and filling my belly. My hunger won as I wandered out of my way, determined to find the wild berries.

I continued to walk but didn't see any berries. A twinge of fear at being lost pricked at me, but I suppressed it. I was fine—if I simply retraced my steps, I'd know exactly where I was.

It was another fifteen minutes before I realized I was in trouble. There were no berries, and I no longer knew where I was. It was stifling hot, and I knew I wouldn't last long without water. My heart pounded at my stupidity. To die in the woods for a few berries, after so many people had risked so much to save me. I sat down hard on a tree stump that smelled of rot, holding my head in my hands.

When I let my hands drop, something oddly cool touched my hand. I peered over and saw something metal and shiny embedded within the bark. I leaned in closer and recoiled: it was a bullet. I lifted my head then, noticing the holes in the nearby trees and the massive mounds of earth surrounding me. There was an odd smell, like rotting food.

I recalled Hans' taunting words. *You might want to try back that way.* He had wanted us to see this.

Graves, I realized. *These are graves.*

I moved the soil with my feet, gently at first. My fear and fury boiling over, I kicked at it harder until I found what I needed to see for myself: bones. I recognized two human femurs, and I stumbled back. Tripping over another hastily dug grave, I lay on my back, winded, staring at the sky. It was a beautiful day, sunny and clear.

I didn't move immediately. I stared at the few clouds that passed overhead and wondered how the sky could look the same when everything here on earth had changed so much.

I was so lost in thought that I didn't hear him approach.

The dog appeared first, running at top speed toward the mounds of earth. Sniffing excitedly, her paws dug wildly through the mud.

"Shatzi," the familiar voice called out to the dog, and I froze despite the heat. "Don't worry, there are plenty of bones."

I tried to rise, but it was too late. The dog was rushing at me, howling loudly to his master.

"Shatzi, what on earth…oh." Hans appeared, a smile playing on his lips when he saw me.

I shut my eyes.

"Well, well, well. If it isn't pretty Maria." Hans came over and snapped his fingers. Shatzi jumped off me immediately, and I tried to sit up again. Hans shook his head and forced me back down, hands firmly at my shoulders. My throat closed with terror, like I was breathing through a narrow straw.

"So, you were looking for the wild strawberries. Open your eyes," he commanded, and, frightened, I complied.

"This is what happens to those who don't behave," he continued, gesturing around him. "You know what happened here?"

"Shot," I whispered, averting my gaze.

"That's right," he said, smiling. He looked pleased. "They were all shot. The Polish mayors and the doctors and the god-damn Resistance fighters. They thought they were so clever. Who's clever now, do you think?"

I said nothing, and he reached over and pinched my thigh hard until my eyes stung.

"I said, who's clever now?"

"You," I gasped. "You are."

"Good girl." He nodded approvingly and released my sore flesh. I breathed deeply, determined not to cry.

"You're a very pretty girl, Maria," he said, leaning in closer. I tried not to flinch at his stinking breath. I felt his hand beneath my skirt then, and cried out, kicking. He pinned me down easily with one arm, using the other to tear at my dress.

"No," I wept, trying to pull away. "Please, no."

There was no one around to hear my screams as he ripped at my clothing, opened his trousers, and forced his body onto mine. My eyes rolled to the back of my head, and it felt as if I had left my body, watching the nightmare unfold beneath me: Hans, on top of me as I thrashed and cried. When he was done, he stood as if nothing had happened and, before raising his trousers, urinated next to my trembling body. It was as if I was inanimate, a tree stump or a pile of rocks. I squeezed my eyes shut at this final indignity, praying he would leave now and not kill me.

He reached into his pocket and pulled out a handkerchief.

"Here," he said, tossing it at me. "You're bleeding."

I said nothing, letting the swastika embroidery of his handkerchief land on my chin. Motionless, I opened my eyes again and stared at the sky. The clouds had moved on, leaving only the sun beating down through the trees.

"Good-bye, pretty Maria." Hans winked at me, as he grasped Shatzi by the collar and headed toward the clearing. "We should meet again soon."

I stared at a pair of birds overhead as his heavy footsteps grew fainter. I could not move until I was sure he was gone. As any trace of noise faded, I continued to stare blankly at the trees overhead. The birds flitted from tree to tree, and I envied them their wings.

I stood up, finally, breathing deeply to curb the nausea that overtook me. The handkerchief fluttered to the ground and I retrieved it. I *was* bleeding, and not just from the earlier scratch to the arm. Dabbing at the blood, I wondered if everyone who saw me would be able to tell what had happened. Stuffing the hanky into my pocket, I held my dress together with my hands, stumbling through the woods. What would I tell Elsbietta? Would Marek find out? I was ashamed.

I would have to leave, I thought, resigned, as I tripped over tree roots and pushed away branches with my calloused hands. I would live in the forest, find the partisans in the woods, maybe. Live off the wild berries that had selfishly drawn me into the woods.

You're a fool, I hissed at myself. *You deserve this.*

When I finally emerged, lurching toward the field where I could see Elsbietta tending the crops, I gave a loud cry before collapsing to the ground. The last thing I remembered before losing consciousness was Elsbietta running toward me, then crouching by my side, her face ashen while I stared again at the sky.

"Oh, my poor girl," she said, crossing herself. "What have they done to you?"

The white clouds faded to black as I welcomed the darkness.

❧

"Maria, Piotr will understand," Elsbietta's pleaded as she hovered over my bed. I tightened my body into the fetal position. I hadn't spoken to anyone other than Patryk in six days. I didn't want to scare him. I couldn't bear even to look at anyone else, let alone speak. Marek and Elsbietta knew, of course—the tears and stains on my clothes made it obvious—and I couldn't stand the pity in their eyes.

"Marek told Piotr you were ill," added Elsbietta. "He keeps coming to check whether you're feeling better."

When I thought of Piotr learning what had happened, I felt overcome with shame. He had warned me not to go home by myself, and I hadn't listened.

I rolled to face the wall so I didn't have to look at Elsbietta's stricken expression.

She sighed and, after a few more minutes of silence, I heard her leave.

"Hasn't said a word in days…will barely eat…won't get out of bed…." The hushed tones of Elsbietta and Marek traveled in fragments through the heavy door.

Marek said something about calling the doctor, something I had adamantly refused. "No doctors," I'd insisted. The thought of anyone else touching me was intolerable. I couldn't have the doctor coming here. I would have to master my trauma and get out of this bed.

"Maybe tomorrow," Elsbietta said. Relieved, I slumped back down. I had another day to figure out how to pull myself together. I told myself I couldn't spend the rest of the war in this bedroom. I would quickly become a burden, and then how long would they let me stay?

I rolled over to face the little dresser where I kept my meager possessions. Amongst them was the little swastika handkerchief Hans had tossed at me. Stained with blood, I had refused to let Elsbietta throw it out. I hadn't said a word, only shaken my head furiously with narrowed eyes. I hadn't expected her to understand, but she did.

"To remember," she whispered. "For revenge…."

Yes, I would somehow, someday, exact my vengeance. Not

just for this, but for all of it. For the bookshop and the ghetto and Rivka and Dov. For Tateh and Lina.

The hours passed as I stared at the ceiling and thought about my next steps. There were partisan fighters in the forest plotting against the Nazis. I wanted to join them. I was older now, almost sixteen. Patryk was older, walking and talking. He didn't need me as much.

"Maria?" There was a tentative knock at the door. "Will you have some soup?"

I cleared my throat.

"Yes," I said.

❦

"I'm going to join the partisans," I said calmly the next day at dinner. I had left my bed and joined the family for breakfast as if nothing had happened. Patryk was delighted, hugging me and planting wet kisses on my cheeks.

Marek shot an alarmed look at Elsbietta. "Maria," he said cautiously. "This is not something you just…do. You don't wake up one day and run into the forest and join the partisans."

It occurred to me then, for the first time, that Marek and Elsbietta might know more than they let on. If they had taken in me and Patryk, they might have connections to the Polish Resistance. It had never crossed my mind before.

"I can't just stay here," I said desperately. "Not after…." My voice trailed off, and my cheeks went red and hot. I stabbed at half a boiled egg.

"Give it some time." Elsbietta reached over and firmly squeezed my arm. "Give yourself some time to recover."

"I'm fine," I insisted, but I clearly wasn't. I began to cry right there at the supper table. Appalled, I wiped at my face, my breathing ragged as I tried to control myself.

"Ria is sad." Patryk leapt from his chair and into my lap. "Still sick?"

I hugged him. "Yes," I said. "Yes, I'm still sick."

After dinner, I went back to my room and picked up the last book Piotr had lent me; a book of fairy tales.

"Maria?" a voice came from the hall, and I froze, panicked.

"Maria?" the voice said again. "Elsbietta's here with me. She said I could come up as long as we leave the door open and she's outside."

"Maria?" Elsbietta spoke now, sounding hesitant. "Piotr just wants to see how you're feeling now that…now that your fever broke. Marek and I have decided it's fine since you still have trouble leaving your bed. I'll wait out here."

I felt helpless, my heart aching. I desperately wanted to see Piotr, but how could I face him?

"Maria." Piotr's voice was pleading now. "I know you've been ill. I don't care what you look like."

I sighed, resigned.

"You can come in."

He entered, tentative at first, then rushed toward me. "I don't care if you're contagious," he said, kneeling by my bed. "I've missed you so much."

I felt a pang of intense sadness. "I've missed you too."

"Was it a fever?" He looked concerned. "Mama says everyone is more likely to get sick without enough to eat."

My cheeks reddened, it was hard to lie to Piotr. Unwittingly, my eyes wandered past him and toward the dresser.

"Yes," I said, finally, but Piotr's gaze had followed mine. He turned to see what I was looking at, and I sat up, alarmed.

"What is that?"

"Nothing." I pulled at his sleeve. "Tell me, what's been happening at the farm? How is Eva?"

He ignored me.

"Piotr," I said. "Piotr, look at me."

As if in a trance, he walked over to the dresser.

"No!"

I wasn't quick enough. Piotr stared at the handkerchief, not touching it.

I put a hand on his back, but he didn't even seem to register my touch.

"What is this?" he whispered. "Why do you have this?"

He turned to me then, and I looked up at him, eyes filled with tears, remembering what had happened to me in the forest.

I couldn't think of anything to say.

"This is his," he said slowly. He wasn't looking at me, but past me, at nothing. His eyes were blank. "He hurt you."

"Who?" I said lamely.

Piotr stared hard at me, finally making eye contact.

"He hurt you!" he repeated. "You weren't sick, were you?"

"I was," I said, and it wasn't a lie. I had been sick—very sick—just not with a normal illness.

"How did he hurt you?"

I said nothing. I grabbed at my nightdress with one hand and his arm with the other.

"Piotr...."

"Tell me!" His voice rose, shaking me off. "Tell me the truth."

He lunged for the handkerchief. Repulsed, he studied the swastika and the blood, and shook it at me.

Elsbietta's voice floated in from the hallway. "Is everything alright in there?"

"No," said Piotr, at the same time that I called out "Yes."

Piotr stared alternately at me and at the loathsome hanky. There were tears in the corners of his eyes and it felt like a knife twisted in my gut.

I did not want to see Piotr cry.

I did not want anyone's pity.

Elsbietta appeared in the doorway. "Piotr," she said firmly. "Piotr, give me the handkerchief."

He didn't move.

"What happened?" he asked. "What happened to her?"

"She had a fever," said Elsbietta firmly. "That handkerchief is Marek's. One of them punched him in the nose then tossed it at him. I must have left it in here, with the laundry."

"What happened to her?" he repeated, ignoring the lie.

"I think you should go," said Elsbietta. "Maria is still recovering. She needs rest."

My eyes met Piotr's. A mutual understanding passed between us. He knew what had happened to me and I knew he knew. We would never speak of it again.

Piotr thrust the handkerchief at Elsbietta.

"I'll go," he agreed.

He cast a final, fierce look at me. I ached to see him go, but he couldn't stay.

"Piotr," I cried, and he froze. He turned back and crossed the room in two strides, grabbing me tightly. He kissed me on the top of my head, and I breathed in the scent of him.

He said nothing and then left abruptly as Elsbietta looked on, ashen.

I didn't know it would be the last time I would see him.

Chapter 18

LINA
Summer, 1943

TO MY GREAT anguish, Masha succumbed to her injuries and to typhoid. We assumed Zofia died too, because she never returned. Without Masha, I felt truly alone. She was the last link to my old life in Warsaw: the last person who had known Anna and Tateh, who had visited our bookshop. She had been strong, so I didn't always have to be. As I wept for my lost, brave friend, I swore to myself I would survive not just for myself and Anna, but to honor Masha for her strength and sacrifice.

I sought out the nurse Irka, who regarded me suspiciously.

"Who sent you? What do you know?" she said sharply.

"Masha. I don't know anything, but I want to help." My voice warbled as I tried to sound brave.

"You're too loud," she whispered, glaring. "Learn to whisper."

"I'm sorry," I whispered back, breathing the words.

"Better." Her mouth twisted. "Are you ready to die?"

I hesitated briefly, thinking of Anna.

She saw it and shook her head, her close-cropped blonde hair moving back and forth. "You're not ready."

"We're going to die anyway," I said roughly. I gestured toward the crematorium. "I'm ready."

She sighed and looked me up and down.

"I am ready," I insisted.

"I'm trying to decide what to do with you." She cocked her head to one side, then rummaged through a drawer.

"Here," she said, thrusting something at me. "Take this to the doctor at the German infirmary. His name is Dr. Berek."

It was a packet of syringes. I felt irritated. I hadn't volunteered to be an errand girl, but maybe this was a way of showing my bravery.

"Give it *only* to the doctor. Do you understand? Into his hands, or bring it back."

I realized then that there must be some sort of coded message inside.

"Yes, I understand."

After that, I ran messages regularly, a conduit of information between enslaved men and women in different parts of the camp. No one suspected me. After Masha's death, I was largely overlooked. Hannelore, who preferred her victims strong and defiant, ignored me now. Relieved, I hid quietly behind the steaming vats.

Jerzy still visited regularly, passing me extra bits of food and information. He knew I ran messages and knew both Irka and Dr. Berek. I wondered how many others were involved, but I didn't dare ask. If I were caught, I wouldn't want to give out names when they held flames to the soles of my feet.

"Lina!" Jerzy called from behind the building as I exited. He appeared from nowhere, a trick of his, and handed me something round and shiny.

"Where did you get this?" I breathed, staring at the apple.

"Eat it quickly," he urged, ignoring the question. "I have news."

My ears perked up as I sank my teeth into the fruit, groaning with pleasure at the satisfying crunch.

"There's been an armed uprising in the Warsaw ghetto led by a handful of young Jews."

"A revolt!" I nearly dropped the apple, but Jerzy caught it and took a large bite.

"Yes," he said, handing it back to me. "It's been three weeks of fighting."

"Three weeks?" Incredulous, I stood frozen, the apple halfway to my lips. "How?"

"Some handguns and rifles, snuck in by the resisters. Gasoline, bottles. It's remarkable!"

I chewed thoughtfully, marveling.

"They can't win though," I said slowly. "Not against the German army."

"No," agreed Jerzy. "But they'll go down fighting, at least."

I nodded, silently taking another bite. We passed the apple back and forth, chewing contemplatively.

"Where did you get this?" I asked again, taking a bite of the core. I wasn't going to let any of it go to waste. "You're not stealing, are you?"

"Does it matter?" He winked.

"I don't want you to get shot!"

"Nicest thing a girl has ever said to me," he said.

"Take the rest of this," I said, thrusting the half-eaten apple core at him.

He polished it off, and I grinned at him. He was kind and funny, and not at all bad looking.

"Do I have dirt on my face?" he asked.

"No. Why?"

"You're staring at me. I figured it was something on my face, but I guess I'm just hideous."

"You're not hideous," I protested, smiling. "Not that hideous, anyway."

He covered his heart with his hands. "Not hideous *and* she doesn't want me to get shot!"

I could feel myself blushing. Jerzy put an arm around my shoulders and pulled me closer to him.

"What would you do if I kissed you?"

Startled, I considered this. What *would* I do? Run away? Kiss him back?

"I don't know," I admitted. "I've never kissed anyone."

"Maybe I should try, then."

I felt suddenly reckless. "Maybe you should."

He touched my chin and looked seriously into my eyes.

"I really like you, Lina," he said. "And one day, I'm going to get us out of here."

He leaned in toward me, and I remembered at the last moment to close my eyes.

❧

The Warsaw Ghetto Uprising did not succeed against the Nazi army, but it was the bravest attempt of Jewish resistance. The makeshift army eventually fell, and the ghetto was burned down by the Nazis. There was now a rumor that those who had survived were being transported to Treblinka. Some said there were only a few survivors of the uprising, that the armed resisters, men and women, had fought nearly to the last person. Others said there were still 50,000 Jews left in the ghetto, but that children were being sent to Treblinka for pelting the Nazi soldiers with rocks and glass. The trains with men, women, and children from the Warsaw ghetto would surely be emptied straight into the gas chambers.

Remembering the brave Resistance fighters in the Warsaw ghetto, I was proud of my own Resistance work. I was running multiple errands a day now. The doctor himself had praised my work, though Irka still wondered whether I could withstand it, if I were discovered.

I continued to dream about escape. I shared an idea with Jerzy to make use of our access to the laundry. We would need different clothes to escape, since we wouldn't get far in our prisoners' striped uniforms.

"Where are the clean Nazi uniforms?" he asked. "Once they've been washed and hung to dry."

"They're picked up and sent somewhere for distribution," I said. "But they sit in piles waiting for collection. That would be the time to grab some."

He nodded.

"I could…," I began, but he shook his head vehemently.

"Don't do anything that would get yourself in trouble," he said sharply.

I scowled, but he touched the side of my face.

"I couldn't bear if anything happened to you," he said softly. "Promise me."

"I run messages every day," I whispered so no one would hear.

"This is different."

"But…."

He cut me off by kissing me, and my irritation melted away.

"Let me help," I said again, when we came up for air.

"You already have." He shook his head. "You don't have to be leading the charge to be important, Lina," Jerzy said. "Your ideas are just as important."

Wistfully, I remembered all the ideas I'd had before the war, all the stories I had planned to write. I hadn't held a pen in so long.

"What are you thinking about?" Jerzy looked at me curiously.

"I used to have ideas." I smiled faintly. "I wrote stories. I dreamed of being a famous author."

"Why 'used to?'" He narrowed his eyes at me.

"I haven't held a pen in ages."

"You can still tell stories," Jerzy pointed out. "When this is over, you'll write it all down," said Jerzy. "You'll tell the world what happened here."

"Maybe," I said doubtfully. I tried to imagine myself after the war.

A whistle blew somewhere in the distance, and we both jumped.

"I'll find you tomorrow morning," he promised, kissing the top of my head.

❦

At night in our sleep barracks, Halina curled up beside me, her face pressed into my back.

"He's handsome," she said, but I could hear the laughter in her voice. I gave her a good-natured kick, and she squeezed my side in return.

"Don't you mind that he isn't Jewish?"

Startled, I realized I hadn't even given that a thought. Before the war, I would never have dreamed of being with a man who wasn't Jewish. I'd barely even interacted with boys like Jerzy. Our worlds were entirely separate.

"It means a lot to me that he knew my sister," I said instead. "She used to leave the ghetto in search of food for us. He helped her. This seems more important to me right now." It was true. Though it was important to the Nazis to know who was Jewish, it now felt less important to me.

Halina poked me. "Is he a good kisser?"

I giggled. "I think so. But I don't have anyone to compare him to."

"I had a boyfriend before the war who slobbered like a dog when he kissed," said Halina.

We laughed.

"What happened to him?"

"I don't know," she said softly. "He went missing. He was a pilot. I'm happy for you, Lina," said Halina sincerely. "You need to take your happiness where you can find it here."

"Thank you," I said quietly.

"And if we ever get out of here, I want to be at the wedding. But please don't have it until we've all grown our hair back and put on some weight so we have breasts to fill out our dresses."

I dreamed that night of a wedding, only it wasn't me beneath the *chuppah*, the traditional wedding canopy. It was Masha, her face stained with tears. Jerzy, handsome as the groom, was also in tears. Anna stood off in the distance, not facing the celebration.

"I miss her so much," Masha whispered to Jerzy. "Poor Lina."

Then Jerzy melted into Hannelore, and I woke with a frightened start.

※

"What was that?"

The ground in the laundry shook momentarily. Then the shouting began.

"Silence," shouted Hannelore, but she sounded alarmed.

Several soldiers appeared, looking harried. There was some whispering in German, and I managed to catch the words "bomb" and "train" and "prisoner." Then Hannelore and her assistants abruptly left with the soldiers.

"Do you think one of the new prisoners set off a bomb?" I asked. "Someone getting off the train!"

"Maybe someone from the ghetto? From the uprising!" someone answered.

There was excited chatter. With no soldiers or guards around, no one was working. I wandered quietly over to where the Nazi uniforms were hung to dry.

I yanked a dry uniform down and folded it quickly into a small square. No one was paying attention to me. All the prisoners were milling about trading theories. I stepped out the back, pretending to use the latrine and crept behind the barracks. Preoccupied with the bomb, no soldiers were around to spot me. Heart pounding, I shoved the uniform into a small crevice under the building, then kicked over some rocks to cover it. Satisfied, I stepped back, nearly colliding with another prisoner I didn't know.

"Taking a piss?" she asked me.

"Yes," I said automatically. I fussed with my garment appropriately.

She nodded, then retrieved something from her pocket—a cigarette.

"Want?"

"No, thanks." I started to leave, but curiosity got the better of me.

"How'd you get that?"

She laughed. "There are ways. This will speed things up," she said, waving her hand in the general direction of the noise.

"Speed what up?"

"The ovens," she said, shrugging. "They'll want to kill more of us, more quickly. There will be hell to pay."

She was probably right. I thought of Jerzy and hoped the plot was nearly ready.

In the distance, there was more shouting, followed by a series of gunshots. The other prisoner watched impassively, smoking her cigarette.

"Best to go back inside," she said. She stubbed out the cigarette and pocketed the remains. "They'll be back and on the warpath."

Hannelore didn't return that day. The guard who came to replace her seemed content to whack the sides of the vats and shout a few times before settling down with a cigarette and a magazine. She seemed indifferent to us, and I couldn't believe my good luck.

Halina sensed my enthusiasm. "Maybe she's dead," she said hopefully.

I winced. Even now, I found it hard to wish for more death and violence.

Halina saw my hesitation. "You're so soft," she scoffed under her breath, rolling her eyes. "You don't want her dead?"

"I just—I just can't think like that," I said lamely, cursing my own cowardliness.

I met Jerzy later in our usual spot, hungry both for news and his touch.

"The bomb," I said urgently. "Do you know what it was about?"

He nodded, glancing around nervously. "Prisoners from the ghetto blew it up in the undressing area. Getting off the train."

Delighted, I clasped my hands together. "They smuggled in a bomb!"

"A grenade of some kind. Everyone is going mad here. The soldiers are terrified and angry."

"They're afraid? Of a few Jews?"

"Yes." He didn't look entirely happy, though.

I thought of the girl with the cigarette.

"They'll speed things up with more gassing?"

"Exactly." Jerzy looked grim. "We need to escape and soon. It's time, I think."

I felt a thrill of panic mixed with anticipation. "When?"

"I'll have more information soon."

He pulled me into him, and I relaxed against his chest. His lips brushed against my hair and I tilted my head back, allowing him to kiss me properly. He tasted of mud and salt, the muck of the camp and the salty taste of blood from his dry, cracking lips.

"Jerzy," I whispered. "I hid something."

He looked around warily, past the barracks and toward the barbed-wire fences and patrolling guards. "You didn't take a uniform, did you?"

"I did," I breathed the words. "Under there."

Jerzy sucked in his breath and let out a stream of curse words.

"You're very brave," he said seriously, grasping my hands. "Foolish, but brave."

"I could only risk taking one," I whispered.

"Shush!" He kissed me again, harder this time.

"Soon," he said. "It will be soon."

Chapter 19

ANNA
Summer, 1943

PIOTR DISAPPEARED without a good-bye. His mother, distraught in her kitchen as she braided Eva's hair, explained he'd returned from our house that night and gone to bed. In the morning, he'd failed to come to breakfast and they found his bed empty. He'd left two notes, one for them and one for me.

"I don't know what that boy was thinking," said Piotr's mother. Eva let out a small cry as Mrs. Kowalski yanked too hard on one of her braids.

"What will we tell them, when they come with the medicine? What will we do about Eva?"

"I'm fine," said Eva stubbornly. "I don't need the medicine."

"Shush," snapped her mother, and Eva looked miserable.

"They'll stop coming if he's run off to the partisans. We'll all be punished." Mrs. Kowalski finished the braid and wrung her hands.

"We'll say he's gone to my brother's," said Mr. Kowalski. He chewed on the end of a pipe, looking pensive and worried.

"They needed help with their farm."

"And when they find out the truth?"

"We'll deal with that when it happens," he answered simply. "What else can we do?"

I held the letter in my hands, staring at my name on the outside. "Maria," it said in small letters. I couldn't bring myself to read it.

"He said nothing to you, Maria?" Mrs. Kowalski's face was pained. I felt it was my fault.

"No," I said in a small voice. "I had no idea."

This, at least, was true. I had no idea that Piotr would run off and join the partisans without me.

"Did something happen?" Mrs. Kowalski studied my face, searching. "Did you quarrel?"

"Enough," said Mr. Kowalski sharply. "It's not Maria's fault."

"Maria wouldn't argue with Piotr," piped up Eva. "They're always kissing."

"Eva!" Mrs. Kowalski looked scandalized. "Go play outside."

Scowling, Eva stomped through the kitchen and out the back door. I looked at Mrs. Kowalski, helpless.

"His letter said he couldn't stand living under the Germans anymore," she said. She put her hand on a kitchen chair for support. "But why now, so suddenly? I just don't understand it."

"We should let Maria read her letter," Mr. Kowalski said gently.

I tried to say thank you, but nothing came out but a tiny warble like I'd swallowed a small bird. I burst into tears.

"Oh, dear." Mrs. Kowalski began to sob, too. "I'm sorry, Maria. This must be hard on you, too...."

I unfolded the letter slowly.

Dear Maria,

I know you will be angry with me, and I know it is wrong to leave you right now. But I cannot look at you knowing what he did to you and that he is still alive. I need to find him. When he is properly dead, I will come back and I will take you with me. I promise. Please, look in on my parents and Eva for me. Please talk to my father. I could not write this to them—but it may be best to pretend I am dead. Otherwise, the Germans will realize where I have gone and they will punish my parents. Eva needs the medicine. Please.

I love you, and I will be back.

Piotr

I swallowed, staring at the paper.

"What does it say?" She leaned toward me. "Did he say why?"

"He said why in our letter," said Mr. Kowalski gruffly. "I understand why."

Mrs. Kowalski whirled at him, flushed and furious. "But Eva! The medicine! Why would he do this to his sister?"

I felt so guilty I couldn't look up.

"We'll say he's at my brother's farm," said Mr. Kowalski brusquely. "You'll say the same, Maria. If the Germans ask."

"Of course," I said nervously.

"They'll check," snapped Mrs. Kowalski. "Those Germans, all they do is keep records. They'll go to the farm and find he is not there."

"Well, I don't have any other suggestions." Mr. Kowalski looked as if he had aged two years in two days. He ran his hands through his wiry gray hair, agitated.

I took a deep breath.

"What if we—what if we tell them he died of an illness? They hate disease, they'll stay away."

Mrs. Kowalski let out a choked sob. I wondered if she thought I was callous.

"It was his idea," I added hurriedly. "He couldn't bring himself to write it to you."

"Good idea," Mr. Kowalski replied slowly. "We'll say he died quickly, and we'll pretend one of us is ill too. We could have a funeral and pretend to bury him in the church cemetery. But we don't have a body. They'll probably check that out."

A body. I thought of the woods, of the mounds of dirt, and of Shatzi digging for bones.

"I know where we can get one to put in a coffin," I whispered.

❧

I wasn't allowed to help. Mr. Kowalski and Marek were adamant that I stay home, and I was still too weak to fight them.

They went that night, and I couldn't sleep. What if Hans was there with Shatzi? Would he shoot them both so that they were just two more missing Poles, two new fresh mounds of earth? It would be my fault.

It *was* all my fault. If I had gone straight home. If I had hidden the handkerchief. If I'd been a better liar. *If, if, if.* What if they didn't make it back? I rolled over and buried my face in my pillow, screaming into it soundlessly.

They did return, filthy and exhausted, but alive. Before dawn, the moon was still visible overhead, both men collapsed at the kitchen bench, accepting a shared boiled egg from an exhausted Elsbietta. In hushed tones, they told us of the body they'd unearthed. The right size, but they'd needed to shave the head. Piotr's hair fair and the poor dead man's a dark brown.

"You don't think they'd…dig it up?" Elsbietta looked aghast.

"I would not put anything past them," said Marek darkly.

Outside, the wagon was waiting, old blankets and burlap sacks and bundles of hay layered to cover what lay beneath.

"We need to hurry," said Mr. Kowalski.

Elsbietta hung back at the doorway, distressed. "What if they ask what's in the wagon?"

"Hay," said Marek grimly.

The adults all exchanged worried glances. Everyone knew this was a poor answer. I shut my eyes tightly and said two prayers.

The body was prepared and put into a closed pine box. The priest was called and told that Piotr had died. Elsbietta wondered if the priest might have guarded our secret, as he had always seemed like such a good man. Marek pointed out that these were scary times and no one could be trusted.

They buried the body in the church cemetery. Word spread in the village that Piotr had died and his mother was confined to bed. Only a few braved the chance of infection to join our families at the funeral.

When the funeral mass concluded, the priest said a few words in Polish about Piotr. Empty, generic words that conveyed nothing of who he really was and how he made people feel. I grew angry and tearful until I remembered Piotr was not, in fact, dead. My head swirled with confusion. I'd barely eaten in days, and I found myself grasping to remember what was real and what was not. I was not Anna but Maria, an orphaned Polish girl. Piotr was dead, not off with the partisans. Patryk had once been Dov, a baby born in the Jewish ghetto.

The priest droned on, and Elsbietta, experiencing her own grief over Piotr's departure, sobbed openly. Eva cried too, having been warned by her parents that if she breathed a word of any of this to anyone, the Nazis would not only find and kill Piotr, but quite possibly them as well.

The service ended, and people scattered. The men shook

hands with Mr. Kowalski, gruffly conveying their sympathies. It wouldn't be easy to run a farm without a son and they offered to help however they could.

I went over to Eva and pressed the book of fairy stories Piotr had lent me into her hands.

"This was Piotr's," I said. "He would want you to have it."

She nodded, her eyes red. "He used to read them to me."

❧

After the "funeral," Marek, Elsbietta, Patryk, and I returned with the Kowalskis to their house. In the distance, a familiar figure climbed the hill toward the church, and my pulse quickened. It was the older Nazi, the one who brought the medicine for Eva. I looked past him, frantic, but there was no sign of Hans or his dog.

"It's the German," breathed Marek from behind me.

We all froze in place at the soldier's arrival.

Mr. Kowalski sucked in his breath and walked toward him. His shoulders shuddered, either due to fear or grief.

The German put out a gloved hand, and Mr. Kowalski accepted it stiffly.

"I am sorry for your loss," he said sincerely. "A terrible thing, to lose a child."

"Yes," said Mr. Kowalski, staring at the ground.

The German turned his attention to Eva. "I am sorry about your brother," he said solemnly. "He was a good boy."

Eva bit a trembling lip. "I miss him."

"I understand," the German said gravely. "I lost my older brother, as a boy. I missed him terribly. I still think of him all the time."

I blinked, surprised. Yes, this man had been kind, bringing medicine for Eva. Yes, he seemed a decent sort. But it was still hard to think of him as a real person. I tried to imagine him as a little boy, grieving the loss of a beloved brother, the idol who'd taught him to kick a ball or read a book. I had not previously contemplated that a Nazi was also human.

I watched him pass a brown paper bag to Mr. Kowalski and pat Eva's curls and then turn away, back down the hill. Only when he was well out of hearing range did I hear Mrs. Kowalski exhale loudly, as if she had been holding her breath the entire time.

"I need to lie down," she said, her voice shaking. "I thought he was going to exhume the body."

"I don't think he's like that," I found myself saying. "I think he may be a good person. For a German, anyway."

"I suppose no people in any country can be entirely good or bad," mused Elsbietta, and Marek nodded in agreement.

Patryk whined then suddenly, pulling his thumb from his mouth with an audible pop. "Home," he said. "Home now."

He reached for Elsbietta, who gathered him in her arms and kissed the top of his head, and we made our way back to our farm.

❦

My plan was to join Piotr.

The question was where to find him. How had Piotr known where to go? Had he known someone in the partisans? Had he simply ventured off into the forest? Every day, I hiked a bit further into the woods, using little pebbles to mark my path. For weeks, I found nothing and no one, though I did pass by the site of the mass graves at least twice. Each time, I picked a few nearby wildflowers and laid them carefully on the mounds of earth.

"I will remember you," I whispered, as I lay a posy of daisies on the ground. "I will avenge us all."

I became preoccupied with revenge, and my temper grew short. My rage boiled over regularly, and I found myself arguing with Elsbietta and even irritated by Patryk. I stomped up steps and slammed doors.

Marek and Elsbietta were patient with me, but I heard them whispering worriedly behind my back. I spent long stretches of time in the woods without them knowing where I was. It made them anxious and cross, but I had stopped caring. My only thought was to find Piotr and join the partisans to fight the Nazis.

And then one morning, everything changed.

"Maria?" Elsbietta hovered outside my bedroom door, hearing the noise.

I couldn't answer. I retched again, but nothing came out. My hair was damp with sweat.

"Maria? Are you ill? I heard something." Elsbietta knocked tentatively.

"Come in," I rasped, resigned. I couldn't hide from her if I was sick.

"Oh, dear," she said, taking in the scene before her. She laid a hand against my forehead.

"No fever," she said, half to herself. "How are your bowels?"

Embarrassed, I looked away, still holding the basin. "Fine," I muttered. "It's just nausea. Could it be something I ate?"

"Possibly, though no one else is sick." Elsbietta was staring at me with an odd expression, and I felt uncomfortable.

"I'm sure it's just a stomach flu," I said, inhaling slowly. The air felt good. I reached back to braid my hair but was hit by another sudden wave of nausea. I heaved violently, but my stomach was empty.

Elsbietta was still looking at me warily.

"What is it?" Was it something contagious that could hurt Patryk? I mentally shuffled through my medical textbook.

Elsbietta shut the door, then sat down gingerly on the bed next to me.

"When did you have your last period?" she asked quietly.

"My—oh." Stunned, I sat back, winded. "I—I don't remember," I said faintly. "Before—before Piotr left. Before it happened."

Elsbietta didn't look at me.

"Did you and Piotr ever…?"

"No," I said quickly, miserable. "No, never."

"It could just be a stomach flu," she said after a long moment. "We could be jumping to conclusions."

I didn't say anything. I couldn't speak. The thought of having that monster's baby growing inside of me made the nausea worse.

"If Piotr returns, I'm sure he would help…."

"No!" I said fiercely. Piotr could never know. Desolate, I thought of our plan to go to America together. That would never happen now. I would hide until I had the baby, and then what? I imagined a baby with Hans' evil face and recoiled.

"We will take it." Elsbietta put an arm around me tightly. "Marek and I. We will pretend it is ours. No one ever need know. I will pretend I am pregnant and we will hide your pregnancy. It will be our secret."

I glanced at her despairingly, thinking of the huge bellies of all the pregnant women I'd known.

"We'll say you are ill," she said, thinking. "You won't go out. You'll stay inside."

"Hans," I whispered.

"You are contagious," she said firmly. "He won't come. He'll never know."

"It will be a monster." I grabbed her hand. "You can't live here with a monster."

"Don't say that." Elsbietta's tone was reproving. "It's a baby. It has no sins, and it is half you, too."

I didn't answer, instead burying my head in Elsbietta's shoulder.

"Come, darling girl," she said kindly. "Some bread will help with the morning sickness."

Monster, I thought dully, despite her words. I clutched at my belly, digging my fingernails in hard.

Chapter 20

LINA
Summer, 1943

THE NIGHT BEFORE we escaped, I dreamed of Anna.

It was the Anna of our bookshop, my little Anna who had grown up climbing ladders and reading atlases.

We were in a field, Anna running ahead of me to collect wildflowers. She plucked them in fistfuls, laughing. Then, suddenly, we were alone in the camp laundry, Anna playing hide-and-seek amongst the massive vats, a trail of flowers behind her.

"Where are you?" I called out, playfully at first. "Anna?"

"You'll never find me," she laughed. Her voice echoed around the empty room. "You'll never find me, Lina."

"I'll find you," I said, tripping over the discarded daisies. "I'm coming."

I went from vat to vat, circling.

"Anna?" I called out. "Anna!"

"Lina." Her voice was fainter now. "Lina, come and find me."

"I'm looking," I said anxiously. "Where are you?"

"Lina," she cried, frightened. "Lina, why won't you come for me?"

"Stop hiding!" I shouted. "Anna, please!"

I woke with a start, sweating profusely.

"You don't have a fever, do you?" Halina stared at me sleepily. "You were shouting and sweating."

"I don't think so," I whispered, swallowing. My mouth was dry. "Just a nightmare about my sister."

Halina murmured something sympathetic and rolled away, already back asleep. I lay awake, worrying over Anna.

In the morning, I kept my head down, trying not to yawn.

"You look terrible," someone said.

"You woke us all with your screaming," Halina chimed in.

"I'm sorry," I said, abashed. "Nightmares."

Halina grimaced "Sleep should be an escape. It should be filled with fluffy blankets and fresh bread and chocolate pastries."

"Butter," said someone else dreamily. "Lots of butter."

"Lemon ices," I said wistfully, thinking of my sister.

We passed out the meager breakfast ration, a small morsel of stale bread. I closed my eyes as I ate just outside the door to the laundry, pretending it was a chocolate pastry.

"Lina," someone breathed in my ear.

I jumped, then relaxed; it was Jerzy. He was quick and stealthy, like a cat. I never saw him coming, he would just appear at my side.

"Lina, listen." His voice was urgent. "It's today."

"Today?" My eyes went wide.

"Yes. Around four in the afternoon."

I looked around nervously, but no one was watching us. "What…?"

"Shush," he whispered. "Meet me there and be ready."

I nodded, swallowing my fear as he squeezed my shoulder briefly before disappearing. Ready for what? To run?

Could I run? I stared at my legs, pale and skinny from starvation and hard work. Would I make it, or would I slow Jerzy down?

"You must be tired," said Halina sometime later, not unkindly. "You're looking at the clock like it might offer you a hot tea and a pillow."

I gave her a small smile. "Remember tea?"

"With honey."

"A bit of milk."

She sighed, closing her eyes, and I tried to focus on the laundry. My eyes frequently flickered to the clock. The seconds passed like hours, and I waited anxiously.

At quarter to four, there was a loud bang.

"What was that?" someone asked.

"Maybe it's another bomb," another said excitedly.

"Maybe it's the Americans!"

"The Russians!" Everyone was shouting now. News was slow and unreliable, but we had all heard the rumors about the approaching Russians and Americans.

"Silence!" Our supervisor pulled her revolver and waved it at us.

"Anyone else shouts out and I shoot. Got it?"

We all fell silent. The supervisor ran from the laundry, and we waited, listening as the shouting in the distance grew.

"I smell smoke," said Halina, sniffing at the air.

In the distance, a siren went off. We all turned toward the loud wailing as if it were a call to prayer.

"She's not coming back. I'm going to see what's going on outside," said Halina decisively.

"Let's go," I agreed. I felt guilty, not sharing with them what I knew. We rushed to the door and scattered outside where we could all see the great blaze.

"Something's burning," someone called out, delightedly. "Maybe it will all burn down!"

There was a resounding cheer. While the others watched, rapt, at the plumes of thick smoke, I snuck behind the building, looking for Jerzy. Where was he?

I looked under the building where I'd hidden the uniform, but it was gone.

Someone nudged my back, and I whirled around.

"Thank God," I nearly cried with relief when I saw it was Jerzy. "What's going on?"

"This is it," he breathed into my hair, and I realized he was wearing the uniform I had hidden.

"You look like a Nazi," I said, recoiling. My face had been pressed up against a swastika.

"That's the idea," he said grimly. He pulled a green card from his pocket. "This is going to get us out of here. I stole it when the bomb went off. We just need it to say I'm transporting you outside the camp. I stole a pen, too." He reached into his pocket.

"I can do it!" I grabbed his arm. "I was a forger in the ghetto."

Jerzy looked surprised and impressed. "A forger? Really?"

"Yes! Give me the pen."

Jerzy covered me while I carefully penned the details, mimicking the German style of handwriting I had perfected in the ghetto.

"This is great work!" he said admiringly.

I looked around at the chaotic scene. The smoke grew closer, and the prisoners were rioting, throwing rocks and debris. The soldiers were angry and restless, and I could hear shots in the distance.

"Don't talk," he said, his expression serious. "Whatever you do, don't say anything. Keep your head down and look like you're afraid of me."

I nodded. It wouldn't be a challenge to look afraid.

"I couldn't steal a gun," he went on quietly, "so we have to pray no one notices I'm unarmed. I'm going to keep an arm in your back that makes it seem as if I have a weapon. Let's go!"

I bowed my head and walked quickly. The shots grew closer and I shook with fear. What if I was shot? Who would find Anna if I died? Should we have waited, if the Americans were coming soon?

I kept walking. My lungs ached from the smoke, and my eyes burned. I willed myself not to cough, to avoid attracting attention.

We were nearly at the gate leading out of Treblinka when a soldier ran over and shouted something at Jerzy. I stiffened, my mouth filled with the metallic taste of fear. Jerzy shouted back in flawless German and reached into his pocket to retrieve the green card. He waved it, and the soldier nodded, waving him along. I nearly cried with relief.

"Just keep walking," whispered Jerzy, his voice shaking. "We're almost there."

At the gate, a gaggle of uniformed guards gave Jerzy a second glance as he waved the green card again.

"Why not just shoot her now," snapped one of them, angrily stomping out a cigarette.

The others jeered in agreement, and one got out his gun and poked it menacingly toward me.

"Those are not my instructions," said Jerzy in careful German. "Perhaps you should raise that with our superior."

The man with the gun quickly pocketed it, turning away. "Go," he said, disgustedly. "And bring back some cigarettes, we are nearly out."

Suddenly, my bladder gave way and I clenched my legs, praying no one would notice. Prisoners were beaten and killed for soiling themselves. Jerzy said nothing. Instead, he shoved me forward.

"She's pissed herself," the guard called out, nudging his comrades. "No better than a dog." But they let us exit.

When I took my first steps past the fence, outside the camp, I could have sworn the air was sweeter. I breathed deeply, wondering if I imagined the smell of fresh grass.

"Keep your head down, just in case," said Jerzy, but I could hear the quiver of excitement in his voice. "Until we're clear of the campgrounds."

I didn't turn around, though every particle of me wanted to jump up and down and into his arms, to scream with joy and kiss the ground.

We continued to walk, veering as far from the main path as possible, heading for the forest where we would be safe.

An hour or so passed, Jerzy still pressing his hand against my back. I wondered if there were still soldiers visible behind us. The thought of being caught now, after an hour of freedom and fresh air, made my eyes prick with tears. I kept my head down and didn't speak, trusting Jerzy's judgment.

More time passed, and finally Jerzy's steps slowed behind me. The grass was high now, nearly to my waist as we grew nearer to the forest.

"Can I turn around?" I whispered, always fearful of Nazi soldiers.

He didn't answer but grabbed me around the waist and spun me toward him. We stared at one another and then I looked beyond him. A vast expanse of tall grass as far as I could see. *Freedom.*

"We did it." Jerzy touched my cheek. "We're free."

❧

We walked through fields and forests. Our destination was a farm owned by a cousin of Jerzy. It would take several more days, maybe a week, to walk there from Treblinka.

Before we'd left the camp, Jerzy had stolen food for us—stale bread and an apple. We supplemented this with wild berries and drank from fast-moving water rather than still streams.

"We'll be sick otherwise," he warned me, pulling me back from a tempting pond. "The berries are safe, but the water isn't."

"How sick?" I stared longingly at the clear water.

"Diarrhea," he said matter-of-factly. "It could kill us. We can't risk it. If the water is moving, it's cleaner."

I didn't argue—I knew nothing of surviving in fields and forests. I didn't want to die of poisonous berries or contaminated water after making it alive out of Treblinka. I wanted to live and find my sister.

"When the war is over, we'll find Anna," he promised, and I remembered the kind social worker and her promise of names in a jar.

"What if we can't find her?" I worried.

"First, we'll find Jolanta, who will lead us to Anna," he said confidently. "But for now, we just need to get to my cousin Witold's farm."

Along with the stale bread, Jerzy had the good sense to steal a map.

The days were long and exhausting. I peered over Jerzy's

shoulder as he navigated and taught me the basics of orienteer-
ing without a compass.

"Moss grows mostly on the north side of trees." He walked
me around a tree, pointing at the heavy growth on one side
versus another. "See?"

I took turns with the map, committing entire sections to
memory. Jerzy was impressed. "You have quite a memory," he
said admiringly. "You must have been a great student."

"Yes." I thought wistfully of my school days long ago. "I
miss it."

"Not me." Jerzy made a face. "All that sitting down. It
was so boring."

I laughed. Jerzy still had trouble keeping still. At night,
when I was happy to collapse into makeshift mattresses of
leaves, Jerzy twitched and tossed and turned, visibly agitated
by his desire to keep moving.

On our third day, Jerzy caught and killed a rabbit and I
wept as he snapped its neck; the poor thing, with its listless ears
and mussed fur. I had never killed an animal before.

"We need to eat," said Jerzy patiently. "We need our
strength."

I nodded, feeling silly. I'd lived through Treblinka and I
was crying over a rabbit? What was wrong with me? Jerzy built
a fire and skinned the sad creature with a stick. My mouth
watered at the smell of cooking meat.

"I've never eaten rabbit," I said.

Jerzy turned the rabbit on a makeshift spit. "It's good," he
assured me. "The French eat it in fancy sauces."

"Do they?" I imagined a restaurant beneath the Eiffel Tower. "I've always wanted to go to Paris."

"Why Paris?"

I turned away, embarrassed. "I once dreamed of being a writer in Paris."

"Tell me," he said. "Tell me about what you wrote."

I stared at the ground, leaves crunching beneath my feet as I shifted them back and forth. "Nothing of any importance. Some stories. Poems. They're all gone now."

"One day you'll write our story. At a café, with the Eiffel Tower in the background."

I smiled. "That's what I pictured when you mentioned the rabbit."

"People in berets with little lap dogs?" He grinned.

"Exactly."

With our stomachs full, we lay together in the grass, our hands intertwined. Relaxed, we talked of our childhoods in Warsaw, the grief of losing a parent young. We learned we both had a sweet tooth and that we'd liked the same candy shop.

"I can't believe you used to go to Grodsky's too!" He rolled over onto his side. "Do you think we ever saw each other there?"

"Maybe." I closed my eyes and pictured the shelves and bins of sweets. "Maybe I pushed you out of the way to get at the lemon drops."

We laughed and he moved toward me. I closed my eyes and enjoyed the kiss, our first real kiss in freedom. I pulled him closer to me, sliding my hands under his shirt.

His breath hitched as he looked at me, gently touching my face. "Are you sure?"

I nodded. "Yes," I said with conviction.

"We don't have to. We can wait…."

I pulled him firmly back to me, meeting his mouth with mine. We shed our clothes and enjoyed the feeling of skin against skin. We slept intertwined, and when I slowly woke to feel him curled around me, I felt truly alive for the first time since the ghetto days.

Jerzy predicted another two days before we reached cousin Witold's farm. Before we fell asleep, he described the farm to me, memories drawn from summers spent there as a boy. I imagined a small but well cared for plot of land and an idyllic little stone house in an isolated patch of countryside. I imagined cows, though Jerzy said the Germans had probably taken them.

When, after days of walking in silence, we were descended upon by a bedraggled group of men, my first thoughts were that they were Nazis. I dropped to the ground, cowering.

"Please," I begged in Polish and then German. "Don't shoot."

"It's alright, Lina." Jerzy fell to my side, hugging me protectively. "These are partisans."

"Partisans," I repeated, uncomprehending.

"Resistance," he clarified. "Resistance fighters, in the forest. We're safe."

"Partisans," I said, my brain slowly thawing. My face broke into what I imagined was a silly grin. "Partisans!"

"Yes." He pulled me to my feet, his arms still around me. "We're going to be okay."

Chapter 21

ANNA
Fall, 1943

THE DAYS WERE long, as all I did was lie in bed, staring at the ceiling.

There were cracks in the ceiling, fine ones that resembled a map or an old woman's face. I imagined that each crack had its own story. One was from a snowstorm that caused the roof to splinter. Another from a cat that always landed on the same spot.

Other cracks were from Marek, working on the roof to keep out the rain and protect his family.

Still others were from Elsbietta, whose sorrow at not being able to have children of her own was a force that spurred its own little tears in the plaster.

A lifetime of actions and reactions told in a tangle of tiny lines. Some days I was sure I spotted new ones, and I knew those were mine. One for Piotr leaving, one for Hans. One for the monster that grew inside of me.

I remained in bed all day long, every day. Elsbietta tried

to talk me into having the baby in my belly. "It's innocent," she said over and over. She promised she would take it. I couldn't picture it as anything other than a monster, and so when she would say this, I imagined Elsbietta swaddling and cradling a horned swamp creature, singing Polish lullabies to it.

The nausea kept me in bed as much as my own misery. I had never felt so sick. Elsbietta brought me bread and I ate it hungrily, only to bring it back up a short time later.

"It's normal," Elsbietta assured me. I wondered how she knew, but it felt cruel to ask.

When I wasn't staring at the ceiling, I leafed through the veterinary textbook, lingering on the pages related to bovine pregnancy and delivery.

I stared at the pictures, at the illustrated cow fetuses at different stages. I traced them with my finger, imagining the monster inside me as a version of a fetal cow. *Did the monster have hands yet?* I wondered. Maybe it would be born with a tail. The Nazis thought that Jews had tails and horns. Maybe this one would.

Patryk knew only that I was sick, and he worried in the way that very small children do, by asking the same questions over and over again. Soon, my bed rest grew normal to him. It made me sad, thinking of how we used to run in the fields between our farm and Piotr's.

But Piotr didn't live there anymore, anyway.

After nearly three months, the nausea subsided and I became restless, desperate to go outside. Elsbietta and Marek seemed relieved, happy that I was getting fresh air and moving around. My belly was still small, but Elsbietta had begun letting out my dresses as a precaution.

"It will just look as if you've lost weight," she reasoned. "From being so ill."

At first, I stayed close to the farm, fearful of running into anyone. What if I saw Hans? What if he looked at me and knew? He still didn't know I was Jewish. What if he tried to take me somewhere, to spirit away the baby I'd promised to Elsbietta? We'd all heard of such things, Aryan-looking babies and toddlers snatched from their Polish families, told they'd gone to live with good families back in Germany.

As the nausea dwindled, I began to walk further and further, enjoying the fresh air and the solitude. I offered to resume my work on the farm, but Elsbietta and Marek refused, concerned about my delicate condition. Soon, my belly began to swell, and at night I lay my hands across it and prayed that it would be taken away.

Elsbietta found me with the veterinary book and recoiled, grabbing it from me in horror.

"This is not healthy," she said firmly. She placed the book on a high shelf in the kitchen. I gritted my teeth, frustrated by Elsbietta's actions. I needed that book.

"I need something to read," I said, feeling desperate. "I don't have anything else."

I wondered briefly if Piotr had left his books. I hadn't seen his family since the faux funeral.

He probably took it with him, I told myself gloomily. *He wouldn't have left that behind. Only me.*

"I must have something else for you to read," said Elsbietta. She bent down and rummaged through a cupboard, removing an assortment of bowls and wooden spoons before retrieving a small, dusty volume. "I thought so. This belonged to my mother."

Elsbietta passed me the book. Dubiously, I stared at the cover. It was a guide to the local flora, handwritten and illustrated. "Thank you," I said politely, but I was not that interested in flowers and plants.

"She drew it herself, and there was a local wise woman who could read and write who helped her with the text," Elsbietta explained.

That perked my interest. "A wise woman?"

"Yes. She fixed remedies and poultices and acted as midwife."

I flipped through the book, trying to make out the handwriting. I noticed the berries I'd eaten with Piotr. Their Latin name and "safe to eat" were delicately printed underneath. I turned the page.

"Thank you," I said again. I wandered back outside and lay down on a shady patch of grass, propping myself up on my elbows as I turned the pages of the little book.

Berries you could eat. Berries you couldn't. Plants to use as salves, herbs for colds and flus. Ways to stop bleeding, plants to stop toothaches. It was more interesting than I had imagined. I studied the drawings and the accompanying descriptions, wondering how difficult it would be to find these plants. I stared out at the forest warily and turned another page.

This page had two intricate drawings. Pennyroyal and mugwort. "Herbs to bring on the menses," read the description.

Bring on the menses. A tingling at the base of my skull reverberated down my spine. Reflexively, I touched my belly. "Tea of pennyroyal and mugwort," it read underneath, followed by a recipe. I studied the drawings. Mugwort looked a bit like parsley crossed with garden weeds. Pennyroyal was a roundish flower with wispy purple protrusions. Both looked familiar.

I recalled the midwife from the ghetto who'd delivered Patryk. Rivka had been ill and not ready to give birth. She had given her something to speed it up. A tincture of some sort.

Lemon verbena, I remembered. *Mineral oil.*

Patryk wandered over and sat down, beaming. He pointed at the sketch of pennyroyal.

"Purple flower," he said proudly.

"Yes!" Guiltily, I shut the book and smiled at him. "Purple flower."

"Ria, come play." He pointed toward the fields that ran between our farm and the Kowalskis' farm. "Race!"

I hesitated. I was supposed to be ill. What if someone saw me?

What if Hans saw me?

Patryk waited patiently for my response, his eyes wide and hopeful. "Ria?"

"Yes, of course," I said finally. I stood and swooped him up, tossing him into the air. He gave a delighted squeal and I caught him, stumbling slightly. He was getting big, but he still had the round eyes and apple cheeks of a toddler. I thought of the herbs and what they could do and cringed inwardly.

It's not the same, a small voice inside me protested. Rivka and Dov were married. Rivka was not raped.

Raped. I so rarely allowed myself to think the word let alone recall what had happened.

But Elsbietta and Marek would love the baby as their own, I argued with myself. *You wouldn't have to be its mother.*

But they have Patryk, the other voice countered. *Are you really going to take Patryk from them? Even if this war ends? They're the only parents he knows.*

I watched Patryk run ahead of me, pretending to let him win the race. Laughing, he turned back to wave at me and then took off again before tumbling into a patch of high grass. Wasn't Patryk theirs now? Where did he belong?

In the early days, when it seemed that the Nazis would win the war, I believed that Patryk and I would never leave the Nowaks'. But now that there were rumors about the Allies defeating the Nazis, it was more difficult to keep certain thoughts locked away.

If the Germans lost the war and Lina came for me, what would we do with Patryk? Elsbietta and Marek were the only parents he'd ever known. He loved them, and they adored him. They were wonderful parents to Patryk, and he felt safe and secure with them. What damage could be done in separating such a small child from his parents? And what could Lina and I offer him, other than his Jewish heritage?

Was heritage more important than love and security? Did

it matter that Patryk had been born a Jew to Jewish parents? What would Rivka and Dov have wanted—and did that matter anymore?

I watched Patryk, who called out for me, laughing and waving.

"Ria, where are you?"

"Coming!" The book was heavy in my hands. I stared at the weeds at my feet. Could they be mugwort? I bent to pick one. No—not enough crevices in its leaves. I waved back at Patryk as I imagined preparing the tea, drinking it. I imagined pain and blood—and relief.

I knew I didn't want Hans' baby. I couldn't count on Elsbietta or Marek to help me. I would have to take matters into my own hands.

❧

I snuck into the forest while Elsbietta was busy with Patryk.

The pennyroyal was easy to find. I had been right—there was plenty of it. I stuffed my pockets full of the feathery flower, sneezing as little tendrils of pollen broke free.

The mugwort was trickier. I hadn't grown up in the countryside, learning to distinguish plants and flowers. The landscape was still new to me, and one leaf looked very much like another. Frustrated, I painstakingly held each one up to the sunlight, counting its points and crevices and placing it next to the drawing in the book for comparison. I was close to giving up when a patch near the mounds of earth caught my eye. *The makeshift graves.* I had been hoping not to venture too near there, but it made sense.

I crouched and plucked a leaf and placed it beside the sketch. I counted the points. I studied the crevices.

It was a match. *Death growing atop death*, I thought darkly.

The plants were heavy in my pockets, and I felt the weight of my plan. Elsbietta and Marek would never approve of my decision.

At dinner, Marek described the Russian army coming closer from the east, and I listened hopefully, glad for the distraction.

"The rumor in town is that the Russians are winning on the eastern front and should be here within weeks," he informed us.

I had been quiet, but I spoke up. "All we hear about are that the Russians and Americans are coming soon, but where are they? Nothing ever happens!"

Elsbietta looked skeptical. "The Nazis are still around, Marek. Taking our animals and our food, and worse. And the Russians—I hear they're just as bad."

"The war must end at some point," countered Marek. "And it seems the Germans are going to lose this war, just as they lost the last."

Elsbietta changed the subject to rations, and I stopped listening. Preoccupied with more pressing thoughts, I dropped a spoon. It clattered noisily to the floor.

"I'm sorry," I said, abashed, as Marek jumped at the sound. "I'm just so tired."

"Of course," said Elsbietta, looking sympathetic. "You should go rest. You're excused."

"Thank you." I avoided looking at her. She was so kind, and I was a liar.

Late in the night, I got up and mixed the tea, hovering anxiously over the boiling kettle so it wouldn't whistle and wake Elsbietta. Staring into the darkness, I drank it and waited for something to happen. The book said it might take up to one week for the bleeding to begin, but with every twinge in my belly, I was sure it was starting.

Nothing happened that night, or the following day and night. But on the third night, shortly after falling asleep, I awoke in agony.

The pain was sharp and came in waves. During the lulls, I tried to convince myself it wasn't so bad, that it was a small price to pay. But during the peaks, I thought I might die. The bedsheets were soaked with blood, but I was in too much pain to change them. I dared not move from the bed, clenching my teeth and balling my hands into fists with every cramp.

The hours passed and I weaved in and out of consciousness. I considered calling out for help, but then I imagined Lina peering at me from the ceiling, and I floated up to her for comfort.

I must have cried out eventually, because I have vague memories of Elsbietta screaming for help and Marek rushing into the room. I do not remember anything else, only waking up several days later, weak and sore.

"Water," I croaked, opening my eyes.

"Maria!" Elsbietta flew over from a dining chair in the corner of my room. I wondered why she was sitting there, watching me sleep.

Elsbietta peered at me anxiously and poured a cup of water from a jug at the bedside. I drank it thirstily, still confused.

"Have I been ill?" I frowned, trying to extract my last memory.

Elsbietta's face fell. "You have, my poor girl. So much suffering." She shook her head.

I struggled to remember. I leafed through my memories, searching them like pages in a book.

A book. Plants. Herbs that bring on the menses. Tea and pain. And blood, lots of it.

"What happened?" I asked, my heart pounding.

A tear rolled down her cheek as she grasped my hand. "It was—it was very bad, my darling girl. We had the doctor here. We thought you might not survive." She took a deep breath and continued. "You lost the baby, Maria. And your womb—it ruptured."

Lost the baby. It had worked; the monster was gone. I fell back on my pillow, wondering if Elsbietta could smell my relief in the stale air of the sickroom.

"Maria," she said urgently, squeezing my hand tighter. "Maria, I'm so sorry."

"It's fine," I said, pretending to be brave. "I was raped."

I had never said the word aloud before, and Elsbietta flinched.

"But Maria…." Elsbietta was crying full tears now. "It was a bad miscarriage. The doctor—he said you will not be able to have children."

I blinked, slowly understanding. It had worked, but everything had a price. I tried to muster up some sort of feeling at the news that I would never have children of my own, but all I continued to feel was relief.

I let Elsbietta wrap me in her arms. I rested my hand on my belly and felt a grim satisfaction at its emptiness.

Chapter 22

LINA
Fall/Winter, 1943–1944

EAGER TO JOIN the Resistance, I was joyous when we found the partisans deep in the forest. Jerzy had quickly gotten us in their good graces with tales of his Resistance work in Warsaw, including the gun smuggling that had landed him at Treblinka. This partisan cell was involved in collecting news and coordinating with the British to carry out small-scale attacks and rebellions against Germans. There were no Jews among them—and no women.

The group was divided on whether to allow me to join. "She may be a girl, but she was tough enough to break out of a death camp and make her way here," one young man pointed out. He had cigarettes and was passing them around as we made camp for the evening, deep in the forest. "She deserves to stay, even if she's a woman."

"It's not about deserving," said another. "She's Jewish and that's too dangerous for us. We should find her a hiding place until the end of the war." He turned to Jerzy. "Didn't you say your cousin had a farm near here?"

I sat next to Jerzy, staring hard at the fire. I didn't want to look up, lest they see the hurt in my eyes. I couldn't allow myself to cry, no matter how much I wanted to. I had to look tough. Why had he told them I was Jewish? I didn't want to be separated from Jerzy. I was tired of losing everyone I cared about.

Jerzy put an arm around me, motioning for me to follow him. I rose, letting him pull me away from the fire. He wrapped himself around me, kissing me gently.

"It might be safer for you at my cousin Witold's farm," he murmured into my hair.

I shook my head furiously. "No, please. Don't leave me alone."

"If we're caught, you'll be shot or sent back to a concentration camp," he said. He took my face into his hands, smoothed my brow with his thumb. "What about Anna?"

Anna. Her name still had the power to make me stop short. I froze, my heart beating faster.

"What about Anna?"

"If you're caught or killed, you can't get to her," he pointed out. "Isn't it better to wait out the war at the farm?"

Frustrated, I turned away. It felt selfish to hide when I could be fighting the Nazis. On the other hand, I had made a promise to my sister. When I tricked her into hiding, I swore to come for her as soon as I could.

"But if she's dead, what good am I hidden away?" I threw out my arms and gestured around me.

"There's a reason to live no matter what," he said quietly.

"If I can't stay with you, I'm going back to Warsaw to find Anna," I said.

Jerzy looked at me, incredulous. "You're a lone Jewish woman. You can't go traipsing around the country."

"I'm just—how can I hide at a farm while you're out there fighting? Better I go in search of Anna now that the war seems to be ending. At least then I'll be useful."

Jerzy didn't answer. He was deep in thought.

"There's a partisan group headed toward Warsaw," he finally said. "I'll join them and look for word of Anna. In exchange, you'll stay at the farm."

"But why can't I go with you?" I looked at him, feeling desperate. "Why are you making me stay behind?"

He studied me. "Three reasons," he said slowly.

I crossed my arms against my chest. "Which are?"

"One, if you're caught, you'll die, and I will have to live with that."

"Shouldn't that be my choice?" Frustrated, I kicked at the leaves. "What if I don't care?"

"Well, the second and third are important too," he said, and at that a small smile played upon his lips. "You see, the second is that I love you. And the third is that you're strong and brilliant but you walk incredibly slowly."

"I do not!" I protested.

"I'm sorry to say it, but you do," he said, shaking his head, laughing.

I didn't know whether to be offended or to laugh. "Anna was always the quick one."

"And you?" He took my chin between his fingers and looked seriously into my eyes.

"Bookworm," I admitted, frustrated.

"I have an idea," he said. "Come with me."

We headed back to the fire. The men were still smoking and drinking. Someone had brought out a bottle of vodka and was passing it around. They looked up at us warily.

"Lina is going to stay with my cousin," Jerzy announced, and there was a murmur of relief from the group. I narrowed my eyes at them, glaring, and they looked away.

"But she is going to help in other ways," Jerzy continued. "She can translate and she's a talented document forger. She created false identification cards and passports in Warsaw for the Resistance."

There was another murmur now, this one of approval.

"We could use that," said the one who'd defended me earlier. We exchanged a small smile. "Can she do British passports?"

"She can learn," said Jerzy.

Someone thrusted the bottle of vodka into my hands.

"Let's drink to that," said another of the men. "To Lina, who will learn."

"To Lina," echoed the drunken group.

Jerzy and I looked at one another, then at the bottle. Trying not to wince, I took a long swig.

❧

Since I was a Jew with no papers, Jerzy was firm with his cousin that I needed to be hidden, rather than living in the house where Witold lived alone.

The farmhouse was small and quaint, surrounded by endless fields of tall grass. An isolated refuge, a haven for someone who'd been sequestered first in the ghetto and then in a concentration camp. But its cellar was dark and cramped. I dreaded going back into a small space, once again boxed in and sealed off from the world.

"Please, no," I said to Jerzy, when he suggested the cellar. I clutched at him, pleading. "Please, I need fresh air." I remembered the crowded train ride to Treblinka and the claustrophobic laundry and barracks.

"It's not safe," he protested. He and Witold exchanged a worried glance.

Witold spoke up. He was a kindly older man, his face weathered from years spent outdoors.

"You need to be hidden," he said quietly. "Only last month, someone informed on a family hiding two Jewish children in the attic. No one knows how they were found out."

I swallowed. "What happened to them?"

He looked at me gravely. "They were taken."

Taken. He didn't say anything further; he didn't have to. My body stiffened with the memory of the train ride to Treblinka.

"There's the barn," said Witold, nodding. "We'll hide you in the barn. So, you'll have the fresh air."

"Thank you," I whispered, grateful.

"It's not too dangerous?" Jerzy looked worried.

"There's a space where we used to keep the horses." He looked sad, and I wondered what had happened to them. "We'll hide Lina there, and cover the entrance with blankets and hay. No one will see."

"Thank you," I said again, reaching forward to grasp his hands.

"Of course," he said simply. "But you must stay completely silent and out of sight. We must be vigilant."

"I'll be silent," I promised.

"Lina will be forging passports," Jerzy informed his cousin in a low voice. "She's a counterfeiter."

Proudly, I reached into my pockets to show off my work. As if by magic, the partisans had brought me pens and paper and a stolen British passport, and I was already hard at work practicing my skills. Witold nodded approvingly, then excused himself to go prepare the barn.

"He can't read or write," Jerzy muttered under his breath to me.

"Oh," I said, mortified.

"Don't worry about it." Jerzy squeezed my arm, then pulled me to him. "We're leaving tomorrow morning, myself and some of the others. Before dawn."

I rested my head on his chest. It seemed my fate to constantly lose the people I cared about. With Jerzy leaving, I had no one left.

"I'm going to track down Jolanta for you," he promised. "One of the others said he thinks he knows where she is."

"Be careful, Jerzy. I couldn't stand to lose anyone else."

"Don't worry. I'll return in three weeks," he added. "Someone from the partisans will bring you more documents for your forgeries."

Jerzy stayed with me that night in the barn. Hidden by a mountain of hay, we kept each other warm beneath a heap of woolen blankets and promised each other to be safe and stay alive.

When I woke, he was already gone.

⁂

The days were long and lonely. Witold couldn't risk coming in more than twice a day to bring me food. With the animals all gone, there was little reason to be slipping in and out of the barn.

I looked forward to Witold's visits for company and conversation even more than for food and water. I had become used to doing without those, but I would never grow used to feeling alone. I longed for news about the war, and for the simple soothing sound of another person's voice and comforting presence.

"How is your work going?" Witold crouched beside me, adjusting the hay bales and placing a small bowl of soup and a lump of bread in front of me. He looked older than he was, all stooped shoulders and weathered skin and wiry gray hair. I would have guessed him to be well into his sixties, but Jerzy had said he didn't think he was more than forty-five. The war had been hard on all of us.

"Going well, I think." I thanked him for the food, my stomach growling appreciatively. Rations were small and food scarce, but it was still much more than I'd been fed in the Treblinka camp and I was starting to put on a bit of weight. My breasts were returning, as were the beginnings of hips. Two weeks had passed since Jerzy had left. He had said he'd be gone three, and Witold kept a count for me on his calendar. Witold was good company, but I longed to be held and touched. Even in the camp, I had the comfort of the other girls' bodies pressed up against mine at night. The nights were colder now, and the hours of daylight were shrinking. It was frightening to be alone in the dark and the cold.

"Any news?" I asked Witold. "The Americans?"

"Any time now, they say," he informed me. "The Germans are pulling back on the eastern front."

Sometimes I wondered if any of it was real. Were there even Americans? What proof did we really have? Sometimes the Americans felt like a myth or a fantasy, a bit like how people talked of angels.

I spread out my work and described it to Witold, explaining the words to him without making it obvious I knew he couldn't read. He studied everything closely, bringing the papers close to his face and staring intently. His son was in a prisoner-of-war camp somewhere in Germany, but I only knew that from Jerzy. Witold never spoke of it and I never pressed. I knew how it felt to have your secrets.

When he left, I returned to my work, eager to make the most of the remaining daylight hours. My skills had improved, and I felt a sense of pride over my workmanship. I wrote and sketched, shaded and inscribed. I was intensely grateful for something to pass the time, as well as to make a contribution to the Resistance.

I completed one set of papers and set it aside, rising to stretch before I started the next. As I sat back down, my weakened legs buckled suddenly beneath me and I tripped, skinning my knee. Wincing at the pain, I noticed the smear of blood on the papers I'd worked so hard to complete.

"No," I hissed. All that hard work ruined in a moment of careless clumsiness. Despairing, I tried to wipe away the red stain, but it was no use. It was wrecked.

I clutched the paper and my pencil, rocking back and forth, eyes stinging. I bit my lip and decided the paper should not go to waste.

I wrote a poem.

It had been so long. I hadn't let myself compose them, not even in my head, convinced my dreams of being a writer were best put to bed. But now, presented with paper and pencil, I couldn't hold back. For the first time in years, I felt almost like the girl I used to be.

They say the angels are coming
Angels at the gates, angels of red and blue and stars
and stripes
But no one comes and we are hungry

And to stop believing is to give up hope
So we believe
And we hope
And we wait.

Witold came in the morning with bread and a precious bit of milk. He noticed the paper immediately and pointed.

"This one looks different."

I chewed hungrily. The more my body remembered what it was like to eat, the more it wanted food.

"I ruined it," I said sadly, turning the page over to show him what had happened. "I was clumsy."

I pointed at my scraped knee, shaking my head.

"I'm sorry," he said gravely. He looked at my knee. "Does it still hurt?"

"No," I shook my head again. "I'm just upset."

He nodded, silent for a moment. He still held the paper, looking at the poem I had written.

"What does it say?" he said finally. He didn't look at me, his eyes cast downward, his cheeks red. I felt sad at his shame and reached to take both the paper and his hand.

"I will read it to you."

He listened intently, and when I was finished, he had me read it again.

"It's beautiful," he said. "I want to learn it."

I read it twice more, and he repeated it back to me.

"They're coming," he said, before he left. "I know it."

❧

A day before the three-week mark, Witold came to me clutching a small envelope. He handed it to me with some bread and cheese.

"Can you tell me what it says?" he asked quietly, his face red.

"Of course. What is it?"

"A letter," he said shyly. "From my son. I can see his name at the end."

He pointed at the name "Jakub," scrawled at the bottom of the letter. I wondered how long he had held on to this without being able to read it.

"My wife could read," Witold said, as if reading my thoughts. "She died of tuberculosis early in the war. Jakub doesn't know."

"I'm sorry," I said, thinking of my own father. "My father died, too."

An understanding passed between us, and I cleared my throat.

"My dear Mama and Papa," I read aloud. "I am sorry for not writing more, but they do not permit it and there is a shortage of paper. Adam has died of dysentery. Please let his mother know. Tell her he died bravely and peacefully."

I looked up, questioning. Witold looked saddened by this news.

"Adam was Jakub's childhood friend," he said softly. "Our neighbor."

I nodded and continued to read. "There is little to eat and the days are long and the Germans are cruel. But I am sure you are suffering yourselves during the Nazi occupation. I miss you both very much. I know it is hard to get letters here. But if you could try, I am desperate for news. Have you heard anything from Veronika? Is she well? I await news and pray this war will soon be over. Your loving son, Jakub."

Witold frowned. "Veronika, his girlfriend," he said, making a face. He spat on the ground. "She took up with a German in the early days of the war."

"Oh," I said, feeling sorry for poor Jakub.

"Could you—could you write him back? Maybe Jerzy will know how to get him the letter. When he returns."

I looked down at my reserve of paper. I wished I hadn't written the poem, now.

"I have this for you." Witold pulled a tiny, crumpled, torn piece of paper from his coat.

"That will work." I hesitated. "Do you want him to know? About his mother and about Veronika?"

Witold nodded slowly, thinking. "Yes," he said finally. "Yes, he needs to know."

"I would want to," I agreed.

We got to work.

Three weeks passed with no word from Jerzy. My spirits sank and I worried if something had happened to him. I stared at the bales of hay, waiting hopefully but with increasing pessimism. I worried that Jerzy would not return, that the war would not end. That the angels were not real.

Witold came every day, trying to keep my spirits up. One day he came with a bit of cooked meat—rabbit he'd trapped himself in the forest. It smelled delicious and my stomach groaned at the scent.

"Can you eat this?" he looked hesitant. "I know there are rules around meat. I don't want to offend you."

I stared at him blankly for a moment, then realized he was referring to whether the rabbit was kosher.

I thanked him and told him I'd eaten rabbit in the forest.

"My father used to say, if you need to save your life, you can do whatever you need to do," I told him. "We ate all kinds of things in the ghetto, too."

Witold nodded. "That makes sense."

I hesitated, then spoke again. "I sent my sister to live with a Christian family. She didn't know ahead of time."

Witold gestured toward the rabbit. "Eat," he said gravely. "Eat and then tell me."

I chewed and swallowed, grateful for the nourishment and the pleasure of filling my belly.

"She didn't know," I continued. "She wouldn't have gone. So, I lied."

"You did it to save her life," said Witold. "You did the right thing."

"I don't know," I said. "What if she had been killed on the way there?"

"You did what you thought best," said Witold firmly. "You wanted to save her life. She would have died, otherwise."

I thought back to Treblinka. The children had been sent into the "showers" before being murdered. Would Anna have been considered a child?

"I am worried about Jerzy, too," I admitted. "Do you think he'll come back? He said he would find my sister if he could."

"I'm sure he will do his best." Witold patted my arm. "He's a good boy and he cares for you."

I blushed. I cared for him deeply, too.

"I hope he's safe," I said instead. "They should have returned by now."

Witold sighed. "It's unpredictable out there. The rumor is that the Russians and the other Allies are arriving. We may be close to the end of the war."

"I keep hearing that, but it's hard to believe."

"I know." He sighed again. "I haven't seen any Russians with my own eyes. I just repeat what I've heard."

"It's just like angels," I said, thinking of my poem. "They say there are angels out there, but where are they?"

"I don't know about that," he said quietly. "I've been thinking. What about the angels that got you and Jerzy out of the camp?"

I blinked, contemplating. I hadn't thought of it that way.

"Or you," I said slowly, out loud, looking at Witold. "You're a bit like an angel, too."

"Pfft," he said, waving his hand. "I'm just an ordinary man. A good Christian, doing my duty for another human being."

"Hmmm," I said, but even after he bid me goodnight, I gazed up at the tiny stream of moonlight that peeked through the worn wooden roof and wondered if perhaps there were angels after all.

⟡

More days passed, then weeks, and I began to wonder what had really happened and what had not. Being stuck in the barn all day, never seeing the outside, my mind had begun to run circles around itself. Had I ever been in Treblinka? Had Jerzy really promised to return? Did Jerzy even exist or had I invented him? Sometimes I spoke to the mice in the barn and gave them names.

I ran out of paper and had nothing left to do. I wondered what the point of the forgeries was if no one from the partisans seemed to come back for the passports. I still had my pencils and pens, so I wrote fragments of sentences on leaves, drafted poetry on my arms.

Witold kept my spirits up with stories of American and Russian troops storming the countryside, liberating camps and villages. The word was being passed from person to person, village to village, so the news we got was thirdhand at best. I had gone from thinking of them as angels to molecules, something I believed was there but couldn't see.

I chatted with my mice, telling them stories from my childhood. I described what memories I had of my mother, of the lovely red hair she had shared with Anna, and of her strong personality and intellect. I told them about my father, explaining his pipe and beard in detail, the books in the bookshop, and our apartment before the ghetto.

I wove braids from hay and lamented I had never mastered braiding when Anna was little, when it would have been useful. I turned them into bracelets and kept them in a small pile. I was embarrassed for Witold to see them, so I tucked them out of sight.

"What day is it?" I asked Witold one evening. He had cheese for me, and I ate it ravenously. "How much time has passed since I first arrived?"

"Many weeks," he said evasively.

Suddenly, there was a rustling outside. Witold stiffened, his eyes growing round with apprehension. He placed a finger to his lips, and I nodded fearfully.

"Cousin?" A whisper came from behind the hay, a familiar voice. My heart leapt.

"Jerzy!" I cried out, scrambling to my feet.

"Lina!"

I kicked the hay aside and there he was, bruised and dirty, an angry red scrape on his right cheek and a bandaged hand, but very much alive.

"You're alive!" I said, stumbling toward him. I buried my face in his chest then pulled back, grimacing. "And you stink."

He laughed. "You don't smell great yourself, my love." He held me tightly, then reached into his pocket for a small slip of paper. He pressed it into my palm and closed my fingers around it.

My breath caught. "Is this…?"

"Yes," he said, excited. "I found her. Anna. Her name is Maria Nowak, and I know where she is."

Chapter 23

ANNA
Spring, 1945

THE RUSSIANS FINALLY came, and then the Americans. We caught glimpses of them with their guns and their loud voices. Marek and Elsbietta warned me to be careful, to come directly inside at the sight of any strange men. The Americans were friendly enough, tossing chocolate bars at me and Patryk, but the Russians frightened me.

I had thought the end of the war would feel different. I think there was a part of me that dreamed I would suddenly be transported back to our apartment in Warsaw. Instead, things stayed the same. At night, I peered out the window, wondering if Hans was still out there.

"Maria?" Marek poked his head into the kitchen. "Can you come help with the sheep? Lina has something stuck in her hoof."

"Of course."

"I want to come!" Patryk jumped up.

"Finish your breakfast first," said Elsbietta without turning around. She had developed a mother's instincts and could sense Patryk's cheese and half a boiled egg were untouched.

"But…," Patryk pouted.

"No 'buts.' Eat. You need to grow up strong if you're going to help with the sheep like Maria."

Sulking, Patryk resumed picking at his egg.

I followed Marek outside, where poor Lina was stamping her hooves and making pitiful noises.

"Oh, no," I said, wincing at her obvious discomfort. "It must be bad."

"I think it's a piece of metal," said Marek grimly. "Probably from the soldiers."

"Ah," I said, shuddering. "Poor girl."

I settled down next to the sheep, patting her gently. "Alright, girl," I crooned. "Give me your foot."

Lina whined softly, her entire body trembling.

"Come now," I whispered. "Let's get it out."

We coaxed Lina to the grass. I grabbed her hoof, the bottom was swollen and bloody and I could see something shiny peeking out.

"I need something," I called out, frowning. "Tweezers…."

Marek reached into his pocket for some pliers. "Will these work?"

I nodded and took them, my tongue set between my teeth in concentration. I grasped the metal and yanked before the ewe could move away. There was a howling sound. Cringing in sympathy, I rubbed Lina's head between her ears.

"Looks like a part of a penknife," I said, examining the injured hoof. Marek pocketed it.

"She should be fine," I said. "We'll need to keep the wound clean and bandage it."

We rinsed the wound and bound it tightly. As I tied the bandage, there was noise from the field.

"Soldiers, probably," said Marek, alert.

I wiped my hands on my skirt and rose, studying the figures walking toward us. They didn't look like soldiers. A man and a woman with no uniforms or guns.

I squinted into the sun. There was something familiar about the woman, something in the way she swung her arms when she walked.

Then I heard her voice.

"Oh my God," I said, trembling. "It's Lina."

Marek's eyebrows knitted together in confusion.

"Lina is here," he said, gesturing at the prostrate sheep.

I couldn't speak. I began to run.

"Lina?" I whispered it at first, then shouted. "Lina!"

She looked up sharply.

"Anna!"

We ran toward each other, arms outstretched. Sobbing, we grabbed at each other. I touched her face and her short hair, grasped her hands. She smoothed my hair and kissed me over and over again.

"I found you," she said. "I found you."

❧

I remembered Jerzy from Warsaw, and with marveled shock I demanded he and Lina explain how they'd arrived here together. We crowded around the kitchen table sharing stories and real bread that Jerzy had brought from the city.

"Do you have chocolate for me?" Patryk asked Jerzy, frowning at the bread. "The soldiers have chocolate."

Jerzy laughed as Elsbietta admonished Patryk.

"That's okay," he said, grinning. "I understand. I would like some chocolate too."

"Try this, Patryk," I said, laughing, waving a slice of bread. "It's real bread."

Our wartime bread had often been mixed with hay to compensate for the lack of flour. It was dry and hard.

Patryk took a tentative bite and looked up in surprise.

"It's soft," he said. "It's like a fluffy sheep."

We all laughed. Next to me, Lina squeezed my hand again and I leaned into her. Lina was alive and she was here, but her appearance shocked me. Painfully thin with cropped hair, she seemed like the ghost of my sister.

"Lina," I whispered, while Jerzy chatted with the Nowaks about the American army. "What happened to you?"

"Don't worry about it now." She touched my hair, tucking it gently behind my ear.

"I want to know." I shook my head. "I'm not a little girl anymore, Lina."

"I was in a concentration camp," she said quietly.

I swallowed. "Like a prisoner-of-war camp?"

She wouldn't look at me. "Not exactly."

"Tell me," I demanded.

"Later, Anna. I'm not ready to talk about it."

"I understand," I said, taken aback. "Or maybe I don't."

"Thank God you don't," she said sharply. Then her face softened.

"Look at you," she beamed. "Beautiful and grown up. You've been healthy and safe here, haven't you, Anna?"

I thought of the things she didn't know, and my insides twisted. I opened my mouth to answer, but couldn't. I grimaced.

She understood. "You're not ready to talk about it either."

My hands wandered to my belly, empty now and forever. "No, not yet."

She didn't mention Tateh, which could mean only one thing.

"How did Tateh die?" I asked quietly, so Patryk wouldn't hear. He was on Elsbietta's lap but watching me and Lina with curiosity.

"Typhoid and cancer," she said. "I think. I'm not a little doctor, though, like you. Remember your book?"

I nodded, my eyes welling with tears even though I'd known in my heart the moment Lina appeared without him that Tateh was gone.

"I had another book here," I managed. "Veterinary medicine. I delivered a lamb and did an operation on a cow."

"We'll move to America, or Palestine," said Lina, her eyes fierce. "You can be a vet there, or a doctor. Whatever you want."

"Palestine?" I said, surprised.

"There's talk of a Jewish homeland there. We heard rumors in the city. Most surviving Jews are leaving Poland. There's no future for us here, Anna."

I thought of Piotr with a pang of sadness. We had talked about going to America together. Was he still alive?

Patryk slid off Elsbietta's lap and asked, "Why is she calling you Anna?"

I paused. "That's part of my name," I said finally.

"It is?" His eyes narrowed.

"Yes," I said, nodding, and I knew then it was true. I couldn't go back; I would never be Anna again. She was gone, grown up. But I wasn't just Maria, either.

"My full name," I said, "is Anna-Maria."

Epilogue

ANNA-MARIA
1987, London

"DR. BAR-LEV?"

The conference assistant knocked tentatively at my open door. I was preparing for a keynote address for tomorrow on maternal-fetal medicine and had given strict instructions not to be disturbed unless it was urgent.

"Yes?" I asked, trying to be polite. "Is there an emergency? A call from the hospital in Tel Aviv?"

"No," she said quickly. She hesitated. "It's—you have a visitor. He says he's from Poland."

"Poland?" I wracked my brain, trying to think of a Polish colleague attending the conference. No one came to mind.

"Yes," she said. "He said...well, I think you'd better speak to him."

"Of course," I said, ruefully staring at the still unfinished draft on my desk and stood up. The assistant disappeared and returned with a man about a decade or so younger than me, tall and broad-shouldered with a headful of thick, curly hair. I didn't recognize him.

"Hello," I said politely, rising. "Can I help you?"

The man stared at me for a long moment.

"Maria?" he asked, tentatively. "Is it really you?"

I stared at him, at his eyes, his nose, his mouth. His dark, curly hair. The first baby I'd helped deliver. My brother, who I'd left behind.

"Patryk," I whispered. I sat back down in my chair, my legs shaky beneath me. "Oh, Patryk."

My voice broke as I said his name. I hadn't spoken it for years, burying my choice and that pain deep within me. I had decided it would be best if Patryk didn't know about our past—that he'd be happiest and safest thinking Marek and Elsbietta were his natural parents. He would forget me, I had argued, to Elsbietta's protests. The circumcision was explained as the result of an infection, something during the war. Better not to tell him anything else.

"Ria," he said, choking. He moved toward me, tears streaming down his face. "My sister."

I stood and impulsively wrapped him in my arms, this man who I didn't know, who in my mind was still a small boy.

"Elsbietta told you?" I said finally, pulling back. I felt embarrassed at the hug, but he didn't seem to mind.

"Before she died," he said softly. "She told me the truth. But Ria, why? Why did no one tell me?"

I sighed and ran a hand through my hair, still long and straight but now a silvery color.

"Come in," I said. "Sit down."

He settled down on a small couch. I went over to a half-full coffee pot on the windowsill counter and filled two mugs.

After taking a moment to collect my thoughts, I began to speak.

"Rivka and Dov Levy were your Jewish birth parents," I struggled to explain. "It was 1945 when I left. I thought you'd be safer with Elsbietta and Marek, a Christian family, no memory of me or knowledge of who you had once been. My sister Lina and I decided it would be too dangerous to take you with us."

"But why not tell me?" he pressed. "Later, when I got older?"

I sighed again. "I didn't want to disrupt your life." I paused, then admitted what I hadn't ever said out loud. "I felt guilty, Patryk. I left you behind. It was easier to think you were happy having forgotten me."

"I never forgot," he whispered. "They told me you were a refugee, someone who stayed with us during the war. But I knew you were more than that."

"You do know I'm not your real sister," I said. "Your parents were my neighbors."

He nodded. "I know," he said. "But you're still my real sister."

"How did you find me?" I asked.

"I had letters," he explained. "Letters with your new name. I knew you were a doctor in Tel Aviv, but I didn't know whether to write to you. For years, I did nothing. But then I was at the

University in Warsaw—I lecture there sometimes—and I saw your name. On a conference flyer in the medical school. I knew you'd be in London."

"What do you teach?" I leaned in, curious.

"I'm a veterinarian," he said, smiling shyly, and I began to cry openly.

"I never forgot you. I wanted to be like you."

I reached for a tissue and offered the box to Patryk.

"Are you married? Do you have children?"

"Yes." He beamed, reaching into his pocket for his wallet. "This is Magdalena, and our daughters, Maria and Elsbietta."

I blinked hard at my tears.

"Named for me," I said softly, pointing. "She looks just like your mother. Like Rivka."

"You might remember Magdalena's family," Patryk said. "They lived on the next farm. Their son died in the war."

"The next farm?" My heart began to pound again. "But their daughter was Eva."

"Yes," he said. "Magdalena was born after the war. Piotr didn't come back."

"Piotr died, then," I whispered. I had never asked, and Elsbietta had never said.

"You were friends," Patryk said, recalling. "I remember."

"He was my first love." I smiled sadly.

"Do you have a family?" He nodded at the photos on my desk, three children smiling stiffly in school photos.

"No, I...I was married, but David—that was his name— he died a year ago from a heart attack," I explained.

"I'm sorry," said Patryk, his cheeks reddening.

"Thank you." I gestured at the photo on the filing cabinet, the one of David and me on our wedding day. "That was him. We didn't have children. I—I couldn't have any. From the war. Those are my nieces and nephew. That's Masha—the red-haired one. She's named for the woman who helped smuggle us out of the ghetto and later died at Treblinka."

Patryk flinched, and I continued. "The other girl is Elana, after Elsbietta, for taking us in during the war. And the boy…." My voice caught. "The boy's name is Dov. That was your name, Patryk, before. And your father's."

"Dov," he whispered, sounding it out.

"He died before he ever saw you," I told him. "We gave you his name."

"What were they like?" Patryk asked, his expression both melancholy and curious. "My—my biological parents?"

I thought of Rivka, brave and cheerful until the end. I thought of Dov, who had crumpled like a flower starved of light in the ghetto.

"They were kind," I told him. "Kind and brave. Your mother—she thought only of you before she died."

Patryk nodded. He looked again at the photographs.

"Those are your sister's children?" he asked. "The young woman who came that day. They brought bread."

"Yes!" I exclaimed. "You remember that?"

"I remember a lot," he said. "Lina, right? Like the sheep."

"Yes," I said, smiling fondly at the memory. "Like the sheep. She's a writer now. She writes screenplays for Israeli television."

We smiled at each other.

"Did she marry that boy?" he asked. "The one she came with."

"Oh! Jerzy." I grinned. We still exchanged letters—he lived in Florida and had four daughters of his own. "No, their relationship didn't last because of our move to Israel. Instead, he received a visa to immigrate to New York, and we couldn't get visas to New York at the time. But we still write."

We sat for a long time, just staring at each other.

"Can I ask how you became Bar-Lev?" he asked tentatively. "Was that your husband's name?"

"Actually, no," I said. "*Bar* in Hebrew means 'son of.' Lev was our father's name. We changed it when we moved to Israel. A fresh start, a Hebrew name. Many refugees from Europe changed their names. And I didn't feel like Anna Krawitz anymore—that was my name before the war—and I wasn't really Maria Nowak either. So now I'm both, and neither, if that makes sense."

"It does," he said, looking thoughtful. "It definitely does."

We spent three days together. I told him everything I could remember about the past, about Tateh and the bookshop and my childhood in Warsaw. How we buried the books in the basement. I told him about Lina in the ghetto and in the Treblinka death camp. He told me about his veterinary practice and about his wife, an economist, and their girls who were both gymnasts. I told him about Lina's writing career, about my nieces and nephew. When he left, we promised we'd write and call, and I told him to bring his family to Tel Aviv sometime.

"We have beaches there," I said. "Children love the ocean."

The first postcard arrived two weeks later, full of information and photos of his girls. I read it out loud to Lina, and I smiled as I read, my breath catching on his last words.

"I've changed my name," he wrote. "*Dov* means 'bear' in Hebrew. In Polish, the surname *Niedźwiedź* also means bear. This way, I will always carry my history with me. Love, Patryk Dov Niedźwiedź-Nowak. PS: I am sending a package separately for both you and Lina."

"For me?" Lina looked baffled. "What could he have sent me?"

I hadn't realized the weighty parcel was from him. I thought it was some books I'd ordered from the United States. I went over to the heavy package, tearing at the brown paper.

"Oh, my God, Lina," I cried. "Lina, look!"

The package was full of books—our books from Tateh's shop. Patryk must have tracked them down and unearthed them. When he wrote that he would be going on a short trip to Warsaw, I had given him the address for where we had lived. He'd said he wanted to see the building.

Lina still looked confused. Then I held up a book of Yiddish fairy tales.

"Is that…?" She jumped, eyes wide. "It can't be."

"It is!" Full of joy, I spread the books out across the floor. Shakespeare in Yiddish. A book of Talmud commentary. An old science book.

Lina picked up the book of fairy tales and began to weep.

"The books!" She clutched the volume to her chest. "Imagine, Anna! Tateh's books! After all these years."

We smiled at each other, marveling at the volumes. We'd lost so much, but we'd been lucky too. We had survived and started a new life.

"We'll donate them," I said. "To a museum. So the world will never forget."

"Yes," said Lina softly. "But I want to keep this one." She pointed to the fairy tales. "To show the children. So, we don't forget Tateh."

I leaned over and pulled my sister into a hug.

Historical Postscript
The Holocaust, Treblinka, and Irena Sendler

Six million Jews were murdered in the Holocaust during World War II. There was a systematic deportation of European Jews to concentration camps throughout Poland, Germany, and other parts of Eastern Europe. Many of these camps had the sole purpose of exterminating Jews, Gypsies, and other "undesirables." Treblinka was one of these "death camps." It was the primary death camp for many of the Jews from the Warsaw ghetto.

The revolt during which Lina and Jerzy escape is loosely based on a real revolt at Treblinka in 1943, as are the details of a failed revolt two months earlier (the reference to grenades and explosions when Hannelore disappears). I have used some of the same names (Irka, Dr. Berek) and tried to incorporate some real details.

The story of Lina and Jerzy escaping is fiction, but it is loosely based on two real escapees who fell in love at Auschwitz concentration camp. Jerzy Bielecki was a Polish Catholic social worker. With the help of other Resistance members in the camp, he escaped in 1944 with his Jewish girlfriend, Cyla Cybulska. Jerzy helped hide Cyla at his uncle's house after their escape.

Jolanta, the code name of Irena Sendler, was a real person and a hero of World War II. Sendler was a young Polish social worker who saved the lives of hundreds of Jewish children from the Warsaw ghetto by smuggling them out and finding them new homes with Christian families throughout Poland. True to the story, she kept their new and old names buried in jars in her garden, unearthed only at the war's end. In 1965, she was recognized by the State of Israel as Righteous Among the Nations. Late in life, Irena Sendler received the Order of the White Eagle, Poland's highest honor, for her humanitarian work during World War II.

ACKNOWLEDGMENTS

This book wouldn't be possible without the hard work and support of many, as well as the thoughtful comments and ideas that led to its conception and evolution as a novel.

Thank you to Gillian Rodgerson and Margie Wolfe and the entire team at Second Story Press, for continuing to believe in my work and for publishing quieter books for young adults that have deeper meaning and significance.

Thank you to my editor, Sarah Swartz, without whose thoughtful work this manuscript would not have been possible. I feel lucky to have had someone knowledgeable and ideologically committed working on this with me. Thanks too to copy editor Jordan Ryder for your eagle eyes!

Thanks to Talya Baldwin for designing the absolutely gorgeous cover and to Melissa Kaita for her art direction. They say you shouldn't judge a book this way, but all of Melissa's covers have been outstanding and in my opinion have contributed to their success.

Thank you to the Banff Centre for Arts and Creativity for enabling me to attend and complete part of a writer's residency in early March 2020. While it was cut short because of Covid, it enabled me to complete a revised first draft, something I may not otherwise have been able to do once the lockdowns commenced. I hope to come back again when it's safe to do so!

Thank you to Voytek Roszuk, whose offhand comments about Irena Sendler sparked an idea for this book, and for helping me with some Polish language and culture queries; and to his daughter Anna-Maria, a budding writer whose name I borrowed for this work.

Thank you to the family, friends, and colleagues who always support and encourage me, and who make it possible for me to do things like take weekends to write or take time off to speak to classrooms or to attend a writer's residency: Karen and Howard Gold, Paul, Jess, and Myles Gold, Cheryl Ellison, Dara Laxer, Sarah Lancaster, Adam Farber, Elena Fiadzinu, and all the other OMA staff.

Finally, thanks as always to my husband, Adam Goodman, for always believing in me and my work, and to my kids Teddy and Violet who inspire me every day with their cleverness and spirited ways.

ABOUT THE AUTHOR

JENNIFER GOLD is an award-winning author of several books for young adults, including *Soldier Doll* and *On the Spectrum*. A lawyer and mom of two kids and two cats, she lives with her family in Toronto.